Praise for Jɛ   ̄o ̄
Reversing Over Liberace

5 Angels and a Recommended Read!! "One of the funniest books I've read in ages! It is smart and witty and the romantic oozes from every direction in this story... the chaos is hysterical!... A whole host of laugh-out-loud bits make this book one I won't forget.

~ *Marlene, Fallen Angel Reviews*

Rating: 78 "This story is written in a chick-lit style although the sentiments of love and life are more optimistic here compared to a typical chick-lit novel... I enjoy reading this story because of Willow's interactions with her most amusing siblings... A lively voice and prose."

~ *Mrs. Giggles*

4 Hearts! "Very Bridget Jonesy and a lot of fun... funny first person account of female growth and introspection. Engaging Chick Lit and a really fun read."

~ *Lynne Bushey, The Romance Studio*

Reversing Over Liberace

Jane Lovering

with best wishes

A Samhain publishing, Ltd. publication.

Samhain Publishing, Ltd.
577 Mulberry Street, Suite 1520
Macon, GA 31201
www.samhainpublishing.com

Editing by Anne Scott
Cover by Scott Carpenter

First Samhain Publishing, Ltd. electronic publication: July 2007
First Samhain Publishing, Ltd. print publication: May 2008

Dedication

To everyone who never stopped believing; the school gate Mothers' Mafia, my parents, my friends. To the kids, for keeping out of my way while I was writing and for not asking (too many times) for food.

And most of all, for Kit. He knows why.

Chapter One

"My grandfather's left me his nose. It's in a matchbox."

The whole bar went quiet (except for Jazz who only goes quiet under the influence of veterinary-strength drugs) as my friends appreciated the embarrassment of my legacy. "Okay, well, look at it this way." Katie, best friend and absolutely *the* person you want to have with you in any crisis, including the unexpected bequest of body parts, eventually patted my arm. "You're no worse off, are you?"

She didn't understand. I'd adored my grandfather. I'd even worked with him on some of his more outrageous inventions and stood on more wooden platforms holding electrical wires than anyone not called Igor. I had stitched, stapled, glued and on one memorable occasion even *welded* parts of myself into some of his contraptions in the interests of scientific advancement—and I got a nose in a matchbox? Admittedly he'd not been a rich man, but he'd promised...

"No," I said sadly to Katie, whose benevolent expression was beginning to get on my nerves. "I'm no worse off."

"And at least it was only his nose." Jazz came over, walking carefully in his huge platform boots. His current look was Goth, but the out-of-control hair and enormous shoes made him resemble a member of The Darkness training to be a funeral director. "I mean, how much worse if he'd cut off something else in that bandsaw accident."

"Shut up, Jazz." Katie and I spoke as one. We spent so long telling Jazz to shut up that it was an automatic response.

"You've really got to cultivate that little thing we talked about called tact," Katie said. "It's no wonder you only manage to keep girlfriends for three days. Anyway, Will? Willow?"

But I was suffering from what will be, if they ever make the film of my life, an extremely expensive special effect—the whole bar had receded into darkness, and a tunnel of light was all I could see. A tunnel which began at the newly opened door to the Grape and Sprout, and ended at my feet. It was like a near-death experience, with vodka. I was aware Katie was talking, but her voice had gone far, far away. They may need to use CGI to properly replicate the whole thing.

"Willow?" Now Katie was shaking my arm. "Are you okay? You've gone all pale."

"Delayed shock," Jazz confidently diagnosed. "She needs another drink. Oh, and while you're up, Kate, I'll have another pint."

"It's him," I said, indistinctly because my tongue got in the way.

Now, before I explain about "him", there are a few things you should know about me, in case you're ever casting director when they do my life film. I'm thirty-two, never been married, never had any particularly long-lasting relationships, lived in York all my life, youngest of five kids of hippy parents (hence the name, I got off lightly, you wait until you meet my brothers and sister) and I have this...problem. Cameron Diaz could probably play me if she's prepared to put on four stone, mostly on her bottom, and rub herself with ugly cream. All right. Back to him.

"Him?" Thanks, Jazz. Always ready with the unnecessary link.

"Over there. Just come in. With the two guys in suits. Don't turn round."

Both Katie and Jazz swivelled, although at least Katie did it subtly. Jazz got his long leather coat caught in the rotating mechanism of his stool and fell over.

"Okayyyyy," Katie said slowly. "But you have to help us on this one, Will. Who exactly *is* he?"

"You're looking at the guy in the middle, yes? The one with the cheekbones and the stubble? The one with the violet eyes?"

"You can tell all that from back here? Bloody hell, Will, yeah. That's the one we're looking at."

"His name is Luke. We...I...we were at uni together."

Jazz and Katie looked at me. They raised eyebrows at each other, exchanged one more look then picked me up bodily, hands under my armpits. Then they dragged me, feet flailing against the floor like Scooby-Doo in cartoon retreat, and dropped me outside the Sprout in time for me to be heartily sick down the nearest drain.

"Close one, that time." Jazz mopped his face theatrically and rearranged his hair over the collar of his coat. "You're really gonna have to get help y'know, Will."

"It wears off," I muttered indistinctly from around the large handkerchief I was wiping my mouth with. "It's only the first few times."

And there you have it. The essence of my little problem. Whenever I see a man I find halfway attractive, I start throwing up. Can't help it. It's happened ever since my teens. My doctor says it's stress-related. Oddly enough, it never happens at work—although that might be because Katie and I work in a department of the local paper where the only men are moribund and/or pensionable. But it means that, of necessity, all my friends are women. If you don't count Jazz and I've known him since primary school so I'm immune. Even though people tell me he's good looking, I can't see past the buck-toothed, toad-loving ten-year-old.

Another one of the unpleasant things about my problem—it can give rise to misunderstandings. Following a visit to a pantomime and a case of food poisoning, I had to spend six weeks convincing Jazz and Katie that I fancied neither of the Chuckle Brothers.

"Can we go back in now? It's freezing out here."

"Are you sure?" Katie raised an eyebrow. "I mean, it's been a rough day for you, Will. Wouldn't you rather go home?"

What, and miss the chance of ogling Luke on an empty stomach? "I'm fine. Honestly."

We tried to re-enter nonchalantly, pretending we'd only popped out for a breath of air. "Okay then, Willow. Spill the beans," Jazz said then slammed a hand over his mouth. "Sorry. I meant, fill us in. Details about this Luke, please, and I mean *details*." He waggled his eyebrows in a way suggestive of...well, actually just suggestive. Sometimes Jazz is such a *girl*. That's why we like him.

"There's really not much to say. He did some kind of science degree. I used to see him now and again hanging round the Union bar. He had a job in town, in a record shop, went out with wassername, you know, the girl that married thingy."

"Uh-huh. So *you* never went out with him."

"Um. No."

"But you wished you had?" Sometimes, for all his comical affectations, Jazz can be quite perceptive.

"Um."

"Willow." Katie frowned at me. "Is this the guy you had that enormous crush on? The one who played in that band that you made me go and see about fifty times? Used to be so skinny he made Jarvis Cocker look fat? That guy?"

Yes, Kate, I wanted to say. That guy. The man I lost sleep over, the man who haunted my dreams, who slid his hand down my thigh in my hottest fantasies. "Could be" was what I, in fact, said. "Looks a bit like him."

"Luke Fry." Katie glanced over again and clicked her fingers. "That's his name. He asked me out once, you know."

What! "You never told me that."

"Well, I knew how much you fancied him." The rest of the sentence went unsaid, but if it had been pronounced it would have contained words such as "never even noticed you were alive".

"Did you go?" Despite the churning of my stomach, I let my gaze roam over and rest on the back view of Luke Fry. He was still slim, though the scraggy body had filled out to be merely slender and, in contrast to his friends, he wore stonewashed jeans and a dark blue shirt. Flanked by the two suits, he looked like a rock star being minded by accountants.

"Ha. Did I, hell." Katie turned a thoughtful gaze my way. "Too bloody cocky for my liking. Anyway, I had Dan."

"And you still do." Jazz tapped his watch. "But only for another twenty seconds if you don't get home in a hurry. You told him you'd be back by five, remember?"

"Oh, shit." With much scrabbling around under the table for coat, bag and phone, Katie prepared to leave. "Hope to God he's remembered to pick up the twins. Last time he forgot and they were still at the nursery at twenty to six, like a couple of uncollected parcels. Oh, sod it, where's my phone? Look, I'll call

11

tonight, Wills, yes? Provided the little darlings go to bed all right. An afternoon with their father is usually enough to wind them up beyond all human understanding. If not, you'll be in tomorrow, all day?"

Sunday. Ah yes, tomorrow was Sunday. I'm sure Bridget Jones has pretty well covered the single thirty-something's Sunday angst, so I won't dwell on it here.

"Course. Love to Dan and the boys." But my eyes had swivelled of their own accord to the impeccably tailored back of Luke Fry. God, how I had wanted that man. You'd think, wouldn't you, that the intervening ten years should have wiped out at least some of that longing, the sheer emptiness I'd felt at the end of every day when he had once more failed to acknowledge so much as the space that I occupied. But, here I was, old enough to know better and still, God help me, *still* wishing he'd turn around, catch my eye and smile that particular smile.

"You okay, Will?" Jazz patted my arm. Owing to the enormous weight of silver rings he was wearing, it was like being caressed by a carthorse in full harness.

"Fine, Jazz. Look." My voice was shaking slightly. "I'd better be off home, too. I suspect a family conference is going to be thrown, now we've all found out what Granddad left us, so..." I kept my eyes stapled to his face. Why should I look at Luke Fry? Why should I even want to?

Jazz stared at me. Although he'd dyed his hair black to go with the whole undead thing, his eyebrows were still distressingly pale, giving him the appearance of an unfinished painting. "Sure you don't want to, I dunno, go clubbing or something? Catch a film?"

"Sorry, next time maybe? Only, you know what my family is like." I pulled my jacket on and backed towards the door, my face pink with the effort of not glancing over at the bar. "If you're at a loose end tomorrow, pop over. I'm not doing anything, as usual." I finished speaking, spun round to open the door and collided hard with another body.

There was a sudden smell of expensive cologne, an impression of firmness and the scratch of linen against my face. Then my mortification was completed by a hand under my elbow helping me upright until I could stare into the face of—

"I'm terribly sorry, wasn't looking. Hold on a moment. Don't I know you? Your face is really familiar. Give me a minute. It's Willow. Willow Cayton, isn't it? Good God, that's incredible. Do you remember me? Fry. Luke Fry? We were at university together?"

With deep breathing and an empty stomach, I could just about keep things down and under control, but I hoped he couldn't see the desperate clenching that was necessary. "Oh. Ah. Hello."

"Good grief, after all these years. You look wonderful, Willow. Absolutely..." and he left a pause, during which he looked me up and down quickly enough not to cause offence, but slowly enough to gratify my ego, "...fantastic."

"I...er." Now I was sure I had most of my bodily functions suppressed, I allowed myself to stare upwards and into his face. Oh. Oh, wow. I could *feel* my pupils dilating. I really needed Jazz to rush up, slap me and carry me away to the Land of the Sane. But the best I could hope for was that he'd stump up in his ridiculous shoes and want to be introduced. Jazz was barely ever within hailing distance of the World of Sanity. "Yes. I think I remember you." I dropped a shoulder in a shrug of assumed insouciance. "You were in a band."

"Fresh Fingers. Jeez, yeah, fancy you remembering that." Oh boy. His eyes really were clear violet. He still had

13

cheekbones like a hungry vampire and his hair was the slightly long, slightly curly blueprint of perfection it always had been. Shit. This man had been my mental benchmark for boyfriends for ten years and this was the first time he'd acknowledged my existence. "Well. What a coincidence, bumping into you like this. It's my first time back in York for, what, about eight months, and the first thing that happens is I meet up with someone I haven't seen for ten years. Amazing." His gaze floated up towards my face again, then glanced behind me. "Look, sorry, mustn't keep you. Your boyfriend is looking daggers at me and you're obviously in a hurry." He waved a casual hand (gorgeous, long musician's fingers, no wedding ring, we are talking Jude Law *at least*, casting-wise) at my jacket slung over my shoulder and half-turned away.

"He...it...that's Jazz. Not my. Er, he's not." I scrambled around in my brain for a coherent sentence. "It was nice to. Too. To see you again. Too."

"Hey, then, perhaps we could catch up sometime? I'd really like to find out what the old crowd's been getting up to."

"The old...oh, yes, right. I, I live in York so..." The "old crowd"? Either he'd forgotten that the old crowd had packed themselves so tightly around him that I'd metaphorically been stuck in the turnstiles, or he was mistaking me for someone else.

"You stayed in York? Cool. Here, give me your number." As I took the proffered paper and pen, I hoped he couldn't see my hand shaking. "Great. Thanks. I'll call soon, yeah?"

I could hardly breathe as I fell through the door he held open for me, and my treacherous stomach felt squeezed and heavy like a rubber knapsack full of leaking batteries. Slowly, carefully, I walked home, ignoring the bile which chattered away at the back of my teeth.

Chapter Two

My house used to belong to my parents, but they'd given it to me when they decided to go off on the longest hippy trail in recorded history. None of the others had wanted it. My sister OC and her husband lived in an old rectory (which Ash referred to persistently as The Old Rectum) in a village north of the city. Of my other siblings, Clay lived in Beijing, Bree had a flat over his bookbinding business in Harrogate and Ash, well, of all of us Ash had most inherited our parents' free spirit and tended towards no-fixed-abodeness. Although I gathered that an orderly queue had formed of people only too willing to provide him with a roof over his head and, most importantly, a mattress under his back.

I'd better get it off my chest now, before you meet him. Ash is not only my brother, but my twin. I hate, resent and adore him in roughly equal measures. He irritates me so much that it makes my head itch. He's mouthy, stroppy, sulky and permanently late—absolutely nothing like me. Really.

And then there's the name thing. Our parents, relentless children-of-nature that they are, had decided that they wanted four children to name after the four elements, Earth, Air, Water and Fire. Along in due course came Clay, Breeze, Oceana and Ash. I suppose it was no one's fault, more of a cosmic joke, that their last-born fire-child turned out to be child*ren*. They were a bit stumped when it came to naming me. OC apparently wanted me to be called Cinderella, but she *was* only two at the time. Then someone pointed out that Ash is also a tree and the rest, as they say, is played by Cameron Diaz.

As I turned into my street, I could tell they were all already here. Clay was staying with me until he flew back to China, and his little black hired SmartCar was parked neatly aligned with the front door. Bree's van was in front, OC had borrowed her husband Paddy's second car (a convertible BMW) and parked behind. Ash's current vehicle of choice, a 750cc Yamaha motorbike was corralled in my front garden, bridled with the weeds I hadn't had time to clear from the walls since summer.

They were all seated around the dining table and they were, as usual, arguing.

"I don't know what you've got to complain about, Clay, he's left me Booter and Snag, and what the hell am I supposed to do with a couple of smelly spaniels?" My sister patted her barely visible bump. "This is due in four months!"

"Complain? Oh, now why should I want to complain about being left an allotment on the outskirts of York when I live on a different bloody continent!" Clay shouted back. "What did he expect me to do, fly over twice a week to spray the cabbages?"

"No, but this is different, this is a baby." OC patted her stomach again as though Clay might have missed the point. "Dogs are all germy. Especially those two."

Ash wandered in from the kitchen at the same time as I entered from the hallway and we exchanged our trademark glare before sitting down. Ash had a bottle of wine and was drinking from it without benefit of a glass. He only did it because he knew how much it annoyed me. "Suppose you're happy with what Ganda left you." He pointed the neck of the bottle at me. "At least yours is fucking portable."

"Well, he always said it was lucky." I took the coffee which Clay passed me and smiled at Bree who was, as ever, sitting listening to the tirade.

"How can it be, for fuck's sake?" Ash waved the bottle now. "Tell me in which context it's lucky to carry your nose in a matchbox."

"You're only angry because he left you twelve pairs of rubber boots. You could always open your own fetish-wear shop."

There was a sound of throat clearing from across the table and we stopped quarrelling to await Bree's pronouncement. He rarely spoke, our brother. It was a family rumour that he hadn't uttered a single word until he was four and had then said "balloon angioplasty" and frightened our mother half to death.

"I think"—and Bree looked around at us all, with his mismatched eyes, one blue and one brown—"that we're just disappointed that Ganda didn't leave us any money. That's why we're bickering." Then, as though embarrassed that he'd spoken, he looked down at the table and let his long hair fall over his reddening face. He was a man who'd been born to the largely solitary career of bookbinding and found social interaction, of any kind, acutely painful. No wonder Ash tended to refer to him as "the oldest virgin in York". But he was clever, Bree, and astute. Disappointment was the real reason for this whole gathering of the clan.

"Ganda never had any money to leave, though," I said. "I should know."

They all turned to look at me. Even Bree.

"Yeah," Ash muttered. "We've kinda wondered about that. You were his favourite, you've got to admit, Will, and all he leaves you is a mouldy old body part?"

"Maybe"—heads swivelled again as Bree spoke—"he gave us what he did for a reason."

"I reckon he gave Clay that allotment so that he'd have something to come back to." I looked over at our eldest brother, fussily tidying up the fallen leaves of my spider plant on the window ledge. "You're always saying you'll come back to Yorkshire one day, aren't you? Perhaps he was making a point. This is where your roots are. It's the kind of terrible pun Ganda used to love."

There was a moment of silence. Then I blew my nose and OC rubbed her eyes with her sleeve like a child would. "But Booter and Snag? You have to admit, Wills, they are horrible, even for dogs."

I sensed the movement as three pairs of eyeballs turned towards me. I loved my sister, absolutely (although I'd never quite forgiven her for the Barbie incident when I was six), but her cleanliness and tidiness fetish drove all of us to want to run round her immaculate house wearing muddy Wellingtons. "Perhaps," I said carefully, "it was because you're the only one of us with the time and space for two spaniels." Plus looking after something other than yourself and the obnoxiously self-satisfied Paddy will be good practice, I prevented myself from adding. A well-placed kick under the table made sure that Ash didn't make the point either. Secretly I knew Ganda had thought OC was far too obsessive about her house and he would have delighted in the chaos the dogs would bring. He was probably up there now, chuckling down on our discomfiture.

Ash poked me with the wine bottle. "Okay, yeah, I can go with all that, and let's face it, who else would he have left his books to but Bree—but twelve pairs of waders? What did he expect me to do, take my friends fly-fishing?"

Since all Ash's friends thought that fresh air was a dangerous perversion, this was unlikely to be the case. I shrugged.

"Well, I've got to be going. Paddy will be home at half past six and I have no idea what I'm doing for dinner." OC aimed a quick kiss at my cheek. "Wills, why don't you come down next week for Sunday lunch? Paddy's got some kind of work do on the Saturday, but he'll be back by Sunday morning."

Oh goody, I thought, torn between my dislike of Sundays and my hatred of Paddy. "Sounds nice, thanks."

"And I'd better..." Bree stood up, too. "Bye." In contrast to OC's fussy farewell my brother simply melted into the darkness. Clay had taken all the used cups through to the kitchen, which left me with Ash.

"One less Sunday on your own," he remarked, handing me the bottle he'd been drinking from and picking up his helmet. Ash always had the knack of sensing my feelings. "You really must be down, Will, if you'd rather spend it with Mrs. Housewife and the Champion Prick."

"They're not so bad," I said. "And everyone else is off doing couply things. Not you and Bree, obviously, but Katie's got Dan and the boys, and Jazz's always at band rehearsals."

"I could introduce you to some of my friends." Ash crammed his bleach blond crop into his helmet and raised the visor.

"No thanks." I walked with him to the front garden where he wheeled the huge bike backwards out of the gateway, manoeuvring it carefully onto the road and throwing his leg casually over the saddle. "I'm not quite ready to be a fag hag just yet."

"They're not all gay."

"Name one who's not."

19

He snapped down his visor, ignited the engine and muttered something over the roar. I flicked him the finger and slapped his red-leathered shoulder and he rode off, waving a hand.

"Willow." Clay called from the doorway. "Phone for you."

I took the handset, presuming that Katie had successfully fought her twins into bed. "Hello." Then, noticing that Ash had decelerated to take the corner, I let out a wolf-whistle of the magnitude only truly mastered by someone with older brothers. It clearly penetrated his padded concentration, because he raised two fingers and cornered tightly, knee almost to the pavement.

The phone was silent in my ear for a second. After a moment a male voice said carefully, "Is that Willow?"

Oh shit. "Um. Yes, hello, Luke. Um. I was just..."

"Not interrupting anything, am I? I mean, is this a good time to call?"

I rushed back inside the house and carried the telephone upstairs. "No. Yes, I mean. It's fine." He had the loveliest voice, too, did I mention that? Softly spoken and with a gentle hint of an accent. (His father was Welsh and he'd grown up on Anglesey. Oh, I knew all there was to know about Luke Fry. I could have had him as a Mastermind subject).

"I thought you were talking to someone."

"Only my brother." Oh, be still my heaving stomach. "Actually, could you hold on for one second?" I flung the receiver down on my bed and rushed to the bathroom, teeth clenched, but in the event only managed a couple of retches over the sink before the feeling was gone—but this was still unusual, telephone conversations never affected me—"Hello, sorry about that."

"Look, Willow, I was wondering, if you're not busy or anything, we might have that get-together I was talking about? Maybe tomorrow? If it's not too short notice for you? I thought, perhaps, towards evening?"

Diffident. That in itself was cute. He obviously wasn't one of these drop everything-when I call types, just nicely deferential, but I'd played this game before and knew the moves. Never agree immediately, it makes you sound desperate. Pretend your life is so crammed with wonderful experiences that he'll have to join a queue for your attention.

"Well, I am a bit busy."

But he spoke again, almost over the top of me. "Only I heard you telling that guy in the bar that you weren't doing anything, so I thought, sorry? Did you say something?"

"Me? No, just clearing my throat."

We agreed to meet at the bar by the City Screen at seven, and he rang off, leaving me breathless and dizzy with the speed of it all. Luke Fry. Oh...my...God.

80CR

Later that evening when Katie rang me, having hog-wrestled the twins to bed and sent Dan out with his mates for a Saturday night restorative, I was knee-deep in my wardrobe looking for a suitable date dress.

"I don't want to look too tarty," I explained with the telephone clamped under my chin, both hands busy rattling through the rails. "But then I don't want to look as though I've got librarians in my ancestry either."

"What about your red dress?"

"Too much cleavage."

21

"The purple one?"

"Not enough." I sighed heavily and sluiced an armful of clothing onto the bed. "Honestly, Katie, my going-out clothes make me look like a cut-price hooker and my work clothes make me look like a geography teacher. Why has no one ever pointed this out to me before?"

Katie coughed. "Um, Will, you don't think you might be reading a bit too much into all this, do you? I mean, perhaps he really *does* want to chat about the old days."

"Listen, I would dress up to hear Luke Fry read the frigging weather forecast. I don't care *why* he wants me there, the fact is he wants to talk to me, and I owe it to my past self to at least feel not like a complete minger while he's doing it. Now. What about the white dress?"

"Bit bridal. You don't want to scare the bejasus out of the poor guy. And don't you think it's all a bit sudden? When he, ahem, I mean, you have to admit, Wills, he wasn't exactly receptive to your charms while we were at uni, was he?"

"Well, no, but I have changed quite a bit, Katie." You should have seen me back then. I was a dead ringer for an Afghan hound after a tumble-dry. And so shy, some days I could hardly bear to talk to myself.

"He recognised you though."

Yes, he had. After Katie hung up to go and have a long, uninterrupted piss, as she put it, I rooted through some of my memorabilia until I found the photograph. It had been taken by my then-boyfriend, a gangly streak of spots called Tom who I'd gone out with because he roadied for Fresh Fingers now and again. He'd been nice enough, quite pretty, too, but the spots had ensured that any attractive tendencies were submerged beneath layers of concealer. So my stomach contents had remained safely content and not avant-garde wall decoration.

The photograph showed Fresh Fingers, posing outside York Minster. The three other lads were sitting on the steps, but Luke had draped himself over the stonework of the south entrance, arm around a carved saint, and was glowering at the camera from under hair which must have made up half his bodyweight. On the far *far* left stood the figure of a girl, almost out of shot. She was wearing a gypsy skirt, a loose tartan top, hiking boots and an overlarge black duster coat. An unruly frizzle of blondish hair obscured her face but, yes, you've guessed it. Looking like an explosion in a charity shop, with split ends in need of extensive welding treatment, and so hopelessly, helplessly, heartbreakingly in love with Luke that a negative aura seemed to surround me, even in a photograph. I was like a black hole with bad hair.

I sighed and shoved the photo away. I was no longer that gauche, slightly podgy, badly assembled girl. No, I was a completely different gauche, badly assembled girl and the pudge had transformed into curves, the bad hair into a reasonably sleek shoulder-length style. I waltzed in front of the mirror, embracing a scarlet hook-and-eye-bodiced dress which made me look like a surgical incision, but was, at least, neither tarty nor sternly practical. It was therefore my choice of dress for Luke. Katie had to be pessimistic. She stood as the voice of reason to Jazz and my enthusiastic overreactions. But there was no escaping that not only had Luke recognised me, he'd rung almost straight away. In my book, that meant interest of a more than catching-up kind.

I yelled a "goodnight" to Clay and went to bed, hanging the dress up from my wardrobe door so that I would see it if I woke during the night, and remember that this Sunday was going to be different.

Chapter Three

Sunday evening saw me ready at least three times. I kept making vital errors of judgement, firstly on the makeup front (when I put on so much that if I'd turned round suddenly my expression would have remained where it was), then the shoes (the red dress demanded heels, the distance I had to walk demanded flats). Then, just before I left I realised that the slim skirt made my underwear visible from four counties, and had to discard my big pants for a thong. Which, combined with the heels (put comfort over appearance? Are you *mad*?) made my entry into the bar a mince-wince-fest.

Several people looked up at my entrance. None of them was Luke. I ordered myself a grapefruit juice and sat down by the windows overlooking the river, to give me something to gaze moodily at. I was working on a nice case of stood-up paranoia when there was a touch on my arm.

"Willow? Hello, sorry I'm a bit late."

He was folding away his mobile as he spoke and I noticed what a neat, up-to-date little thing it was, what beautifully casual trousers he was wearing, that his shirt looked freshly pressed. Anything rather than look at his face. Even so my stomach was doing its warm-up exercises.

"Oh, um, hello, Luke."

I managed to keep my eyes below neck-level, but any moment now I was going to have to look up, or be thought terminally rude. I flipped a peek up and straight back down again, hoping he wouldn't think I was fixated with his groin. Despite the supersonic speed of my glance, I noticed that he was smiling at me, holding a chair slightly away from the table.

"Is it all right?"

"Oh, yes, sorry, yes, do. Sit. Yes. Down," I burbled, moving my jacket, bag, the menu, rearranging my glass on the table, anything but look directly at him. "Have you had far to come?" Despite myself, my gaze treacherously slithered upwards and rested on the bridge of his exquisite nose. Oh dear God, but he was gorgeous.

"Not really. I'm staying in the Moat House across the river until I can find a place to buy." He indicated the ridiculously pricey breeze-block pile which loomed over the river like a concrete frown. "How about you? You said you live in York now?"

I struggled to reply coherently. All the while the windmills of my stomach ground and turned, and I fought that grapefruit juice to an internal standstill. We chatted a little more, about university life, the very few mutual friends we had had, including Tom who was now, apparently, a well-regarded glamour photographer. I hoped his spots had finally cleared up.

"I really fancied you back then, you know." I half-raised my hand to cover my mouth then realised that I didn't have to. Amazingly enough, the words had been spoken by Luke.

"You what?"

"Yeah. Christ, I'm still ashamed of myself, the way I used to follow you around. I was too shy to do anything about it, of course."

I coughed, and the grapefruit juice did a little celebratory dance. "Shy? Were you?" Shy? This man—I met his eye for the first time—this man had regularly taken most of his clothes off on stage in front of hundreds (another of the reasons why I had attended just about every gig Fresh Fingers gave) and been famous for his double-mooning trick in the Union bar.

"With girls, yes. Terrible. So. Sorry. I bet you're, what, married now?"

How did I play it without making myself sound like someone who only dated during total eclipses. "Not really. I mean, no. Not married. In fact"—inventing quickly so as not to sound less attractive than a case of typhoid—"I've recently split up with someone actually."

Luke let out a long sigh. "Yeah, know the feeling." We kind of stared at each other for a moment. At least, he stared and I clenched. "Bad breakup?"

"Pretty bad, yes. I caught him with someone else." *What happened there?* I mean, one minute we're in *True Confessions* mode, and the next I'm laying down the 'How I Dated a Serial Cheater' precredit sequence for Jeremy Kyle's new TV extravaganza.

"Shit happens, yeah? Was it the guy from last night? The one with the crazy eyes?"

Crazy eyes? Jazz? Although, now you come to mention it... "Look, do you mind if we don't talk about it? I'm still feeling..." a bit like a lying cow. Why hadn't I simply admitted that my last relationship of any kind had been six months ago? It had ended because I couldn't find model aircraft flying at all fascinating and we'd broken up *sotto voce* on his mother's couch during one of her feted scone and jelly teas. Answer—because I didn't want to look a total tit.

"Yeah, course. Sorry. So." Was it my imagination or did he really look quite sorry to drop the subject of my love life. "What do you usually do on a Sunday night?"

Oh, you know, the usual. There's the laundry. If I'm really feeling like pushing the boat out, I might pumice my feet. "Not a lot. Well, sometimes I sing in a band." Yeah, right. Sometimes, like when Jazz's band is completely desperate and even its last-ditch singer, the one with a squint and no boobs, has got dysentery.

"Hey, that's great. We'll have to get together sometime, have a jamming session." Luke leaned across the table and a waft of exclusive aftershave hit me in both nostrils. "I hope you don't think I'm some kind of weirdo, stalking girls I used to have a thing for. It was completely accidental, but I'd been thinking of you a lot. After so long away, I guess, all the old gang were on my mind."

A sudden, grim thought struck me. "You aren't confusing me with someone else, are you? I mean, we didn't really move in the same circles much." And every time I saw you, you completely ignored me. And I'd noted the words "used to".

Luke gave a grin so hot that diamonds would have gone runny. "Oh now, let me see. You had longer hair, love the new cut by the way, read English, rode around on a bright red bicycle like you thought you were at Cambridge, wore possibly the biggest boots on campus and hung out with Katie somebody."

"O'Connor," I supplied.

"Yeah. I was so crippled up with shyness that I could hardly even bear to look at you."

Now our eyes met properly. His gaze was level and steady. The stomach churning was becoming unignorable and my throat began to constrict, but the eye contact was luscious with

27

promise. If I ran for the toilets now I might never see a look like that again.

I made a quick decision—pulled my jacket towards me and pretended to be having a coughing fit, searching for a handkerchief whilst in reality I was throwing up the grapefruit juice into a pocket. It was short, sharp and nasty, but Luke thankfully didn't seem to notice.

"So then. Would you like another drink? Or"—he waved a hand at the crowded bar—"would you rather go on somewhere else?"

I would have toured the inner circles of hell to keep Luke Fry's attention focussed on me. I mean, how much would it take to make *you* vomit in your own pocket? We ended up walking through the darkening streets, and before I knew it, he was walking me home. It had started to rain at some unnoticed point and umbrellas were erupting around us. The streets shone, colours bleeding into one another as my eyes glazed with sheer happiness. Our heads bent together in introspective conversation, what with the twirling *parapluies*, the neon shimmer and the encroaching hush of Sunday night falling on a suburban area, it was like the closing scene of a Jeunet film. Luke bid me a decorous goodnight. (Although I noted, when he leaned against me to give me a peck on the cheek, the bulge in his trousers indicated that he would have gone for something a lot less chaste.) I did the cliché thing of closing the front door and leaning against it breathing heavily. This ended swiftly in a very unclichéd rush to the bathroom, where I stripped off all my clothes from which a slight smell of sick was beginning to waft.

Chapter Four

"No, I'm sorry, Luke. I can't make it tonight. I have a very important meeting to go to. Perhaps some other time?"

"What'cha muttering about? You goin' bloody loony on us then, Will, or what?"

I looked up from my computer screen to see Neil and Clive, the Tweedledum and Tweedledee of the front office, hanging over my desk. "What?"

"All this chuntering away to yerself, soundin' like you're as barmy as"—a gesture—"the Lady of the Lake down there."

The lady in question, namely Katie, could be heard singing a Killers track from the filing room, which was meant to be soundproof but wasn't because the boys hosted farting competitions in there and the tiles had fallen off. "No, I was just..."

But Neil and Clive had lost interest in me and my amusing foibles and were taking themselves off to annoy Katie. She gave much better value in the irritation stakes since she had a far wider vocabulary of expletives and, because of the twins, was always slightly sleep deprived.

"No, really, Luke," I continued to myself as I absentmindedly typed in the wording for a badly written advertisement. "I am so *terribly* busy. Maybe next month, sometime." And then the telephone rang, making me jump. "Hello, *York Echo*, how can I help you?"

"You can let me take you out for dinner tonight."

"Luke?"

"Sorry, yes. But if it makes it any better, I'm covering for Brad Pitt."

I laughed out loud without thinking, and the rumpus from the filing room stopped. "Bloody 'ell, that's it. She's laughing to 'erself now," I heard Clive mutter.

"Tonight? Are you sure?" I lowered my voice to a semi-whisper.

"Now, let me see, if I move Fearne Cotton to Thursday and put Cat Deeley on hold until next week—yes, Willow, I'm sure. I'll pick you up at seven thirty, okay? I mean, will that be all right?"

I agreed, I must have done, because the next thing I knew the tiny office was full of Neil and Clive and their body odour, with Katie elbowing her way past the lot of them shrieking, "Have you got a date?"

Neil shook his head. "Fuck me, about time." Neil and Clive didn't know about my little problem with men, you see. Oddly enough, I was never troubled in the digestive department by either of them, my tastes running to men whose neck measurements are a fraction of their IQs rather than double it. "Tasty bit like you shouldn't be moping about on 'er own. Tell 'er, Clive."

"Yer. 'S right."

Morecambe and Wise they weren't. When they left, I brought Katie up to speed on the current Luke situation. Obviously she'd had a blow-by-blow breakdown last night when

I'd got in, plus a military-style debriefing over the coffee machine this morning, but I was always up for another round.

"Whoa, two nights in a row? He *must* be keen." Katie sounded almost wistful. "He didn't, um, he didn't remember me at all, did he, Will?"

"We didn't really talk about university much," I lied. Luke had failed to remember anything about Katie apart from the fact that she'd been my friend, until I'd half-jokingly reminded him that he'd asked her out once.

Katie carried on. "I mean, he didn't *seem* shy. Not when he chatted me up. Seemed perfectly at ease, actually. You know, cocksure, like he knew exactly what he was doing."

I loved Katie dearly. As she always said, we had far too much dirt on each other to ever be enemies. So I didn't tell her what Luke had told me. He'd been part of a group of science students who looked down on us arts-and-humanities types and he was too shy to go against peer pressure by chatting me up. One night, however, he'd got raving drunk and had somehow ended up asking Katie out in the hopes that she'd introduce us. Telling Katie he'd only talked to her because he was drunk would go against the whole spirit of sisterhood. Plus, she might hit me.

"Where's he taking you?" Definitely wistful now. Poor Katie. Since the birth of the twins, she and Dan regarded putting the wheelie bin into the driveway as an evening out.

"No idea. He didn't say. I'd better not wear the red dress again."

Katie and I looked at each other. "This might be a case," she said, portentously.

"For the black chiffon!" I finished. Demure at the front, but low cut at the back, it somehow managed to say "I'm pure and untouched" and yet growl "come and get me, big boy". "As long

31

as he wants to take me somewhere reasonably grand. I really can't go into Burger King, not without knickers."

"Well, he's got cash, hasn't he? What was it you said he did, something to do with classic cars?"

"Yes, he and his brother have got a car-import business, bringing classic cars from all over the world. Luke's been in the States for the last year, setting up a franchise in Boston. His brother's out there now sorting it out. They've got another one in Milan and Luke wants to open one up here in York. He's come to check out the competition, look at the market, plus he wants to buy a house here in the city." The words "and settle down" hung in the air, large enough to bang your head on.

"Sounds perfect." Katie picked up another armful of potential filing. "But make sure he takes you somewhere really nice. You deserve it, Will—you really do."

"Thanks." I turned back to my screen with a coy smile to myself. Yes, I *did* deserve it. I deserved Luke Fry and his sexy violet eyes, his beautiful hands and his lovely pert bum. I felt as though I'd been on hold for the last ten years, marking time with nearly-good-enough boyfriends, as if I knew that one day Luke would come back and claim me.

ဆၟ

The illusion of perfection continued into the evening. Luke picked me up in a black BMW at seven thirty on the dot, drove me confidently down a confusing maze of streets whilst telling me how good I looked, and pulled up outside a country house which could have made a living doubling for Windsor Castle.

"Through here, Willow." Luke placed his hand on the small of my back to guide me into a crystal-and-candelabra-filled room. For a moment his hand lingered almost imperceptibly on my pantless buttock and I was sure that it shook slightly. His hand, I mean, not my buttock.

Luke ordered for both of us, in impeccable French (mine is better, but I was taught languages by a drunken ex-Madame from Marseille. Thank my parents), then raised his glass in a toast. "To starting again; it may have taken me ten years to get you here, but I'm bloody glad I made it at last." We'd just taken a first sip when there was an outburst of tiny, tinny music, as though an ice-cream van had driven into the plush hallway and was plying its wares outside the cloakroom. "Bugger." Luke fished in his pockets. "I know it's bad form to leave it switched on, but, ah." With a deft finger he located the phone, sprang it open and glanced at the caller display. "Oh, *shit*."

I stared at the tablecloth, tracing the damask pattern with a fingernail. "It's fine, Luke. Take the call. Our food won't be here for a bit anyhow."

Luke chewed his lip, gazing down at the screen of his phone. People were starting to look. "It's not important."

"It could be though."

"No. It's not." Sudden, definitive. In one swift movement of his hands, as though he were wringing the neck of a troublesome chicken, he turned the phone off and thrust it back into the deep recesses of his pocket. "Business, that's all. James, probably wanting to twitter on about some new deal he's got going down." Luke turned his full smile on me. "He'll be horrified when I tell him that he interrupted my date with the woman I've been thinking about for the last ten years."

"Have you? Really?"

"Really." His hand reached across the tabletop, took mine easily, naturally, as though this was date seventy-five, not number two. "Willow, I—"

"Mr. Fry, sir." Over Luke's left shoulder appeared a man so generically waiter that I couldn't have picked him out of a line-up. Even if all the other linees had been seven-feet tall, dreadlocked and covered in tattoos. "You have a telephone call, sir."

"Me?"

"Yes, sir. In the foyer, sir, if you would like to follow me."

Luke flicked me an apologetic glance as he followed, offering me a shrug and comedy-raised eyebrows. I used his absence to give the menu a quick once-over. This was one of those places where they look as though they'll demand your first-born if you can't pay the bill. I thought that I must recommend it to Katie. She'd gladly hand over both her first-borns for a meal she didn't have to wash-up after. The waiter topped up my wine again and shortly afterwards Luke was back.

"I am *so* sorry, Willow." He genuinely looked it. His mouth was drawn down into a tight line, his skin furrowed across his forehead. "It was just James being a complete pillock about some figures, that's all. It could have waited until tomorrow, but he's a bit of an old woman when it comes to the accounts."

"Well, it must be hard when you're running on different time zones. Must be, what, early afternoon in Boston?"

Luke flashed me an odd look, then shook his hair back and took my hand again across the table. "Anyway. Where were we? I believe I was telling you how great it is to have met up with you, having spent the last decade running through all those conversations we should have had, if only I'd had the guts to ask you out."

As the evening continued, we fell into many of those conversations. Life stories were exchanged, or at least, edited highlights were bandied around. I might have talked up my

English degree a trifle, and I didn't let on that I *knew* Luke was skating over the surface of the truth when he told me his mother had died and left his father to bring up James and himself. As I think I told you earlier, I knew an *enormous* amount about the young Luke Fry, and the whisper had been that his mother had run off to Amsterdam with an Egyptian nude deep-sea diver.

And, do you know the best part? I was only sick once. Between starter and main course, which was even better because I would have hated to have wasted those scallops—they were delicious. I made it to the Ladies in decorous time, pretending I needed to check my makeup. God, could things get any better?

"Goodnight, Willow. I hope you don't mind me not coming in or anything, but I really ought to go and call James, make sure he's over his panic." The BMW pulled up outside my house and Luke leaned across me to open the door.

"No, of course." I went to slide off the leather seat, but he stopped me with one hand on my shoulder.

"I wanted to..." Long fingers tipped my face towards him, lips shaped like the most delectable dessert descended on mine. I closed my eyes and lost myself totally in the elastic kiss. "See you tomorrow, Will," he whispered.

Did I say things couldn't get any better?

Chapter Five

"He sounds a bit iffy to me." Jazz cradled a pint and looked up at me over his Guinness moustache.

"Why? Because he wants to go out with Willow? Why does that make him 'iffy'?" Katie leaped to my defence.

"Oh, I dunno. He just sounds a bit, full on, yeah?"

Now, before you start getting ideas, Jazz doesn't think of me in that way, if you know what I mean. We did have one *extremely embarrassing* moment way back, when we briefly entertained the notion of going out together as more than mates. But that was in the days when we both wore advanced dental appliances, he was still called Jasper, and our combined puppy fat could have built a litter of Great Danes. Since then we have been happy to be friends and give one another the uncensored version of the truth about our chosen romantic partners. Katie actually thinks Jazz fancies my sister, but I like him too much to hope this is the case.

"I mean, you only met him last week and this is the first time we've been able to get you out for a drink." Jazz mouthed another swirl of beer. "I tried to ring you last night and there was no answer."

I'd heard the phone ringing as Luke and I had fallen, giggly and entwined, through the front door, but I'd been a little bit otherwise engaged. "What did you want?"

"Another pint, please, Will, if you're offering."

"Sod." But I went to the bar anyway. It was nice to be drinking with the gang again. "Why did you ring, then?" I asked as I got back.

"Only wondering if you'd be free to sing on Sunday night. We've got a short-notice gig in the Basement Bar."

"But isn't there anyone else?"

"Nah. Big Rosie's off down to Devon for the weekend, won't be back."

"Go on, Will, you haven't sung for ages." Katie leaned forward at me drunkenly. "And, I mean, Luke sounds lovely and everything but"—a quick glance to Jazz for support—"you still need to do stuff on your own."

There was a slow-spreading warmth inside me that had nothing to do with the rapidly ingested beer. Luke had promised to come to lunch at OC's on Sunday. If I had a booking in the evening, he might stay on and watch the band (in my imagination I was shining in the spotlight already) and then, maybe, I might be able to persuade him to stay overnight.

Katie noticed my slight frown. "Wassup, Wills?"

"No, nothing, really. Just wondering, when you and Dan got together, how long was it before you went to bed? Together, I mean, obviously."

Jazz gave a smutty snigger. "About twenty minutes I should think."

"You know, Jazz, not everyone is as sex-obsessed as you." Katie drained her glass. "It was, let me see, we went out on the..." Her lips moved and I felt better. I'd begun to wonder. Was it me? I fancied Luke so much that it was driving me crazy. We'd kissed, quite a lot, and he showed every sign of enjoying it, if you know what I mean. But there had been no attempts on his part to take things any further. I was sure he wasn't gay (see my earlier comment), and from things he'd told me about previous relationships I didn't think he was in thrall to any religious save-it-for-marriage cults. So, *was* it me? "Seventeen hours."

"Does this mean that you and Wonder Boy haven't done the thing yet?" Jazz shuffled his feet in barely suppressed excitement. "Willow Cayton, you have definitely lost your mojo."

"Mojo? Those are little sweets, aren't they?"

"Your 'thing', you know. Your 'it'."

Katie and I looked at one another. "He's so obnoxious when he's pissed," she said. "And don't ask me to take him home. He's got his Frankenstein remedial boots on again. Couldn't pick him up with a forklift."

"Nah, we could just leave him here."

But Jazz unfolded himself to his full, not inconsiderable height and peered down at us. "I shall make my way home under my own sht...steam, thank you, ladies." He drained his glass. "Willow, I will meet you at four in the Basement Bar for a soundcheck on Sunday."

"That's tomorrow, Jazz."

"Sho kind to remind me. Yes. Tomorrow." Gathering his dignity around him, which stretched it pretty tightly, he stalked from the bar.

"He looks like a clothes peg from Castle Dracula," Katie remarked. "But, pissed as he might be, he has a point. Are you and the delicious Mr. Fry not yet making the beast with two backs?"

"We're taking it slowly. After all, we've waited ten years, a few more days won't kill us."

"All right, no need to be defensive." Katie emptied her glass. "Well, better go. Meeting Dan in half an hour, we're off to the pictures. His mum is having the twins for the afternoon. First time in three years."

"Great. What are you going to see?"

"The way I feel, the insides of my eyelids comes top of the list, followed by the contents of Dan's trousers. Anyway. Take care, Will."

Once Katie and Jazz had gone, I felt suddenly flat. Saturday afternoon. Two o'clock, to be precise, and the rest of the day and evening stretched ahead of me as empty as oh, I don't know. Name me something emptier than the prospect of a Saturday night alone with the monotonous silence broken only by my beery pizza burps and early evening TV. Luke had apologised profusely, but said he had to work on Saturday—promised to be at my house in time to drive us out to OC's for lunch on Sunday, so what was my problem? I had, as Jazz so kindly pointed out, seen him every night this week.

I wandered home, couldn't think of anything else to do. British Summertime had officially started last week, so it was raining and cold. Clay had flown back to Beijing so there would be no one to share a takeaway. God, I was miserable. The misery deepened when I turned into my street and saw Ash perched across his bike in full gear, with his helmet on his lap, swinging one foot in the running gutter and obviously waiting for me. Saturday, and *Ash* didn't have a date? I ducked in case the Apocalypse was creeping up behind me.

"Hey."

"What?" I fumbled sullenly in my bag for the key.

"No, nothing. I thought...you doing anything tonight?"

I flashed him a quick look. But apart from his helmet-hair, he looked normal. For Ash. "It's not like you to ask that. What's happened?"

"Happened? Nothing." Ash pushed past me in the hallway and flung himself down full-length on the chesterfield. Leather met leather with a creaking like a boned corset under pressure. "I just wondered if, hell, I've got someone I'd like you to meet, all right?"

I paused on my way through to the kitchen, watching Ash pose. There was definitely something different about him today. "You've taken all your piercings out," I realised suddenly.

"Well, not *all* of them." He grinned up at me. "Only the ones you can see."

I grimaced. I'd been treated, along with Jazz and Katie, to a blow-by-blow account of the agonies of Ash's Prince Albert. (Jazz still couldn't look Ash in the face without tears of sympathy welling up.) "Thanks. I'll have to go and lie down in a dark room to expunge that particular mental image. So, what's happening with losing all the metal? Afraid you were going to fall through the earth's crust?"

Ash shrugged a skinny shoulder. "He doesn't like...look, I just fancied a change. You coming, or what?"

"How far?"

"Up onto the moors. Thirty miles, no more."

"All right then, if you promise to go slowly. You know I hate riding pillion. Oh and I'd better get my gear on, hadn't I."

I heard him snort as I went upstairs. "Yeah! You'd freeze your howdy-doody off in that skirt and I'll be fucked if someone sees me with a girl on the back of the bike. They'll think I've gone straight, and whoops goes my reputation up the PVC Emporium."

Since Ash had been as gay as a neon jelly-baby all his life, this was highly unlikely to be the case. I wrestled myself into a set of his old leathers, popped my helmet out of its box (which always, satisfyingly, reminded me of squeezing a blackhead) and galumphed down the stairs. Ash has skinnier legs than me, which means I can't bend my knees in his trousers and have to walk like I've wet myself. Ash stared.

"Fuck off, you've lost weight, bitch."

"You think?" I did a smug twirl. Going out with Luke was obviously good for me. Good as it might be, I didn't yet feel I could unveil him as a full boyfriend to Ash (who would only ask, with painful accuracy, why the hell he wasn't taking me out on a Saturday night if he was such a catch) or OC (who had merely been told that I was bringing a friend to lunch tomorrow). Fate was, in my experience, not something to be tempted. Rather like Luke then, I thought sourly.

"You'll be prettier than me soon."

"Shut *up*, Ash. Honestly, if you weren't my brother."

"You'd be happy, I know."

Ash and I get on a whole lot better when no one else is there. It's like we don't have to compete for attention anymore. We're the classic case of the observer changing the thing observed.

"Piss off and start the bike." I checked my mobile to make sure Luke hadn't had a change of heart and decided to call me after all. But he hadn't, and so I mounted up behind Ash and wound my arms around his ribcage. So it wasn't quite how I'd envisaged spending Saturday night, but right now it beat the alternatives.

Chapter Six

It was a tiny, hidden valley in the depths of the moors. Great grey drifts of heather heaped themselves like breaking seas at the base of dry-stone walls. The walls combed up the sides of the valley, dividing it into small squares each of which held about half a dozen huddled sheep. "Come on." Ash propped the bike up on its stand and began to lead the way down a tiny lane between two of the walls, carefully stepping over the scatterings of sheep dung.

"Where are we going?"

"You'll see."

Down the trackway we filed, it being too narrow to walk side-by-side. I followed Ash gloomily, wondering exactly what I'd let myself in for. The whole place had an ominous air. Trees overhung the path, making it spookily dark although I couldn't imagine any ghost being desperate enough to hang around here. Except possibly the earthbound spirit of some recalcitrant farm animal.

"Ash?"

"Shh. Nearly there."

"Oh. Wow." The way suddenly widened, throwing up the view of a small whitewashed house perched on the bank of a stream which was tickling its unassuming way between the buttocks of the hills. Green meadows dotted with early white flowers surrounded the house and a goat was grazing, tied to an apple tree outside a shed.

"Who the hell are we visiting? Heidi?"

"Cute, isn't it? Come on." Ash grabbed my hand and we ran down across the fields towards the dinky dwelling, me suppressing a desire to yodel. Around the back we raced, through a little cobbled yard, and on through a door standing open, into the house itself.

It was hideously dark in contrast to the daylight outside and I stopped dead. "It smells funny."

"Yeah," said a voice I didn't recognise. "What do you reckon?"

I sniffed. "Mushrooms?"

"Dry rot," the voice said, glumly. "Or possibly wet rot. Some kind of fungal thing. Knowing my luck the place will probably turn out to have athlete's foot as well."

"Willow. This is Cal." Ash moved away so that a little more light filtered in through the doorway.

There was a note in his voice that I recognised. Pride and a touch of warning, plus a warmth that was usually lacking in my twin. Oh God, Ash was in love.

"Hi, Cal." Outside, the sun suddenly broke through the clouds and bounced off the internal whitewash, revealing the owner of the glum voice in a halo of reflected light. I widened my eyes.

"Hello, Willow."

Certainly a very definite step up from Ash's usual muscle-bound types, I thought. The initial impression was of eyes—huge, brown eyes in a pale face, unshaven and a bit hollowed around the cheeks. The second impression—as he moved forward to shake my hand was "phwoar". He had the looks of a poet who's spent too long staring into the abyss; long dark hair and lines of stress around the mouth. Luckily, as ever when meeting my brother's boyfriends, I had no inclination to vomit on him. Dunno why, but something inside tells me that, however gorgeous, it's not for me and my stomach remains steady. "Nice place you've got here."

"It could be. Would you like a tour?"

"Go ahead, show Will round. I'll make some tea, yeah?"

What, my ludicrously undomesticated brother making tea? "Boiling water. From a kettle," I called, as Ash disappeared into the recesses of the dark.

"Ha. Bitch."

Cal stood smiling curiously at me. "You're very pretty," he said, disarmingly. "Ash didn't tell me."

"Um, thank you," I stammered. I actually felt a bit windswept from the journey over and kept catching sight of a wayward piece of hair sticking out at right angles above my left ear. "Have you known Ash long?"

"'Bout three years." Cal moved forward towards a door which he threw open to reveal a large room, and I could see properly. See, for example, that he was using a stick. See also that he moved in a lurch as though one leg was longer than the other. I bit my lip.

"Living room. Dining room at the back. Over that side of the house is the kitchen and study, which is actually the old walk-in larder. Upstairs"—the stick gestured at the ceiling—"there's two bedrooms and a bathroom so disgusting I'd advise you to pee in the field. I haven't found out where it flushes to, but I bet *that's* not going to be good news."

I half-smiled but was finding it hard to tell whether this man was joking or not. He had a straight face and delivered his words sharply, as though he wasn't used to talking to strangers.

"Um, Cal."

"Willow."

"Why am I here?"

"Ash wanted to bring you. He thought we should meet." Cal shuffled himself around to face me. "And I'm glad we have."

Okay, I had to get this question out of the way, whilst we were still relative strangers. It would be a lot more awkward if his relationship with Ash really took off and I was still skirting around the topic. "What's the matter with your leg?"

Cal tipped his head on one side. "War wound," he said, deadpan. "Got shot up in '45, had to put the old crate down behind enemy lines. All very hush-hush, donchaknow." Still no trace of humour, but a slight brittleness which told me this was his standard reply, a running gag to keep people from intruding. It made me wince on his behalf.

"You don't look old enough to have fought in the war," I replied in kind. If he wanted his privacy, he had nothing to fear from me.

"Oil of Olay, m'dear. Fantastic stuff. I'm actually a hundred and three." I couldn't help myself, and snorted back a laugh. Cal's face brightened. "That's better. You shouldn't take me seriously. And you're even prettier when you smile."

Despite knowing he was Ash's, despite his clearly doing his best to keep me at arm's length as far as personal questions were concerned, and despite the fact that I'd only just met him, I blushed. As I was about to say something witty and snappy and devastating, Ash bounced back into the room with three mugs of something which looked almost like tea.

"Ash, you're going to make someone a wonderful wife." Cal, still deadpan, took his mug. "Can you iron?"

Now it was Ash's turn to blush. I looked over my tea at the pair of them, Ash skinny in his leathers, hair ruthlessly spiked into a bleached Number 2, and Cal unkempt in a check shirt and jeans, tall, thin and dark, dark, dark. Talk about an odd couple.

"Look, I really should be getting back." I swallowed my tea scalding.

"Are you still having trouble with your laptop?" Cal asked out of nowhere.

"What? Laptop? Oh, yeah, loose connection or something. Bloody stupid machines. Better off with a piece of paper and a slide rule."

Cal looked at Ash. "Well, that's me Luddite-ed out of a job."

"Cal's a computer consultant," Ash explained, whilst I watched Cal being quietly amused. "That's why I told him about your laptop. Thought you might want him to take a look at it for you."

"Oh. Sorry. About the slide-rule thing. Obviously. Couldn't, um, do spread sheets with a slide rule."

"Only I could pick it up from you and drop it round to Cal's tomorrow." Ash's voice had a pleading tone. Oh-ho, I thought, still at the looking-for-every-opportunity-to-drop-in stage, eh?

"No, it's too far to bike all the way over here again just for my laptop."

"No, it's fine. Cal lives in York. Works from home." Normally if I'd asked Ash for a favour such as, say, picking up my dry-cleaning you'd have thought I'd asked him to mud-wrestle Madonna, but now it seemed he couldn't do enough.

"I just inherited this place," Cal said calmly, as though the intimated early-morning presence of a sex-crazed Ash was a well-known occupational hazard to computer consultants. Perhaps he was looking forward to it. "My great aunt died. Well, obviously. Inheriting from the living is something of an extreme sport, I should imagine. I used to spend summer holidays here and she knew I loved the place, so." A little catch in his voice there. Again, that touch of vulnerability, quickly glossed over. I was beginning to see what Ash saw in Cal—apart from his total shaggability of course.

"My grandfather died, too," I found myself saying. "He left me his nose." And then I realised that this was the first time I'd actually said it aloud. "My grandfather died," I said again. I hadn't even managed to say it to Luke. It was almost as though if I didn't say it, it hadn't happened.

Cal nodded. "Takes a while to get used to, doesn't it? Almost like they've been around so long, they can't just *stop* being. Maybe they have to, kind of, wear away in our heads."

On the ride home, tucked down low to avoid the pull of the wind, I thought about this. Had Ganda left me his bodily remnant to ensure that he never "wore away in my head"? Or as a good-luck charm? He'd always sworn that, after the accident which had removed said nose, his luck had changed. Nothing that made his fortune, but enough to pay for materials, workspace, horrible baggy tartan trousers—all the sort of things that are necessary to mad inventors. All right, yes I had to admit it. Much as I had loved...*still loved* Ganda, much as I had enjoyed being his favoured grandchild and helping him with his creations, I had known all the time that he was completely barking. And look at his legacies. A ton of dusty books, a pile of mouldering rubber boots, half an acre of sandy soil and two spaniels?

Once home, I fetched the matchbox from the cupboard and pulled open the inner tray. There lay the nose in question, looking even more mummified than I remembered, round with a dividing crease like Tom Thumb's backside.

"Honestly, Ganda," I said. "What were you *thinking*?" My grandfather had known he was dying, had a few weeks warning to get his affairs in order, so it hadn't been a mad whim. I closed the tray up. The nose was padded in place with a wad of paper so it barely moved. "Maybe I'm supposed to wish on it. Like a star." I was speaking aloud, glad that there was no one to overhear. Wishing on a star is pathetic enough, wishing on your dead grandfather's nasal organ has to border on the pathological. "All right." I shook the box again. "I wish...I wish..." A mistimed snatch of my fingers and the inner tray of the matchbox flew free, sailed across the kitchen and deposited Ganda's nose deftly into the plughole of the sink. It caught on the trap for a moment before my careful attempt to pry it free with my fingernails sent it plunging into the cabbage-scented depths of the U-bend.

As I sprawled under the sink attempting to unscrew the pipe, I found the paper wadding from the matchbox tray. It was thicker than the tissue paper I had thought stuffed the box, and its flight had caused it to spread half-open revealing the lettering which covered one side. I wiped my hands on my legs and ironed the paper down on the floor. The words I read sent me flying to the phone to call Katie, all thoughts of the renegade nose forgotten.

Chapter Seven

Sunday can best be described as a contained disaster. You know those days when, through nobody's fault, you are desperate to be somewhere else but are forced to go on with a kind of ritual? Katie said that summed up her wedding day to a T. I couldn't tell Luke or OC what I'd discovered hidden in the matchbox, not yet. Not until, well, not yet. In consequence I was a bit distracted. OC was cross with Paddy who hadn't yet returned home from his conference, which left poor Luke the only one of us fit to hold a civilised conversation. But, on the plus side, he really hit it off with my sister who, when she'd stopped clutching her bump and complaining that Paddy's absence was causing her Braxton-Hicks contractions, hissed to me over the sprouts, "Don't let this one get away, Wills."

"What do you suggest, a high-pressure containment field?"

"You know what you're like with men. They're there one minute and gone the next."

"I don't exactly release them into the wild."

OC made a face and passed Luke the potatoes. "Will never has much luck with men," she said.

"What *is* this? Just because Sophie and Iain aren't here, you feel that you have to go all parental on me? For God's sake, OC, next thing you're going to be showing him photos of me having my nappy changed."

(Sophie and Iain are Mum and Dad. They brought us up to call them by their given names. Sickening, isn't it? I blame the parents.)

Under the table, Luke squeezed my knee. "Well, I'm not going anywhere."

I had to dash into the garden room and be sick. I blamed it on the dogs.

And then it was Sunday night and I was on stage, wearing the band uniform black and white, belting out eighties' classics, feeling all warm and powerful with my boys behind me (best place for Jazz who, in defiance of the whole androgynous-Goth thing, was growing a goatee and therefore looked like a penguin with its dinner round its mouth) and Luke somewhere in the dark audience in front of me. I mean, *forget* releasing an album and have it enter straight at number one, this was what I was in music for.

We finished with "Do You Really Want To Hurt Me?" and exited to applause. Luke was waiting for me. "Will you be all right to get home?"

"Yes, in a bit. Got to give the lads a hand with the equipment first."

"Oh. Right. Good." Then he gave me a swift kiss on the cheek. "I'll see you tomorrow then. About eight?" Without waiting for an answer, he was gone. I stood and gawped after him, watching his trendily cut blond hair as it walked off out of the bar. "But," I muttered to myself, "but." What had I done? What had gone wrong? All right, so I'd not actually got round to asking if he'd stay over, but, was it me? Did I look, in my white lacy top, less like a celebrity and more like a set of net curtains? Did the black and white ensemble make him think of some ill-advised liaison with a waitress? Or a Friesian cow?

Sadly I began helping the band pack away their instruments, coil wires and box amps.

"Wonder Boy gone then, has he?" Jazz appeared at my elbow, parts of his keyboard over his shoulder.

I thought about lying, but not seriously. I might manage to get away with fibbing to Jazz, but Katie would get the truth out of me in seconds. "He had to go." I drooped, but rallied quickly. "He'll have loads of work to get on with. He and his brother have found some premises and they're dead keen to start shipping some cars in."

"Has he shagged you yet?"

"Ah, this will be the famous Jazz tact and diplomacy." I half-heartedly rolled some wire in my hands, before Bob, the bass player, snatched it off me.

"He hasn't then. Only three reasons I can think of, he's married, he's gay, or he could be gay *and* married I suppose, or he belongs to some religious sect that doesn't believe in sex and thinks everyone should be smooth plastic below the waist. You know, like Action Man and Gareth Gates."

"Action Man and Gareth Gates? Members of a religious sect?" I was baffled.

"Smooth plastic. Well, nearly smooth, just this kind of seam thing."

"You're weird, Jazz."

"You're sex-starved. I know which I'd rather be." With that he hefted his synth into his arms and walked off. I think he might have been grinning, but that could have been his goatee slipping.

৪৩

Date: Monday morning. Time: Nine fifteen. Place: Council offices—Roads department. I know, not exactly glamorous, not exactly *Mission Impossible*, but what were you expecting? If you're looking for people jumping out of aeroplanes and defusing bombs, you are *so* in the wrong place.

I was sitting on a badly designed chair, swinging my legs. Katie had gone in search of a coffee machine, and when the door opened, I thought it must be her coming back. I'd ordered a Kit Kat and was beginning to pine.

But it wasn't Katie. It was a woman I vaguely recognised, carrying a pile of buff files, which she lowered onto the desk and turned, with an expression which only missed being loathing because she didn't have the right kind of face for it. She had one of those pretty-pretty insipid faces which start off when they're young being peaches and cream, but rapidly degenerate into whisky and ginger.

"Oh my God, it's Nadine, isn't it? Nadine Mitchell?" The face stared back. Although she showed no sign of acknowledgment, I had the feeling she recognised me. "You were up at York with Katie and I. We did English and you were doing Drama. Remember that performance of *The Crucible*? When everyone got riotously drunk and Tituba fell off the stage?" Still absolutely nothing. Behind me Katie came back in.

"Oh! Hello, Nadine. I haven't seen you since that night at St. John's. Did that poor guy ever get his wig back, do you know?"

To my horror, Nadine's eyes were suddenly overflowing. For a couple of seconds, she stared at Katie and I, tears making canal tracks through her stiff makeup, then she flung an arm against the pile of filing and shot out of the office making little snuffling noises.

"Whoa, distressed pig alert." Katie handed me the long-overdue Kit Kat.

A woman came into the room and eyed us suspiciously, as though she suspected us of having poked Nadine until she cried, in some bizarre local-government testing experiment. "Miss Cayton?"

"That's me."

"My name is Vivienne Parry. I apologise for Nadine. She's been a little unwell lately. Very highly strung. Now, what can I do for you?"

I unfolded my paper. "My grandfather, Mr. Edward Cayton, he left me this, in his will." I pushed the crinkled sheet forward. "I was wondering, can you tell me what it's about?"

Vivienne Parry, who was the approximate shape and colour of a cottage loaf, bent her head over the page, then reached behind her into the filing pile and pulled out one of the card files. On it was my grandfather's name, crossed out, and mine written over the top. She opened the file.

"Again, I can only apologise," she said. "Nadine has typed up the letter, but clearly forgotten to post it to you. Here, maybe this will answer your queries."

Together Katie and I hunched over the headed paper, scanning and then reading the words properly, letting them sink in. After the third time, Katie let out a little squeal.

"God, Will, looks like you're a rich bitch!"

I couldn't get the words to settle in my head. As soon as I thought I'd made sense of them, another paragraph would come along and panic them all into the air again, whirling and twittering. "I think it says that I *could* be. Eventually. When they finish testing?"

The gist, because I know you'll be agog to find out, was this. My grandfather had patented a new form of road-surfacing material. It was simple, easy to produce and, above all considerations for local councils, cheap. As far as I could tell from the associated paperwork, it seemed to consist of a substance like sequins being introduced to the tarmac before laying, which caused the entire road to reflect oncoming headlights like millions of tiny cats' eyes. The council was currently testing the material, and was prepared to pay an initial sum of (and this was where my eyes swam around) fifty thousand pounds. Upon successful completion of said testing, they would pay an additional four hundred and fifty thousand pounds for the rights to produce and market the material. Preliminary testing, continued the letter, looked extremely encouraging, with night visibility on treated surfaces being increased by up to thirty-five percent.

"Gah," went my mouth.

"This is soooo *cooooo!*" shrieked Katie, as though the previous twenty years had never happened and she was twelve again. "You've got loads of money, Will—what are you going to do with it?" Then a short pause for oxygen before "Well, we'll clean out the designer shops, obviously. Ooh, and there was that bag, that pink one, remember, the one you said you'd give up eating for?"

I couldn't seem to process it, was still waiting for the catch. Still waiting, I suppose, for the gift horse to turn around and bite my hand off.

"We can transfer the initial payment into your account today." Vivienne was businesslike, despite having an overexcited mother-of-two gyrating around her office. "You only have to sign some paperwork. Most of the formalities were dealt with by Mr. Cayton before he...er...passed on."

"Um, all right," I couldn't get rid of the feeling that this was all a huge joke. When she handed me a pen I stared for ages into the ballpoint end, waiting for a little flag to pop out with "sucker" written on it.

Nothing, as they say, continued to happen.

"I thought you were going to refuse to sign in there for a minute," Katie said afterwards, as we enjoyed a celebratory pack of Thornton's Toffee-Chocs on a bench in the middle of town. "What were you waiting for, divine guidance?"

"I don't know. I was thinking, I suppose."

"Thinking? Someone says here's a cheque for half a million and you say, hang on, I need to think about it? In what universe is that normal behaviour?"

"It's not half a million, it's only fifty thousand." Then I grinned at her, a lunatic grin. "Listen to me, 'only fifty thousand'. What am I like? That's more money than we'd make in, what, three years? Even if you take off tax and my overdraft and these Toffee-Chocs, I'm still left with..."

"Loads." Katie stuffed another sweet in her mouth. "So, what *were* you thinking about?"

"The others."

"What, the film?"

"No, the *others*. My brothers and OC. What are they going to say when they find out that Ganda didn't just leave me that nose, that there *was* real money, and they didn't get any of it?"

Katie chewed thoughtfully. "Well. For one thing, we don't know that what he left them didn't have any money attached. I mean, maybe those books that Bree got will turn out to be worth millions. Has he tried eBay?"

"Bree thinks eBay is a place in Bermuda."

Jane Lovering

"All right, but you never know. And that allotment, maybe there'll turn out to be oil, or diamonds or something underneath it."

"Katie, I think all this talk of money has turned your brain. Even *if*—and it is an if so enormous that you probably can't even comprehend its size—that did turn out to be the case, I don't think that anyone would pay anything for Ash's boots. And the dogs...cute, yes. Crufts winners, no."

Katie shrugged and tossed another ball of chocolate into her mouth. "Okay then." She cudded like a bovine for a few seconds. "So, are we dossing off work then, or what? I mean, come *on*, Willow, there is a time and a place for sensible discussions and family loyalty and I am here to tell you that right now is *not it*."

"What, not go in? How will they manage?"

"Wills, darling, you're the ad sales manager at the local free paper. One where the headline 'Man Finds Cheese' once ran for three weeks. They will manage, trust me. Neil and Clive will cover for us."

Her enthusiasm was catching and, do you know, once I'd started spending money it became a lot easier. We didn't exactly clean out the local shops, but we left a lot of clear floor space and bare shining chrome in our wake. I bought Katie some clothes, and then we hit Mothercare and I splashed out on the twins, bought myself a gorgeous leather jacket which I'd coveted secretly for months, had an enormous lunch in a bistro neither of us had dared enter before, but did so now with our Monsoon bags held up like status badges and I rolled home just before dark. My arms were full of fresh flowers from the market. Their smell was enough to send my spirits soaring, let alone the knowledge that, even when this lot came off my credit card, and with all the other considerations taken into account, I was still going to have an indecent amount of money left. Plus, and I hardly dared even to whisper the prospect to myself, if Ganda's invention went well, there would be *another four hundred and fifty thousand pounds*. Dear God, I'd never have to work again. I pushed open the front door with my shoulder. I could run off to some Greek island and sell shell creations on the beach, or buy myself a little cottage in the Highlands and write a bestseller. Or—I began sorting through the flowers, grouping them into vases—I could buy that smallholding I'd always been on about. Only the need to earn a living and pay the bills had forced me to stay at the paper. Ever since I'd seen *The Good Life*, aged about ten, the idea of being self-sufficient had called to me. Having chickens and geese and growing herbs to sell, and wearing flowing dresses and big sunhats and wandering dreamily barefoot through an orchard of flowering cherry trees with an impossibly perfect man on one arm and an immaculate and silent child on the other.

There was a knock at the door and my dream bubble took flight. Standing alongside a pristine convertible Morgan, bearing a hefty amount of flowers, was Luke. I had completely forgotten about him.

"Oh!"

"Sorry, did I take you by surprise? I'm a few minutes early, I know, but something's come up and...are you all right?"

"Umm, yes. Luke, I've had some news."

But Luke didn't let me finish. He pushed the flowers forward at me. "I'm really, frantically sorry about this. These are for you, by the way. But I have to fly out to New York first thing in the morning. James has had some kind of emergency and, look, I won't bore you with the details but..."

He looked perfect, with his hair artfully disarranged, pale linen jacket over cream chinos. So perfect it almost hurt.

"Doesn't matter," I said. "'S okay."

"No, Willow, it's not." Luke stepped up close, pressing the flowers against me with his body. The smell of crushed rose petals was almost overwhelming. "That's why I, God, I hope I haven't taken the most awful liberty here, but, look, I've booked a hotel. For us? Next weekend? In the Lake District? If, and *please*, tell me if I'm really out of order here, if it's all right?"

A picturesque breeze ruffled his hair and lifted the edges of some lilies. They brushed against my wrist like a kiss. "I think that would be perfect," I half-whispered.

Then he had to dash off, something to do with paperwork and visas and suchlike, but it didn't matter. I was practically orbital, hugging the bouquets to me and whirling around the living room, scattering bits of foliage as I went. Next weekend! A hotel, double room, I hoped. I mean, a man wanting to go away for the weekend was hardly anticipating brisk walks and nightly cold baths, was he? And, even better, I had a whole week to prepare. *And*, even *better*—in fact I nearly wet myself with how sensationally brilliant the timing was—I had enough money to buy some quite staggeringly lovely clothes. Underwear, shoes, oh, and I must buy some gorgeous perfume so that, even naked, I'd be classy.

I wandered around, dazed by the faultless synchronicity of it all, and slightly stupefied by the flower scents in the air. The dining table looked like a florist's practice room, with half-made-up bunches and vases solely filled with daffodils or catkin stems. And some of these flowers had been bought for me *by a man*. A proper, good-looking, affluent man, who I fancied and wasn't sick on all the time. God, life was good.

A sudden roar from the road outside indicated that life was about to get worse by a factor of ten, as Ash pulled his bike up onto the pavement and came stomping through the open front door. "Willow? Oh, fuck, did somebody die?"

"Shut up, Ash. So, to what do I owe the total nonpleasure? Don't tell me, you forgot to take the power cable for the laptop this morning."

"Nah. Well, kind of. Cal wanted to have a word with you about the laptop, that's all. Reckons there's more to it than just a faulty connection."

"Have either of you ever heard of the telephone?" I wanted to be left alone to hug my secrets to me, possibly to ring Katie and hold a hushed, wondrous conversation about designer knickers.

"I was on my way over there, thought I'd pick you up as I came past."

"All right," I sighed, and thrust some floppy stems into the sink. "Just a minute." Then a thought struck me. "Ash, have you moved in with him?"

"Who, Cal?"

"Well, I hear the Archbishop of Canterbury's spoken for."

Ash looked coy for a second. "Weeellll, early days yet. But, fuck me, he's gorgeous though, isn't he? And cute with it. I mean, don't you just love the way his hair is all kinda over his face and he's got those huge eyes? He's a bit thin though, needs feeding up. Some tender loving care."

"And you're the man to give it to him?"

Ash smiled a secretive grin. "I hope. Look, I didn't come over here to tart about, are you coming?"

"I suppose."

੪੦ଓ

Cal's flat was not what I'd expected. He lived over two shops in a select, pedestrian area of York, in what at first appeared to be an open-plan room. The parts of the floor not occupied by computer things were piled high with books and magazines, all science fiction. It looked like Nerd Ground Zero.

I stood awkwardly behind Ash as we came in. There was something relentlessly male about this flat in a utilitarian, everything-has-a-function way. Although it looked untidy, I bet Cal could put his hand on a memory card or a modem without a second thought.

"Cal!" Ash bellowed. He'd let himself in with his own key, I noted. Cal might be good with computers, but he was obviously a sucker for a blond. "Callum!"

"Hey." Cal emerged from another doorway. "I'm here. Do you want something to eat?" In his own environment, Cal's limp was less noticeable. Though maybe it was the reason for all the empty space. As he led us inside, I could see that he didn't use a stick here. "Hi, Willow. I was in the darkroom. Do you want to have a look?" Through another door we entered a tiny room, windowless and illuminated only by a dim red bulb overhead. It looked like the bedroom of a light-sensitive prostitute. "Right. I don't usually go into small, dark rooms with women I've not been formally introduced to, so you'll have to forgive me if I get a bit overexcited." Cal rummaged around among some papers. "Now, what do you think of these?" He handed me a sheaf of glossy photographic paper. "I just developed them. What do you think they are?"

"You mean you took photos of something without knowing what it is?"

"Well, duh. Of course *I* know what it is—I want to know if you do."

"If this is pornography, I warn you, my brother has a black belt in karate and will defend my honour with his dying breath."

Cal chuckled. "Willow, your brother couldn't get a black belt in sushi, I don't think he gives a stuff about your honour, and why the *hell* do you think I'd bring you in here to show you porn?"

"Um, I don't know. Maybe you got a bit overexcited?"

Cal gave me a huge grin. It lit up his glorious eyes, made him look less tired. "Aha! *Now* you're getting the hang of humour. What do you make of it?" He indicated the paper in my hand.

The photographs seemed to be images of a cityscape. Tiny beads of light shone out in complicated patterns scattered randomly across an otherwise dark surface. Smudged streaks of glow could have been the lights of cars captured in motion. "Is it New York? From a helicopter?"

"It's a motherboard." Cal took the pictures from me.

"A...?"

"Motherboard. The thing that makes a computer a computer. Lots of chips, all stuck together on a board. I take pictures of computer parts from unfamiliar angles, close-ups, that kind of thing. I've got a great one of a USB port, looks exactly like the Channel Tunnel."

"Why?"

"Just a hobby. I don't..." He hesitated. "I spend a lot of time at home, what with..." He stopped again, dropped his eyes, then his head.

"Yes, I imagine the old war wound must make life a bit awkward," I supplied.

A grateful smile crinkled his eyes and the corners of his mouth. "Precisely. I've had to resign myself to never dancing salsa again."

"Bet mountaineering's a bit tricky, too."

"Ah, dear Everest. How I miss her cloudy heights."

I decided that I rather liked this odd man. "Please, tell me that none of these pictures feature intimate portraits of my laptop."

"Not at all. I have special machines to pose for me. Yours is in the living room, the coy little thing. I think you might have a problem with your fan. It could be overheating that's making it cut out."

"Can you fix it?"

"Do you want me to?" The red light made his face all angles, deep shadows under his eyes and cheekbones, like a Halloween mask, but a sad one.

"Please."

"Then, my dear young lady, I shall be only too delighted. Now, let us leave here, before I become overexcited again and you call for your brother to sort me out using only his exquisite black belt."

Cal held open the door of the dark room and we went back into the suddenly too-harshly-lit hallway. "I'll have it mended by the weekend. You can come over and collect it, if you like."

"Great. Oh, I'm away this weekend. Monday?" Just the thought made me tingle.

Cal made a face. "Yeah. Sure. I'll chuck a blanket over it on Friday, use it as a picnic table." Then he gave another of his sudden enormous grins. "Come Monday. It'll be fine."

"I'll look forward to it." I surprised myself by meaning it. Cal was strange to the nth degree with a weird kind of hyperactive melancholy, but he was fun, charming and seemed to like me. This was at least three points up on Ash's previous boyfriends, who'd either been illegally odd, suicidal or had hated me in the kind of bitchy, supercilious way that some gay men do so well.

Ash decided to sleep over on Cal's sofa. (Yeah, like I was going to fall for *that* one. What did they think, that I've never watched *Queer as Folk*?) So I made my own way home. The streets were dark, the road dull and bleak under the tyres of passing cars and I wondered what Ganda's invention actually looked like.

His voice echoed in my head. "Remember, Willow, you have to see the whole picture," he'd always said, whilst inventing. "Don't just think in the here and now, try to think forwards. You don't have to think about what people *want*, you have to think about what people *need*. Sometimes, they don't even know themselves."

All very well, Ganda, I thought as I headed down my own familiar road, but it's hard to think about what people need, when you don't even know what *you want*.

Chapter Eight

I was surprised at how much I missed Luke. In little over a week I'd somehow come to rely on his presence every evening, his phone calls every morning. The lack of these things made his absence more profound.

"Are you falling in love with him?" Katie asked. She and Jazz had joyfully reclaimed me for after-work drinking sessions and were gaining any amount of vicarious pleasure from asking deeply personal questions such as this. "I mean, you haven't really known him very long."

"And you haven't shagged him yet," pointed out Jazz. "No point in getting all droopy-eyed over the guy if he turns out to be hung like a vole."

"Oy, size isn't everything. And, no, I'm not 'falling in love'. I just miss him, that's all."

"I read somewhere"—Jazz took a deep mouthful of his Guinness while we expressed shock and surprise at the fact that he could read—"that you can make someone fall in love with you, just by being in contact with them at the same time every day."

"In that case," Katie retorted, "the barman in here must absolutely adore *you*."

"Maybe he does," Jazz replied evenly. "I'm only saying, that's all."

"You are *so* cynical. I think it's lovely that Will has got herself a gorgeous bloke, and if I didn't have Dan I know I'd be raving jealous. That Luke is a real ride."

Jazz and I stared at her. "Is there something you want to tell us?" I said, eventually.

"About how you know he's a good ride?" Jazz put in.

"Oh, sorry. I was slipping into the Irish vernacular there, guys. I meant ride in the sense of being a shaggable bloke."

We forgave her for not being British and ordered more drinks. Despite my newfound wealth, Jazz and Katie shared the round-buying, which showed that the status quo was still exactly as it had been.

"Have you told the others yet about the money?" Katie asked, over another bottle of white wine.

"Um. No. Not yet."

"Don't you think you ought to?"

You see what I mean about the personal questions? "I'm still trying to think how to put it. OC should be fine, Paddy earns enough to buy Mexico. I don't think Bree will be bothered, as long as no books were harmed in the making. Clay's got bootloads of cash from doing whatever it is he does for foreign banks."

"And what about Ash?"

"He'll probably scratch your eyes out." Jazz snorted. "Or ignore you *very ostentatiously.*"

"I think Ash might have other things on his mind," I said carefully. Ash had taken to coming round after I'd gone to bed, slamming doors and playing music far too loudly. I hoped he soon got over whatever bothered him because living with a thirty-two-year-old teenager was trying my patience.

And then Friday night arrived and Luke turned up at the door in the Morgan, wearing a scrumptious blue shirt which made his eyes look purple. I Audrey-Hepburned down the front path (skipping slightly, swinging my bag in a girlish fashion in kitten heels) and Luke opened the car door for me.

"Had a good week?"

"You cannot imagine." I grinned. "How was yours? How was New York?"

"Big. Noisy. But I did some great deals, I hope. Fingers crossed everything will pan out all right, just as long as the cash flow holds up. Anyway, let's not talk shop. We're going to have a great weekend. Ever been to the Lakes?"

I had, just once, on a family holiday when I was ten, and my memories of crowded streets with brief glimpses of water, torrential rain and Bree coming down with chicken pox had rather prejudiced me against returning. However, returning in a convertible next to a stunning man was altogether a different matter.

It was dark, but I could sense a stupendous view and the hotel itself was worth the journey, crying out for the adornment of a couple of huge hairy dogs and a squire with a shotgun asserting his *droit de seigneur* with the housemaids.

"Is this all right?" Luke asked, as our bags were carried into our room. Yes, *our* room.

"It's beautiful." I walked over to the huge open fire flaming away in a stone grate.

"No, I mean"—he waved an arm to take in the canopied double bed looming in the middle of the room like a small bungalow—"this."

"Oh. Um. Yes. I think...yes. It's fine."

"I didn't want you to think...if it's not all right, there's a couch, look, or I could book another room, I'm sure they're not full."

"It's fine, Luke. Wonderful."

"So, shall we go down to dinner? Or did you want to change?"

I put my head around the door to the ensuite bathroom, which had the largest shower I'd ever seen, a whirlpool bath, and towels the size of Manchester. "I think I'll change first, if that's all right." Yeah, I'd bought enough clothes to spend the weekend with the Queen and I was bloody well going to wear all of them. God knows this was probably the only outing they'd get. Modestly I shut myself in the bathroom to strip off, leaving Luke changing in the bedroom. I couldn't believe it, I was nervous. Ten years, more, of wishing for a sight of Luke Fry in his underpants, and I'm locking myself in the bathroom like a virgin on her wedding night. What was wrong with me? Apart from the obvious, I thought ruefully, as I dry-retched over the shell-shaped sink.

Dinner was fabulous, although I drank rather more than I should have done, and we lingered happily over brandies in a sofa'd drawing room.

"Okay?" Luke smiled at me, draining his glass and putting it decisively on the table.

"Yes, thanks. Fantastic."

"Then, shall we?" He held out a hand and helped me to my feet, curling a protective arm around my waist. "I'm looking forward to that huge bed."

We rocked together, slightly drunk, up the stairs and into our room. The covers had been turned down on the bed, a handmade chocolate was carefully centred on each pillow and a small, atmospheric lamp glazed the room a light pink.

I was suddenly shy. Caught by the reflections in the window, I went over and pretended to gaze out into the night, arms along the windowsill. I felt the hairs prickle on the back of my neck as Luke stood close behind me, his breath swirling the air warmly at my nape.

"Willow," he said, and I turned. Instantly he had me, lips on my mouth, hand entangled in my hair, fingers trembling over the buttons on my shirt. The air came chill against my body as first my shirt and then my skirt fell away, but I was almost unconscious of it. Luke's heat drove any other thought from my head. His fingers traced my shoulders, then his lips did the same. He kissed me again so hard that the air fled from my lungs. Whispering to me all the time, things he wanted to do, things he *had* to do or die, teasing me and taunting me. Then, when he had me pinned beneath him, the embroidered canopy of the bed swinging over our heads like the roof of heaven, he began to undress himself.

God, that man was sexy. His body was every bit as stupendous as I had imagined. In fact, it was probably better now than it had been ten years ago, muscled and taut where it had been spare and skinny, a raft of pale hairs drawn between his nipples and down the line of his stomach. As his hand went to his belt, he looked at me quizzically. "Are you sure?"

"Oh, yes," I breathed, a phrase I was to repeat quite frequently from then on, with variable punctuation. "Oh, *yes.*"

There was a kind of frenzy about Luke in bed—oh, nothing kinky. You're not getting any tales from *me* about handcuffs or spanking competitions. (Even if it *did* happen I wouldn't tell you. We don't know each other *that* well.) A very *concentrated* approach to sex, as though he was blocking out the whole of the rest of life while he made love to me. It made me feel as if I was the centre of the universe, the most desired, the *hottest* woman in the galaxy, watching the man I'd always wanted giving himself up to me on waves of pleasure and afterwards collapsing in my arms with sweat glazing his body.

"So then." I lay on my side and traced the outline of his ribs. "How was New York?"

"Busy. Loud. Dirty." Luke rested on his back with his arms behind his head. "Much as you'd expect. Have you ever been?"

"No." I waited for him to say "we'll go together", but he didn't. "What did you get up to over there? Apart from work."

"Apart from work, nothing. I'd had the heads-up from James about a car, thought I might be interested in it, so I flew out to take a look, had a bit of a poke round some others while I was there, came back. End of story. So. How was your week?"

He turned his head to look at me, his eyes lazily clouded with sex, and I gulped to prevent lunch reappearing. "Um. I...well, I had a good time, actually. I..." I'd been about to mention my legacy but when he looked at me like that my mind went a complete blank. "I...oh *God, Luke...*"

Later, we tried conversation again. This time Luke initiated. "It's a bloody shame I couldn't buy that Caddy over in New York, you know. You would have looked absolutely amazing in it. You do have the most incredible breasts, by the way, did I mention?"

"I think you did say something similar, yes," I said, rather breathlessly. "Was it not for sale after all?"

Luke began kissing me. "Yeah, but I've got a bit of a cash shortfall at the moment, until I get the business up and running this end. So I had to say 'no' to it. Pity, but there you go, that's business. Can we just try...?"

The man was insatiable.

Chapter Nine

When Luke dropped me off at home on Sunday, I flopped down on the sofa feeling slightly guilty at how thankful I was to be able to lie down without being leaped upon. Lack of sleep had left me a little bit cranky and six months worth of sex in two days had left me with what Katie would have called "a fanny like a nail file" so when the phone rang I didn't exactly leap to answer it.

"Hello."

"Oh dear. I thought you were away for the weekend?"

"Cal, if you thought I was away, why did you ring me?"

"I mean, I thought you'd been away and would therefore be all sparkly and rejuvenated."

"Yeah, I'm sparkly. That's me, sparkly. Like Barbie's party frock."

"Barbie is an alien invader from the planet Busty. Now, do you want to know why I'm ringing?"

I smiled down the phone, suddenly less tired. "All right. Why are you ringing?"

There was an answering smile in Cal's voice. "Because I'm very bored. Oh, and to tell you that I've fixed your laptop."

"Well, that's good. Can I still pick it up tomorrow?"

"Of course. I'm looking forward to it. I've descaled the kettle in honour of your visit and built a rather nice little gazebo out of the limey bits."

"I thought you had to have a garden to have a gazebo."

"Windowbox gazebos are in this year, you know. So, I'll see you tomorrow?"

"I'll be there." I was still smiling when I put the phone down. Cal really was the weirdest creature, but he did make me laugh. That was the one thing lacking in Luke, I thought, starting to unpack, wondering whether these expensive clothes could be machine-washed. It would be unfair to say that Luke didn't have a sense of humour, although he was the kind of man who thinks off-the-wall refers to a dado rail. But then—I winced as I sat down too quickly—Luke had many other compensations, some of which more than made up for a lack of chuckles.

The telephone rang again and for some reason I expected it to be Cal. "Hello," I answered cheerily. "Still bored?"

The line whistled and shrieked like a haunting. "Hello?" said a distant voice, eventually.

"Hi, Clay. What's up?" Clay never rang unless there was a problem.

"I'm coming back, Will. Can I stay with you again?"

A minor twitch of irritation. "I suppose. Why?"

The line wailed as my words twanged off the satellite and bounced back down in China. "Fed up," I made out, as the reply floated back. "Decided to take time off, find out what"—crackle crackle—"really want to do."

Sod. So not even a flying visit then. Good job I hadn't bothered changing the sheets from his last visit. And, a large plus, Clay's room was in the attic, with its own bathroom. That put three doors and a well-insulated ceiling between us, should I decide to, ahem, *entertain*. Whilst I hadn't actually been planning nights of noisy debauchery with Luke, I wasn't going to let the presence of an older brother in the house put me off. "Of course, it'll be fine."

But the line was dead, he'd gone. Whisked back into the world of the merchant bank, which was clearly not all it was cracked up to be. It would be exactly like the old days, brothers hanging out of windows watching my every romantic move. But this was his home as much as it was mine. I could hardly come over all Lady of the Manor and deny my siblings shelter, could I? Bugger it.

ಬಿಚ

Monday morning. Katie and I huddled in my office with a supply of chocolate biscuits, the phone on divert and a sign on the door warning Neil and Clive what happened to the last man to interrupt us.

"So? What did he say about the fifty grand?"

"I didn't get to tell him. Every time I started to say something... Let's just say, we didn't really do much talking this weekend."

"Was he any good?"

I thought. "Oh, Katie, he was *fabulous*."

"Lucky cow. *And* you got the Lake District. I only got a Saturday night in Blackpool out of Dan."

"Could have been worse." I got up to boil the kettle again. "Could have been Bognor."

"Yeah, but I came back pregnant with twins." Katie sighed and stood up. "Better get on with what we laughingly call 'work' then." She walked to the door and stopped. "Will, can I be nosy?"

"Why break the habit of a lifetime?"

"No, it's...what *is* it with you and Luke? Is it a casual thing, or something else? Are you falling for him?"

I gave a rather superficial smile. "Why the interest? I've only known the man a couple of weeks."

"Just wondering whether I should be buying a hat or a huge stack of Kleenex, that's all. Do you want it to be a relationship? Because if you do, then it's about time you did a bit of talking, Will. If he finds out that you've been sitting on all this cash and not saying a word about it, it might give him the wrong impression about you, don't you think?"

After Katie had gone out and I'd put the phone back, I thought about what she'd said. Not about the talking part, talking could wait as far as I was concerned, but the falling-in-love part. *Was* I falling for Luke Fry? Casually, I let the memory of him wash through my mind. An image of him sitting on the grass as we picnicked, head thrown back as he laughed at my impersonation of a duck, shirt slightly untucked, collar open to show golden skin.

Phew. I fanned at my face until the hot blush receded. So there was no doubt I was in lust with the man, but love? *Did* I love him? *Could* I love him? Was I even capable of loving someone? After all, with my little—well, we decided we'd call it my little problem, didn't we?—I'd not had a lot of practice at loving men. I loved my parents, wherever they were, and my siblings—sort of. As long as they didn't interfere, or patronise me, or poke holes in my posters of Duran Duran, the bastards. But falling in love with a man was something else entirely, territory not exactly uncharted, but one with a map drawn on the back of a Mills & Boon cover in purple crayon.

I walked from work to Cal's to pick up the laptop. At last the sky was the pure blue of a boiled sweet. Tulip and daffodil stems were pregnant with blooms and birds were beginning the annual round of gang warfare in the hedges, so my step was jaunty as I bounced my way up to the flat and leaned on the doorbell.

Cal must have been waiting, because the door swung inwards as soon as I rang. "Hey, Willow, good to see you."

"Hi." I went in. "Is Ash not here then?"

For a second his face clouded. "No, not at the moment. Come on through. Hungry? I just made a mushroom stroganoff. Yeah, it looks like puke on a plate but, hell, it tastes good."

"Sounds great. Yes, I'd love some, thanks, Cal." I hadn't intended to stay. I was going to grab the laptop, maybe have a cup of tea and rush off home for an early night to try to refill some of the bags under my eyes. But there was something about the combination of the sun slanting in through the long windows, the creamy smell of cooking and the general air of stillness in the flat that made me think "sod it". "Ash has been a bit weird lately. Did you and he have a tiff or something?"

Cal paused, mid-stride. "You'll have to ask Ash, okay?"

"If you say so. I usually avoid asking Ash anything." I looked out of the window, for some reason struggling for something to say. "It's a beautiful evening."

"Thank you." Cal gave me a mischievous half-smile. "Do you have any idea how hard it is winching the sun into that particular spot in the sky? I was at it all morning."

"What with that and the gazebo I'm surprised you found time to cook." We were standing in the kitchen area now, a bare-floored room with exposed brick walls and a surprisingly large and professional-looking stainless steel cooker on one wall. Seating consisted of a big sofa with a low table in front, angled by one of the tall windows.

"Yeah, I had to invite a tiny vicar to tea, to justify building it. Anyway, he fell off the window box, and it's two storeys down. We haven't found him yet." Cal gave me another grin. "Do you like red wine?"

"Um, yes."

He took two glasses from a shelf and put them on the table, then grabbed a bottle and corkscrew. "Do the honours then."

I set to opening the bottle as Cal competently moved from stove to fridge and back, adding, stirring, his limp hardly noticeable in this confined space. I wondered exactly what my feral brother had in common with this gentle, domesticated man. But then attraction, I guess, moves in mysterious ways. I mean, look at Luke and me. I knew precisely what I saw in him, but what did he see in me? Apart from my more obvious charms, which I stared at, then jiggled.

"What on earth are you doing?" I looked up and saw Cal watching me, a newly poured glass of wine in each hand.

"Only, um, looking at my breasts."

"Puberty caught up with you, did it? Nasty that. I once got an attack of adolescence, but I just drank until it went away. Cheers." He handed me my glass and drank from his own. There was a bit of a pause.

"So." I sat with my glass perched awkwardly on my knee. "How did you meet Ash?" In *loco parentis* interviewing mode, even though Iain and Sophie had never shown the least inclination to interview our prospective partners and were, I always felt, slightly disappointed that only one of us had turned out gay.

"Does it matter? Llama racing, reading the news, over the frozen turkeys in Tesco—what's the difference?" Cal put two plates down on the table and handed me a fork. "Eat up. Thousands of innocent mycelium were dragged screaming to their deaths to bring you this dish. The least you can do is enjoy it."

Side-by-side we ate and drank red wine, until the plates were empty and the glasses wore only a tidemark. "Where did you learn to cook like that?" I sat back, replete, and tried to burp genteelly. "That was stupendous."

"Ancient Rome. All that philosophy and art, and they were buggers for a well-cooked bacon sandwich." Cal leaned over and turned on a lamp, the room was quite dark now.

"Do you ever answer a question seriously?"

For a moment, in the half-shadow, he looked almost scary, eerily lit from one side, which highlighted his cheekbones and eyes. "That depends," he said, and the words were heavy as though a weight of sadness lay upon them, "on who's asking."

"Me." The wine had made me brave.

"Oh, well, in that case, no." He stood up, clearing the plates away into what looked like a cupboard but turned out to be a concealed dishwasher. "Would you like coffee? Tea? Rosewater poured from the brows of virgins?"

Feeling rebuffed I said, "I'd better get home. Thanks for fixing the laptop, send your invoice to the office, will you? Oh, and thanks for the food. It was lovely. Really."

Cal stopped stacking dishes and straightened up at the work surface with his back to me. "I won't charge you," he said softly.

"Oh, but—"

"And it's cerebral palsy. My leg. It affects my arm too, but only slightly. I was born too early, you see."

"Cal—"

"Right, now you'd better be off. I don't want my reputation ruined by the presence of a woman after dark. Besides, you don't know what I turn into when the moon gets up, so you ought to hurry." Brisk now, no nonsense, he turned back around, no sign on his face that he'd been anything other than joking. Unless, if I looked closely there were lines of strain around his eyes that hadn't been there a few minutes ago.

"The moon's up already."

"Is it? The tablets must be working. Right, here's the laptop. I've checked it and it's running fine, but any problems—you know where to find me, don't you?"

I found myself hustled out of the door and went out onto the street with a feeling that something rather odd had happened, but not sure what it was.

Chapter Ten

The week continued to give the illusion of spring, and after he picked me up on Wednesday evening, Luke suggested that we should go for a drive to the coast. This we did, and ended up sitting on a beach in a secluded cove.

"Are you all right? You've been a bit quiet this evening." I nestled myself closer to Luke against the chill of the incipient night.

"Yeah, I'm fine. It's just, oh, work, money, stuff like that. You wouldn't be interested."

"Try me." I pulled his jacket around the pair of us, leaning into the smell of Aramis and snuggling into his shirt. His body was very warm.

"It, ah, it's stupid stuff. You know how it goes. All the cash is tied up in Boston with James. *I* want to start looking at houses here in York but there's nothing available to buy with until I start the business up and running, and I can't do *that* without cars, which there isn't any cash to buy because it's all tied up in Boston. D'you see?" Luke looked down at me and curled his arm around me to pull us closer together. "Stupid stuff, as I said."

"How much cash do you need?" My mouth was slightly dry.

"Oh, I dunno. 'Bout ten grand I think. Nothing amazing, only a bit more than the bank is prepared to lend, on top of the business loan we've already got. They're saying maybe we should relocate where the stock might shift a bit faster. D'you know, yesterday my bank manager suggested that I'd be better off setting up the showroom down south, somewhere-on-Thames? Bloody cheek. I promised I'd think about it, but I reckon it's a stupid idea. There's plenty of classic car salesmen down there already. Still, if that's what it takes to get the extra, maybe I *should* think about it. Always room for another Lamborghini in London."

All right, I admit it. I panicked. He was thinking about *leaving*, for God's sake. I'd only just got him, and he was thinking about moving on. What was I *supposed* to do? "I could let you have the money," I said.

Luke smiled and kissed the top of my head. "Ah, sweetie, I know you would if you could, but it doesn't matter. Things will turn out for the best eventually."

"But I *have* got it."

I explained, fairly briefly and without reference to allotments, spaniels, books or boots. Luke's mouth fell open and his eyes went very round. "I don't *believe* it."

"So if we're only talking about ten thousand pounds, then I could get it for you tomorrow." I paused. "Or, at least, as soon as the bank can transfer it."

"No." Luke shook his head. "I can't let you, Willow. It's not fair. James and I already owe our dad fifteen thousand for money he's put in. We've got round that by making him a silent partner in the business, which means he gets a share of the profits, when we make any, but..."

"Then make me one," I said quickly. "A sleeping partner, or whatever. Then I know I'll get my money back eventually. It'll be like investing it. Oh, go on, Luke. Please."

"Well." Luke ran a hand through his hair. "I don't know, Will. It's a lot to ask and you realise you've got no guarantee of getting the money back if the whole thing goes under?"

"It's only money." I grinned. "I didn't have any before. If I haven't got any afterwards, then at least I will have had fun in the meantime."

"You"—Luke kissed the side of my neck—"are a very special woman, do you know that?"

"Uh-huh."

"And I know we've only been together a few weeks but I'm very afraid..." his lips trailed down and his fingers released buttons on the way, "that I'm going to have..." my groan nearly drowned out his final words, "...to marry you."

I pretended not to have heard. I didn't react. Not to his words, anyway. My body I couldn't control so well and we slid together on the sand under the cover of his jacket. Cold, salty skin, lips tasting of the sea and pounding pleasure like the waves on the rocks. I was given the added edge, of course, the reassurance that Luke wanted more than this. He was thinking of the future, a future which included me.

ജ്ഞ

"And we had sex on the beach and I've never done that before."

Jazz rolled his eyes and Katie gave me an arch look. "Next you'll be telling us that you've never had sex on the backseat of an Austin Allegro, and I know for a *fact* that you did with Darren Simmonds, after Heather's party when we were in the sixth form."

"No. 'S true. Never on the beach."

Jazz grunted. "Might as well rub your knob with glasspaper," he said getting up to buy another round. "How about you, Kate? You ever done the sand 'n' shag?"

"Two words, Jazz, Blackpool and twins. It's not an experience I'm in any hurry to repeat. But yours sounds absolutely *incredible*, Will! Did he really propose?"

I lowered my voice. "I'm not sure. I mean, he never mentioned it again, so maybe it was just something that slipped out."

Jazz gave a smutty guffaw.

"In the heat of the moment. Don't get me another, Jazz. I'd better go."

Katie made a face. "Oh, why? I thought we were going to sit here and analyse your sadly unexperimental sex life."

"Fascinating as the topic is, I've got a brother at home having a nervous breakdown in the attic, another one that's gone missing completely, a sister who spends hours on the phone every evening trying to persuade me to bring Luke for dinner again, no doubt so that she can recount the cute story of how I poohed in the bath when I was three. And if that isn't enough, I've got Ash's boyfriend ringing me up and being professionally weird."

"And a boyfriend of your own who might want to marry you. You think. Unless you misheard."

I wondered, on my way home, what Luke could have said that I might have misinterpreted. I'm going to have to—carry you? Bury you? In any event, I wouldn't have been human if I hadn't popped in to WH Smith and picked up, quite casually you understand, the latest copy of *Brides* magazine. Oh, and *Your Wedding*. And a marriage special from one of the glossy monthlies and, to my consternation, *Horse and Hound*, because there was an article in it about hiring carriages. Cut me some slack here, please. I'm thirty-two and this is the nearest I've ever got to a wedding. Oh, apart from when Katie and Dan got married and I was the hideous bridesmaid. So leave me alone for a bit with my fantasies of Vera Wang silk sheath dresses and the veil-versus-tiara debate, all right?

I read all the magazines, carefully, and then put them in a heap under my bed where they wouldn't be found by any rogue brothers. Although, come to think of it, Clay hadn't come down from the attic for a couple of days, and all I'd heard from Ash was a postcard from Prague where he was, even now, roaming the streets "conducting an in-depth body-piercing survey". I bet. I wonder if Cal knew?

ଚ୍ଚେ

It took a few days but I arranged for ten thousand pounds to be paid into Luke's account, at which he was grateful, but not pathetically so. "When I get the rest of the money from Ganda's invention, I can always put some more into the company, if you want," I said as we left the bank.

"Well, only if *you* want to." Luke took my hand. "I don't want it to be said that I'm trying to part you from your cash. I hope you've told everyone that you're doing this of your own free will."

"Of course." I smiled pertly.

Chapter Eleven

Katie had raised eyebrows. "Are you sure he's not just after your money, Will?"

"How could he be? We've been going out together since way before I had any, since before I even knew I was *going* to have any."

"Oh. Yes."

"And stop sounding like Jazz. Luke wants me for me. It's nothing to do with the money. He's not a gigolo, you know."

"What's a gigolo?" asked Clive, looming into sight over the top of the filing cabinet.

"Musical instrument, innit?" Neil replied.

"Don't you two cvei do anything independently?" Katie looked up from her typing. "Wills, phone call for you."

I waited until the boys had gone before I took the receiver from her. "Is there really, or did you just want to get shot of them?"

"No, there really is. A man. Not Luke either, before you ask."

"Hey there."

"Hello, Cal." I sensed Katie pricking up her ears, so I mouthed "Ash's boyfriend" at her and she shrugged and went back to typing. "What's up?"

"Ah, nothing. Just got the megrims, that's all. I had to perform a tracheotomy on a Powerbook and things aren't good, although I have to admit that I do look *sensational* in scrubs. How are you?"

"I'm good."

"Right. Deep breath here, Cal, and try not to dribble, the lady doesn't want to hear the sound of your bodily fluids trickling down the line. Thing is, Will, I wondered if you'd come down to the old house with me at the weekend."

"The farm?"

"That's the baby. I need to make a few decisions and, well, you seemed to like looking round and, all right, I admit it, I need someone to handle the goat for me. She's out in the orchard and a neighbour is keeping an eye on her, but I'm going to have to shift her over into the big paddock and she scares the shit out of me if you want the truth. The goat. You didn't think I meant the neighbour, did you?"

"Er."

"She's got an evil temper on her and she's got the hang of knocking me over."

"This is still the goat."

"Yeah, right. So, just wondering, you know, if I pick you up? Thought I'd check now in case you were planning to be away again?"

"No. No, I wasn't. Sounds like...I don't suppose 'fun' is really the word."

"Well, it's *a* word. But so is 'cantankerous'. And 'evil'. And, incidentally, 'quadrumanous', but that's irrelevant. Oh, and she smells completely vile. That *is* the neighbour. Bye."

"He is *so weird*," I said, staring at the phone as though I expected Cal to come bursting out of the mouthpiece at any moment.

"Oho." Katie turned her chair to face me. "I sense storytime."

"I told you about him. Ash's boyfriend. Or, probably, ex-boyfriend, if Ash is laying himself down for his country in Slovenia or wherever Prague is these days. Unless they have an open relationship, which I really hope they don't. Cal deserves way, *way* better than Ash."

Katie merely raised her eyebrows at me and went back to typing.

Later that morning, on the pretext of picking up some milk, I popped over to the Roads department again. Vivienne Parry, Bread Woman, was manning the desk this time and there was no sight of the lachrymose Nadine.

"Hello. I'm—"

"Willow Cayton, yes, I remember."

"I just wondered if—?"

"No further news yet about your grandfather's patent, sorry."

Had this woman been casting the runes? "Oh. I thought I'd ask."

"I hear that testing is still going well. They're into the final stages now before they release for commercial production." She smiled at me and her cheeks formed perfect burger-bun circles.

"That's wonderful, thank you. Oh, by the way, how's—?"

"Nadine? Taking some time off, at last." Vivienne shook her head slowly. "Poor girl. Boyfriend trouble, apparently. Put your foot down, I said. Don't let him run rings around you."

As I left, I wondered if any man had ever had the stamina to attempt running rings around Vivienne Parry. Mind you, with her gift for knowing what I was about to say before I spoke, she'd probably have any man with ill intentions crated up and shipped to Basrah before he opened his mouth.

I sighed and leaned against the parapet of Lendal Bridge, staring upstream to where the railway crossed the river, and beyond the city boundary to the fields. In the hopeful spring sunshine, people were walking beside the river with their dogs and pushing toddlers in buggies. There was also someone waving at me from a bench.

"Hey, Willow." It was Luke, sitting on a riverside seat with one long leg crossed over the other, wraparound shades keeping the sun from his eyes. "Come down and join me."

"I should be getting back to work," I puffed, having jogged down to reach him. "I only came out for some milk. They'll think I'm persuading it out of the cow." But the relaxed presence of Luke and the glorious sunshine made me linger. Plus I couldn't see the point of hurrying back to a headline which read 'Local Cat Wins Show'. It wasn't exactly Pulitzer Prize-winning material.

"So, what are you doing with yourself today? Thought you were sorting out that showroom?" I squinted up at the sky.

"Yeah, sorted. No, I was looking across the river there." Luke pointed at a new development of riverside apartments being sold at extortionate prices. "When, sorry, I mean *if* of course. I realise I haven't done the deed formally, as it were. *If* we get married, then we'll need somewhere to live, won't we?"

"Um" was all I could think of to say. My mind was busy doing a little celebratory dance that I hadn't, after all, wasted fourteen quid on magazines.

"Good a time as any, I suppose." Without removing his sunglasses, Luke slouched off the bench and crouched down in front of me, balancing on one knee right beside a large dog turd. "Willow, would you do me the great honour of agreeing to be my wife?"

I looked around to see if anyone had noticed, but there was only a single rower hauling heftily on his oars, as if trying to pass by before anything more embarrassing happened. "Yes, all right" was my less-than-effusive answer.

"Good. I'm glad that's over." Luke straightened up again. "Hard on the old Paul Smith, all that on-bended-knee stuff." He tweaked at the leg of his trousers accordingly. "Well, then. Would the new future Mrs. Luke Fry like to see what I've been looking at?"

I walked with Luke back across the bridge, savouring the name. Mrs. Willow Fry. Willow Fry and her husband, Luke. Following Luke down a narrow strip of boardwalk, I had to stuff my knuckles into my mouth to avoid myself squeaking aloud. Mrs. Fry—oh my God, I was going to marry him! I admired the back view of my husband-to-be, his hair coiling into loose curls just over the collar of his jacket, a jacket which fitted to absolute perfection across his slim shoulders and tapered down to not quite cover his delicious buttocks. Not, of course, that these were visible to the naked eye, but *I knew they were there*, which is what counted.

We stepped out of a glass lift, which had carried us to the second floor of one of the blocks of apartments, and into a light, airy hallway. Luke opened the door to one of the flats with a key he had in his pocket. "I asked the agents for this, so that I could look around. Now. Do you want to see the kitchen first, or the bedroom?"

As proudly as if he was already the owner, Luke showed me around. The flat was small, one ensuite bedroom, another bathroom, kitchen and living room, but it had phenomenal views of the city, a balcony hanging over the river, bare wooden floors and pale painted walls like a colour supplement ad. "What do you think? I know it's probably not quite what you had in mind, but it's convenient for both of us for work and it's extremely prestigious."

I was in a mental void, I literally did not know what to think. I had only just come to terms with the fact that this man wanted to marry me and now I had to get my head around the whole new life that this would entail. "It looks pricey," I squeaked.

"Ah, yes. It's not really. Not that bad, at any rate, for what it is. And, of course, we don't have to decide anything here and now. That would be stupid. It's only that"—Luke looked a little crestfallen—"I fell in love with the place when I saw it advertised and, moron that I am, I kind of thought that you would love it as much as I did. But it's okay. I mean, we can look at places *you* like, too." He gave a deep sigh.

"Oh, Luke, no. It's lovely, really it is. I hadn't considered...I mean..." I looked around at the flat again, seeing the nicely proportioned rooms, the superb fitted kitchen with top-of-the-range fixtures, the railed balcony which would catch the summer evening sun. "It took me by surprise, that's all."

Luke put his hands on my shoulders and looked deep into my eyes. "Are you sure? You're not just agreeing with me to keep me sweet, are you? Because, Willow, I don't sulk. You should know that about me by now. If I can't have what I want, I learn to live with it."

"You don't have to," I said. "I love the place, Luke, honestly. But how would we afford it?"

Luke massaged the base of my neck with his thumbs. He was breathing quickly, I noticed, and there was a sheen of sweat on his forehead. "For now we only need the deposit, that'll reserve it for us, until we can get a mortgage sorted out and that shouldn't be a problem at all."

"How much is the deposit?"

"Twenty." Luke leaned back against the immaculate wall, his eyes still fixed on mine. The sun slid over him. He looked like a David Hockney painting.

"Twenty thousand?"

"Yeah, but it's not so bad. I've got about four grand I can put down now, cash."

"But."

Luke stepped up to me again, cupped my chin in his hand and raised my face to his. Kissed my mouth softly. "It'll be worth it, Willow. In the end. You and me, here. Of course, if we decide to have children we'll have a place with a paddock, ponies for the kids, few chickens scratching around. For now, though, don't you think this will be the perfect start to married life? Imagine, waking up on a Sunday morning." He turned me by the shoulders until I was gazing out of the porthole-shaped window. "Lying in bed and being able to see the raindrops falling in the river. Newspapers spread all over the floor, place smelling of fresh coffee."

"And a sofa, here." I pointed to the space next to the balcony. "So we can sit and people-watch."

A smile spread over Luke's face like butter on a crumpet. "I *knew* you'd go for it." The hand around my shoulders tightened into a hug. "Things are going to be great, Willow. I can feel it. You'll forgive me if I don't buy a ring straightaway, won't you? I think all the money we have should go into the business and this place."

I pulled free of his embrace and walked in what I hoped looked like a taking-in-the-view way to the balcony, where I projectile-vomited over the rail, narrowly missing the solitary rower who was making his way back downstream again.

ঔৎ

"You only went out for bloody milk!" Katie shrieked, when I enlightened her on the reason for my prolonged absence from the office. "And you come back with a fiancé and a flat. You only took a pound, for God's sake. It's a good job we didn't send you with the whole petty-cash tin. You'd probably have come back with Prince William and the Taj Mahal."

The speed of it all had overwhelmed me, too. "It was incredible. He did it all properly, down on one knee and everything, and he'd already got the flat lined up for me to look at. It's just...*amazing*, Katie, the whole thing."

Katie shook her head. "So, when's the big day? And what are you going to wear? Oh, please, can I be matron of honour? I've never been one before. I'll do anything, I'll wear purple, I'll have visible tan lines, anything."

I shrugged again. "We haven't really talked about the actual wedding yet."

"Will you get one of your brothers to give you away? Ash could do it. He looks great in a suit."

"Look, Katie, right now you know as much as I do about the whole thing. As soon as there's any breaking news, you will be the first to know. But at the moment, can I get on with these ads?"

As soon as Katie went out, I hugged my arms around myself in a tight circle of glee. That had been the performance of my life, trying to be cool and not scream with delight and head for the Yellow Pages to discover the whereabouts of the nearest bridal-wear shop. Let me calm down, have another therapeutic flick through the bridal magazines, and then I'd invite Katie over for an evening of wine, chocolate and detailed planning. For now, life consisted of me and Luke, our home-to-be and enchanting daydreams about our future children.

Chapter Twelve

Clay was on the sofa, hugging a cushion and watching *The Simpsons* when I got home. "Good day?" he asked, leaping up to make me a cup of tea.

"Pretty good, yes." I glanced around the living room. It was scattered with scraps of paper, all bearing pencil drawings. "What have you been up to?"

"Ah, nothing. Just fiddling. Designing my perfect house, actually. Do you want a biscuit?"

"No, I'll do myself something on toast in a bit. Have you eaten?"

"I had some scrambled egg earlier. Ash rang, by the way. Said he'll call you back later."

"Fine." I sat back and took the mug Clay offered me. It struck me then, suddenly and horribly, that this was probably what married life would be like, and I had to sit very still until the palpitations went away. Surely Luke and I would never descend to this level. Clay and I had known each other all our lives. We were entitled, indeed *expected*, to have conversations like this. I was hardly likely to come home to be greeted by him suggesting sex in the garden before dinner. Urgh, nasty thought, nasty thought. It took ten minutes with a furtively bought copy of *Young Bride* (yes, all right, I *know*, but some of those brides weren't *that* young) in my room before I got rid of that image.

"I'm going out in a bit, Clay," I called over the banister. "If Ash rings back, tell him I'll be around tomorrow."

"Okay." Clay came halfway up the stairs. "Are you meeting up with Katie and Jazz then?"

"No. Well, yes, maybe." I certainly wasn't about to tell my brother, in his fragile, midlife-crisis state, that I was going out for a frenzied evening of passion with my new fiancé. Clay had begun to recover, slowly, from the shambling, questioning heap that had got off the plane a few days ago, swearing never to go nearer to any financial institution than the local ATM. I didn't want to rub his nose in anything by pointing my own good fortune at him.

"Great. Enjoy." He went back down to sample early-evening TV a little further, while I changed into a stunning little asymmetrical tea dress and pink heels to celebrate my first ever outing as an affianced woman.

Luke turned up driving a huge black car which looked like the Batmobile. "What *is* this?" I climbed into the passenger seat, wide enough to accommodate even the bottom of Vivienne Parry.

Luke grinned. "An investment is what this is. There's people queuing up to buy this honey, so I thought we'd be the first ones to take her out for a spin."

I felt a tremble of excitement start somewhere near the base of my stomach. "It does look pretty sleek."

"Yeah. And there's plenty of room in the back, too, for any extra-showroom activities, if you see what I mean."

The tremble turned to something of a sinking feeling. I had hoped that our first sex as a proper couple might have been somewhere more salubrious than the backseat of a car. "We could always go back to mine," I said. "If you want. I mean, why don't you move in for a bit? It'd save on all those hotel bills, until we can get the flat sorted out."

Luke put his foot down and the car sleekly responded, growling its way out of town. "Well, you've already got your brother staying, haven't you. Besides"—he turned the car so we were heading north—"the hotel is a tax-deductible expense. Patience, Willow, things will come together soon enough. Anyway I'm really looking forward to christening this gorgeous hunk of metal somewhere quiet. There's a spot above Pickering, looking out over the moors. There'll be no one there this time of evening. How about it?" He grinned manically.

The tremble was back, this time an unmistakeable craving. "Mmmmm." I slid down in the leather seat so that the dress rode up and showed my thighs. "Definitely."

"And after that"—almost without looking, Luke reached across and put his hand on the smooth skin above my knee— "there's a great restaurant out that way. Been meaning to try it."

I wriggled again, aware of his gaze leaving the road to play hotly over my exposed legs. Slowly and deliberately I bent one knee and rested a high heel on the edge of the seat so that the dress fell away to reveal the tiny thong I'd chosen purposefully to go under it. "Sounds delicious."

We broke the speed limit all the way to Pickering.

Chapter Thirteen

When Luke dropped me back at the house, it was past midnight, and Clay had gone to bed, which was just as well. My asymmetric dress was now far more asymmetric than it had been when I left, more creased and crumpled, too. My knickers were in my bag and one of the pink heels was decidedly wonky. But it had, all in all, been a very satisfactory experience.

As I turned to push the door closed behind me my foot slipped across the doormat and I sprawled untidily into an attack of the splits. Hauling myself to my feet, I found that I had stepped onto an envelope, the resulting lack of friction being the cause of my skid.

It was plain brown, no name or address, the sort of envelope pushed through unwary letterboxes by door-to-door double-glazing hitmen, or those selling unspecified insurance, although those missives were usually unsealed and addressed to The Householder. The absence of any identifying name made me wonder, so I slid a finger under the flap and tore it open.

"You don't deserve it."

That was all the sheet of paper said, the words written in large, curly letters, like the handwriting of a fifteen-year-old girl who has only recently stopped dotting her i's with little love-hearts and forming the lower loops of g's and y's into spirals.

Paranoia bit deep. What didn't I deserve? Yeah, I'd got the money, but that was properly mine. The only other thing I had was my job, but not even the very bitterest of disillusioned hacks would hold that against me. Managing ads for the local free press is a bit like pole-dancing, but without the healthy exercise.

My hand shook. I felt a kind of shame at receiving such an obvious and tangible form of someone's hatred, and I had the urge to tear the paper into tiny pieces and flush them down the toilet. Then, as I became numb to fear, it was replaced by a curious elation. Why, exactly, did I assume this note was for me? But then, that begged the question, who was it for? Had Clay's sudden urge to throw up his extremely lucrative Beijing post and replace it with skulking under a skylight and playing The Smiths been the result of a misplaced love affair? The script was feminine, but that didn't rule out any of Ash's scorned exes. A little voice in my head whispered that I'd never seen Cal's handwriting, although I couldn't imagine anyone less the type to send anonymous letters than Cal.

No, I decided. No one could be harmed by a note they hadn't even seen and I became surer by the second that it wasn't aimed at me. In fact, I thought as I lurched up to bed in my one-and-a-half stilettos, maybe it wasn't even aimed at this house. Neither we, nor next door, where three young science teachers lived in a hotbed of physics intrigue, had conspicuous numbers. By the time I'd showered and fallen into bed, I was absolutely convinced that the whole thing was a complete mistake.

Having been spark out at one a.m., I was a bit confused to find myself wide awake and sweating at three.

I was getting *married*? How the hell had that happened? My treacherously antisleep brain replayed the proposal moment over and over again, with added close-ups. And I'd *said yes!*

Now my reading material was made up of articles on outdoor catering and big pictures of spot-free women wearing whipped cream and curtains.

I turned onto a cool patch of sheet.

We'd only been dating for, well, since we only usually met in the evenings, but factoring in the weekend in the Lakes, *hours*. But he said he knew, said he'd known from the moment he set eyes on me again in the Grape and Sprout, that I was the One. And how could he *not* be the One for me when he'd been my obsession throughout my twenties?

My heart was steadying now. After all, it wasn't some nobody from the back of beyond. It was *Luke Fry* asking me to marry him. He of the violet black eyes and the sexiest little bottom this side of an Angel DVD. How could we fail? He loved me with, let's face it, quite a lot of passion. And I loved him with...*did I?* Oh, yes, I loved him. Of course I did, with a ten-year back-catalogue of longing. The sex was great, we laughed at more-or-less the same things, we both wanted our lives to be a success—compatibility was assured.

With this thought comforting my mind, I turned onto my side and floated off into fluffy dreams of white dresses and rose petals and Luke inexplicably taking close-up photographs of me.

Chapter Fourteen

The next week further advanced my opinion that Luke and I were right together. He rang me at work several times a day, and the real clincher was that *he didn't ring to say anything.* I got the collywobbles every time the phone rang now, thinking of him standing in the midst of the showroom renovation (apparently the place was a wreck) thinking of me enough to whip out that little silver phone and dial, to say hi and exchange no factual information at all.

Katie, of course, was mad-on jealous and now refused to answer the phone on the grounds that it was bound to be some limpid-eyed man wanting to simper at me, which was unfair because the only men ever to call were Luke and occasionally Cal. Whom she'd never met, and was therefore not in any position to pass opinion on the limpidity of his eyes, which I had at first taken to be an insult until I got home and wrestled my dictionary down from the shelf, to find that I had been thinking of limpets.

"What on *earth* would I be meaning, saying 'limpet eyes'?" Katie asked. It was Friday night and we were well stuck into anything that came in a bottle in the Grape and Sprout. Which was rather a lot. Jazz swore they sold bottled spit to visitors.

"How should I know? That's just what I thought you said."

"Could be kind of, you know, sticky, hanging on to you like limpets hang on rocks." This was Jazz's contribution.

"Luke does not have sticky eyes," I pouted. "He's wonderful. In fact, he's taking me away for the weekend again in a few weeks, that's how wonderful he is. Cornwall, before you say anything."

Katie made a face. "So, how come he's never around at weekends? He's all over you all week and then come Friday night he vanishes, unless he's whisking you away to some expensive hotel, where the only view you get to see is the bedroom ceiling."

Jazz made a "that's not fair" noise in his throat, his mouth being full of beer.

"He works all day at weekends." I poured myself a hefty glass of wine. "Sometimes he goes back to Wales to visit his dad." Katie and Jazz gave each other A Look, and I turned down the corner of my mental page to bookmark this for future reference. "Or sometimes he has to go to Boston to check up on James. He knows that I've got stuff that needs catching up with at weekends, too. So we've agreed, for now, to keep our weekends apart."

Katie sniffed. "When Dan proposed to me, I wouldn't let him out of my sight until we'd got up that aisle."

"Yeah, but you were living in that tiny little house in Acomb at the time. He *couldn't* get out of your sight, not without climbing into the understairs cupboard."

"So why aren't you and Luke moving in together yet? Surely you're not going to marry him without living with him for a while first? That's so old-fashioned, it's..." She groped for the right word. "Well, actually it's quite sensible. That way you're safely hitched before the disillusionment can sink in."

"What disillusionment? He hasn't got a two-inch dick, has he?"

"Jazz." I spluttered my wine.

"Well?"

"No!"

"That's all the disillusionment I can think of. Nothing worse than getting a guy into bed and finding out that he's got a knob like a matchstick."

Katie hiccupped. "I meant, like finding that he uses the sheets as a hanky in the middle of the night, and that he hums all the way through *Desperate Housewives,* and that if there's no toilet roll left when he has a shit he doesn't bother to wipe, and—"

"Stop!" shouted Jazz and I, as one. "Jesus, Katie, we've got to look Dan in the eye again sometime."

"Oh. Sorry, yes. I didn't mean... It's not all Dan, if that's what you were thinking. I kind of amalgamated previous fellers."

"So then, you two. Why the funny look when I mentioned Luke's dad?"

Jazz took another enormous mouthful of beer, leaving Katie to answer. "You haven't met Luke's father yet, have you?"

Jazz swallowed noisily and then nearly choked himself trying to do a Darth Vader impersonation, hissing into his beer glass, "Luke, I *am* your father." He'd clearly reached the stage of drunkenness where we could expect *Little Britain* quotes at any minute.

"No," I said, ignoring him.

"Hasn't Luke wanted to introduce you? Or hasn't Luke told him yet that he's got a fiancée bobbing around in York? And"—she rounded on Jazz—"how do *you* know there's nothing worse than getting a guy into bed who turns out to have a micropenis?"

Jazz pointed at her with the end of his glass. "*I* listen to women. I am a New Man." Then he burped resonantly, grinned and fell off his stool.

"Luke's waiting until his dad has got over his heart surgery," I explained to Katie. "He's been really poorly and Luke wants to wait, rather than mention it when everything is all oxygen tents and monitors."

"Fair enough."

"Three, two, one...you're back in the room," came from under the table and I stood up.

"Right. I'm off. Going over to Cal's tomorrow and I wouldn't want to tangle with him if I was hungover." Beneath the table there was now the sound of an enthusiastic amateur Scissor Sisters impersonator murdering "Take Your Mama Out". "He's all yours, Kate."

"Gosh, thanks."

Due to Jazz's prodigious consumption of alcohol causing the evening to end a little earlier than usual, I found myself at a bit of a loose end. I could have gone home with Katie but, although I adored her twins, I frankly found them completely exhausting. So I found myself wandering around York, through the narrow, picturesque streets in the Shambles area, heading towards the river, along with most of the jogging population of the city. The smell of muscle spray filled the air, and the hissing and cracking of water bottles being sucked echoed off the concrete of the embankment like the sound of a Dalek life-support system.

I looked up at the windows of our flat-to-be. On impulse I crossed the bridge and went through the glass and metal foyer to stand in the hallway which led to the lifts. People had already started living in some of the flats. I could tell by the lights which shone onto balconies and the shadowy figures moving about within. Anticipation nudged its way around my heart like a dolphin in an aquarium.

Soon two of those figures would be mine and Luke's, cooking dinner together, flopping on the sofa with a glass of wine and a DVD, deciding on a colour scheme for the bedroom. All things I was totally unpractised at, comfortable, domestic things. Our lives seemed to run along parallel to one another, with occasional passionate collisions and exciting interludes in hotels or on beaches—very romantic, but hardly real life. I thought about Luke's reasoning, that moving in with me wouldn't exactly be a gentle initiation into what married life could be, but more a baptism of fire—what with Clay, Ash, and the vagaries of our working lives—frenzied, and we'd hardly ever see each other.

I walked outside, into the freshening breeze, and gazed up at the building. We'd got the deposit together between us and Luke was going to the estate agent on Monday to put in the offer. Once the flat was secured, we could go ahead and set a date for the wedding, and then the wagons would be rolling. Although rolling was probably not the word, more like accelerating rapidly downhill. My wedding had been planned in great detail since my first boyfriend had twanged my bra strap. Now it really only remained to weed out the place settings for the relatives who had since died.

I was considering dress styles, lengths and appropriate materials (was raw silk a little too *passé* or could I get away with it?) when I arrived home. The house was quiet, in that buzzy kind of way which meant that there was nobody else home, rather than the hushed-quiet-with-background-stereo which might indicate that Clay was hanging upside down in the loft, or whatever it was he did up there. Maybe he'd got a Friday night date. Or maybe he was roaming the streets with his apotheosistic face on, sketching unwary buildings. Anyway, who cared? After being out almost every night this week, I was in the mood for a long, soapy bath, candles and an early bed.

There, accusingly direct on the mat, sat another brown envelope. I felt a curious sense of violation, as my heartbeat sprinted blood through my veins and the back of my neck tingled with a feeling that something malevolent had put a dark mark on my home. After all, who thought they were entitled to tell my family we didn't deserve what we had?

I tore open the flap and flicked the single sheet open. "You don't deserve it." Again the same handwriting, the same graphic approach to indefinite one-liners. Did they think that this cloak-and-dagger approach made it better somehow, more palatable? And there was something laughable in the repetition. My stalker couldn't even manage originality.

As I had done with the last letter, I scrunched this one up into a ball and dropped it into a drawer in the hall dresser. There was simply no point in getting angry over such vague hints which couldn't be said to amount to a threat, was not much more than a simple point of view, unattributed and unattributable. So why did my thoughts keep coming back to it?

౸౬

I was still shambling around the house in dressing gown and slippers when Cal turned up at the door next morning.

"God, you're early." I let him in and shuffled back through to the kitchen for more strong tea.

"Great thinkers never sleep."

"Do they drink tea?" I brandished a mug.

"All the time. Noted for it. No milk, two sugars and I could slaughter a piece of toast."

"Bread. Toaster. Butter. Marmalade. Teapot." I pointed as I spoke, my arm jerking randomly around the kitchen. "I'm going to get dressed."

By the time I came back down, wearing my best goat-proof clothing, Cal had made a stack of toast, which leaned dangerously over the edge of the plate, defying gravity only through the adhesive powers of marmalade.

And then he ate it. All of it. I watched, with my jaw becoming more and more slack, until the final crust was chewed and swallowed, and he noticed me.

"What?"

"You're so *skinny*! How can you eat so much and be so thin?"

"Genuinely interested, or is this a women's comment type thing?"

"No, I really want to know. I mean, do you have worms or something?" I heard the sound of footsteps on the stairs and unthinkingly poured tea into another mug, holding it at arm's length just in time for Clay's entrance into the kitchen. Cal glanced at Clay and carried on talking to me.

"I am, in reality, incredibly fat. I have an enormous pleat which runs down my spine. Observe how I never walk *away* from people, only towards them. This is to prevent them noticing that said pleat stretches into Lancashire."

Clay, decidedly less deific at this time in the morning, looked puzzled. "Who the hell are you?" And then, a misplaced sense of realisation dawned. "Oh, right. You're, um, with Willow, yes?"

I broke the embarrassed silence by dropping Cal's toast plate into the sink. "This is Cal. He's a friend of Ash's."

"Oh. Is Ash back then?"

"Er, no." I grabbed a jacket from the back of the kitchen door. It didn't look very goat-resistant, but I wanted to get out of there before Clay really got started. "See you later, Clay, okay?" I hustled Cal, as swiftly as he would let himself be hustled, to the front door.

"And Clay is?" Cal stopped on the doorstep, rummaging in pockets.

"My brother. Eldest."

Cal brandished a set of keys. "Right."

I stared at him. "You're driving?"

"Well, yeah. It's a bloody long way for a piggyback."

"No, I just..." I managed to shut myself up.

"You didn't think I'd be able to drive, did you?" Cal waved the key fob and across the road the lights on the tattiest Metro I'd ever seen blinked in response.

"It's not that." I bridled at the implication, "I kind of assumed you'd have a bike."

"A *bike*?" This said in Lady Bracknellesque tones.

"Yes. Like Ash."

"Oh, a *motor*bike. I see. No, sorry to disappoint any fantasies you might have about slipping your leg over my tank. If it makes you feel any better I could strap you to the bonnet?"

Since the bonnet of the Metro looked semipermanent at best, I declined his kind offer and wriggled my way into the passenger seat, negotiating three Aero wrappers, an empty sandwich packet, a full bag of crisps (cheese and onion) and a lone sock on my way.

Cal was the worst driver in possession of a full licence that I'd ever sat next to. In complete silence, because his concentration was almost palpable, we ricocheted through the streets of York, along the road north and up onto the moors, where we were overtaken by several curious sheep and a bunch of octogenarian walkers. At last we pulled in to the top of the path to the house and got out. Cal was almost immediately disadvantaged.

"Sorry," he said. "It's the bloody mud. Can't get my balance. One of the reasons why I don't reckon I can hang on to the place."

"You could tarmac the path as far as the first field, then have a kind of gravelled parking area and it's not so much of a stretch to the house."

Cal looked at me sideways. "You've clearly thought about it."

"Well, when I was here with Ash, I wondered how you'd get a car down. How did your great aunt manage?"

Cal turned his attention back to the path, down which he was edging slowly. "Oh, she carried everything. On her back. Built like King Kong, my great aunt, thighs like a set of welding equipment."

"Cal," I warned.

"Oh, all right. She had a pony and trap. The ultimate in four-wheel-drive."

We rounded the last bend and stopped, by silent agreement, to take in the sight of the tiny white cottage stamped in the green field. A few late daffodils fluttered flags of yellow in the grass, puffs of cloud scratting about overhead. "Wordsworth would have wet himself," I said.

"Wordsworth never had to pick up the maintenance bill for picturesque." Cal gave a sigh and leaned against the gate. "If any of the Romantic poets had ever had to contend with damp courses, they would have taken to writing obscene limericks."

"I dunno. I always suspected Coleridge would have been handy with a routing tool." I leaned alongside him, arms on the top bar, chewing my lip. "Cal, are you sure you want to sell?"

"No. But, ach, sometimes everything's wrong, you know?" Briskly he pulled himself off the gate. "Right. Let's go and find the old bitch, shall we? Are you going to be all right? I mean, she's hefty, and she's got a whole circus of tricks up her...what I shall have to describe, for now, as a sleeve."

"If you'd really thought I couldn't handle her, you wouldn't have asked me to come along, would you?" I asked with impeccable logic. "Lead the way. If not the goat."

We found the goat, a Toggenburg improbably enough named Winnie, grazing in the orchard next to the house. It was a fairly simple matter to grab her by the leather belt she wore around her neck and haul her through the gateway. Throughout the whole experience, Winnie maintained a typically goatlike expression of aggrieved surprise and only tried to injure me seriously once. I, however, had trained up on small, evil ponies, every one a semiprofessional in maiming, and steering a goat presented few problems to a woman who has once rolled a Shetland down an embankment.

"That was incredible." Cal spoke from the safety of the sidelines, as Winnie, with a look of execration in her satanic eyes, peed all over my foot, then trotted to the river, managing to drink whilst still staring at us from under her eyebrows.

"Thank you." I squelched my way out of the field. "And for my next trick, I shall smell of goat's piss all the way home."

"You don't have to. If I get the Aga lit, you could have a bath."

"Have you got a towel?"

"In the car. Oh, and if you're going up, there's a cool bag in the boot with some food and drinks in."

"Anything else? I mean, if I say I fancy listening to some music, are you going to tell me that you've got the Manchester Philharmonic in the glovebox?"

"Er, no. But there is a digital radio under the passenger seat."

"Oh, aren't you the well-equipped one."

"Never had any complaints yet," Cal said, archly. I rolled my eyes at him and started the soggy-socked process back up the hill towards the parked car. The sun was shining through the leaves, lime green with newness, which made it feel as though I was walking along the bottom of a river, a feeling which the silence and the occasional stickleback dart of small birds only enhanced. In the time it took me to riffle through the vehicle's contents (loads of clothes and CDs, two bottles of beer, an unopened packet of condoms and more rubbish and wrappers than I would have believed a Metro could hold), only two cars and a tractor passed the lane end.

I trotted back down to the house with the fluorescent pink cool bag under one arm and a striped beach towel under the other, to find that Cal had managed to fire up the ancient farmhouse range which occupied the kitchen like a rusty squatter.

"Give it an hour or so, then we'll have more than enough hot water for you to get clean. Pass me the lunch, I'll pop the bottles in the stream to cool down."

While he was gone I had an in-depth look around the little house. Okay, it smelled of damp and cabbagey old ladies but... "This really could be a lovely place," I said, descending the vertical, and bannisterless, staircase. "That front bedroom with those beams, it's perfect."

"Used to be mine, when I was a kid. If you open the cupboard in the corner, there's a secret set of ladders leading to the attics."

"And the views. How much land comes with the place?"

Cal looked at me quizzically. "Why the interest?"

I was suddenly ashamed. Whilst I'd wandered upstairs my imagination had taken over and I had seen the master bedroom all fitted out, the smaller back room painted pink, carpeted and with a tiny cot taking pride of place. Outside I could almost have sworn that I had seen my future self trailing a lazy finger over knee-high herbs in an area currently occupied by the spitting-mad goat. Even the archaic bathroom fixtures had a kind of *Country Living* charm. "I think the place has potential, that's all."

"Yes, it's potentially a house. Slightly unfortunately it isn't one at the moment. Look, I've got some work to do. Would you like to cruise around the acres for a bit? I won't be long and then we can have some lunch."

"Do you need a hand with anything?" There was a short pause during which I had time to wish I could bite my tongue off.

"I'll be fine." Cal spoke a little stiffly. "I'll give you a shout when I'm done." And he walked carefully and precisely out into the courtyard, around to one of the little barns, went in and shut the door with a kind of "bugger off" finality.

I went back upstairs and became slightly disenchanted with the bathroom. Then I further explored the bedrooms, finding the cupboard Cal had mentioned and ascending the rickety ladders to the dust-haunted attic beyond. A dormer window let more light in up there than any of the lower rooms could boast, and the view across the valley to the purple hills beyond was spectacular.

Jane Lovering

The place was absolutely and totally the house I would have picked for myself, mouldy floorboards and all. It had everything, seclusion, outbuildings, cosy rooms with open fireplaces. The range sitting in the kitchen could have comfortably cooked a meal for forty, and heated enough water to wash it all up in. And, as instinctively as I knew that I could happily live here, I knew that Luke would hate it.

I sighed and looked out of the window which opened onto the courtyard. There was no sign of Cal and the barn door was still firmly closed. From the field beyond, the goat gave me a narrow-eyed look of hatred, and I was sure I could hear the music from *The Exorcist*.

"Sod it." I was bored now, and hungry. The barn door was invitingly ajar as I crossed the yard. "Cal? Sorry, I just wondered..." I pushed the door open slowly and put my head around, in time to catch Cal whipping off a pair of headphones and starting to his feet.

"Oh, fuck it. Come in here, Willow, and shut the bloody door!" I was taken aback by this uncharacteristic ferocity. Cal was usually laid-back and so indirect that you needed a map to get his point. In here, though, he seemed to have become someone else. His hair was tied behind his head, his gaze direct and incisive. "Sit over there for a second, I'm nearly done." Indicating a bale of straw in one corner of the barn, he was already turning to the screen in front of him, replacing the headphones and sitting on the ergonomic seat with the keyboard set on the table attached.

I could only stare. In contrast to the charmingly unmodernised cottage, the barn was, well, shit hot. A machine even *I* recognised as a state-of-the-art computer was humming away to itself on the wall, a green light flashing on and off beside it. Cal sat before a screen the thickness of a credit card, tapping on the keyboard at rattling speed, every now and then
110

speaking into a microphoned headset. Two laptops were running, set on the side of an old hayrack and the air smelled of technology.

A couple more snapped remarks into the microphone and Cal snatched it off, shutting down monitors and shushing noisy units with a well-pressed button. A flick of a master switch and all the lights went dead, leaving us in the windowless dark and new silence.

"Well," said Cal, and there was a slightly different tone in his voice.

"Well?" I realised that I was trapped here, in this barn, on this nameless farm, with a man I didn't know. And someone had been sending me anonymous letters. And no one knew where I was. "Well," I repeated, and my voice had a little wobble to it.

"Well, I don't know about you, but I'm bloody starving. Come on." The big door was pulled open and sunlight spilled like butter through the gap. Cal loosened his hair from its ponytail and was back in the land of the vague again. Even his eyes lost their focussed expression. "I would race you, but we all know about the tortoise and the hare, don't we, and I wouldn't want you to have to bear the humiliation."

Almost bursting with questions, I followed him down a pretty little garden path which led between low-growing beds of alpine phlox and thrift to where the garden seemed to fold in upon itself. It was an almost obscenely sexual place.

"It's like having lunch in a porn star, but there you go. My great aunt, bless her, wasn't the most perceptive of people and she liked the shape of the garden here. The stream was an accident, but I'm afraid the judiciously planted ferns were her doing." Cal nodded towards a group of feathery fronds jutting pubicly just above the stream's trickle. "Have a sandwich. Just thank God it's not sausage."

I snorted and took one. It was egg and cress and delicious. Then I had four more. Cal opened a bottle of wine which had been dangling in the green water and we shared it and some strawberries and before I knew it, I was telling Cal all about Luke, the engagement and the flat. I moved on to Katie and Jazz, my family and then I was pontificating about Ash.

"And, d'you know the stupid thing? Now he's prannying about in Prague or wherever, instead of being here. An' he should be here, really, shouldn't he? I mean, really. Go on, you can tell me." It was dawning on my system that we were at least halfway through a second bottle of wine and maybe now was the time for me to shut up. But sounding off about Ash always overrode the system.

"Do you know where I met Ash?" Cal asked suddenly, lying on his stomach facing away from me.

"No."

"We were both in therapy."

"Therapy? What, you mean lying on a couch telling everyone how unhappy your childhood was?"

"More or less." Cal poured me some more wine, then he took a deep breath. "Ash was there because of his family relationships. Did you know that?"

I shook my head. "My brother never tells me anything. I think he hates me." My lip trembled. I'd reached that stage down the bottle.

"Uh-huh." Cal was a little uncoordinated too. "He was in therapy because he felt he was living in your shadow, that you were the bright one and he was just Ash, I suppose. You got a degree, the house and a life and he's got nothing."

"I thought he liked it that way." I downed the wine in one gulp because it was beginning to taste like paint-thinner. "Why were you in therapy? You seem really sorted."

"Sorted? Me?" There was an uncharacteristic bitterness in his voice for a second. "No, I was in therapy because I was mad. Totally, unalterably mad, you see." He added a little cackle for effect. "But I'm fine now. I have come to terms with the fact that I'm Napoleon."

"No one ever imagines that they're plain old Mrs. Biggins, do they?"

Cal rolled over on his back. "I don't think it quite works like that, you know." He laid an arm over his eyes to block out the sun. So I couldn't see his face when he asked, "Have you set a date for the wedding yet?"

"Not yet. Luke's still getting the showroom up and running, so he's hopping over to the States a lot. We have to wait until that settles down before we can finalise details."

"Hmmm."

"What's that supposed to mean?"

"Nothing. But he's okay, this Luke, is he?"

"He's...yes, he's fantastic. Totally gorgeous. I mean, he probably wouldn't do it for you. He's nothing like Ash after all. But he's got a great body. Not that I'm commenting on Ash's body, you understand. I mean, yuk, but—"

"What do you mean, 'he's nothing like Ash'?"

"Well, he isn't. Ash is kind of gawky and angular while Luke is—"

"Yes, I get that. But what I meant was, why would I want to compare him to Ash, for God's sake?" Cal uncovered his face and sat up to look at me.

"Because I know you gay guys usually go for a type, that's all." I sat up, too, although it made my head swim a bit.

"Hang on. *I'm* gay? When did that happen?"

"What do you mean?"

"If I *were* gay, I think I might have noticed, don't you? I mean, there's all that business with the buying the right clothes, hanging round the right bars, the attitude and, oh God, I don't think I've got the *time* to be gay, let alone the inclination."

"But you have to be gay!" We were practically forehead to forehead now. "You and Ash, you were... Can you do that if you're not gay?" He really did have the most remarkable eyes, very brown, with lashes so dark they looked like the reeds on the ponds of the netherworld.

"You haven't spoken to Ash lately, have you?" Cal wasn't moving back either, his eyes flickering as they took in my face. "I really wanted him to tell you because it was a bit of a...I was going to say 'cock up' but that would only compound matters, wouldn't it? But look." His fingers cupped my chin and curled up onto my cheek. "If I was gay, then I wouldn't want to do this, would I?" The gentlest kiss fell on the side of my mouth. Instinctively, like a baby searching out food, I turned towards it and felt his lips fasten onto mine for one brief, thunderclap moment.

The next second he was flat on the grass again, arm blocking the sun, leaving me half-crouched and breathless, wondering whether the whole thing had been an alcohol illusion. "You're *not gay*," I said wonderingly.

"Nope."

"Shit."

"Sorry."

"No, I meant..." And before I had time to move, I was voluminously, copiously, dramatically sick all over his shirt, his jeans. I think I even managed to fill his pocket and get it in his hair. It was truly the most impressive of vomits. To his credit he didn't pull away or act shocked. He simply waited for the retching to stop, then sat up and offered me a handkerchief.

"Here. Do you want a drink of water or something?"

"Please." The tiny voice was all I could manage, forced over the broken glass of embarrassment.

"Ash did tell me that you had a bit of a problem with your stomach." Cal handed me a chilled bottle of mineral water and I used it to rinse my mouth, although I really wanted to pour it over him and eliminate the chunks of recycled picnic which clung to his clothes. "Have you ever tried getting help?"

"The doctors told me it was just stress and I'd grow out of it. They couldn't explain why it only happens when I meet a man I..." *Oops.*

"A man you...?"

"I quite like." I busied myself blowing my nose and sluicing my face with water from the stream. Anything but meet his eye. "Do you think there's any chance the water will be hot yet?"

Cal glanced down at himself, dripping regurgitation. "Oh, I hope so," he said, fervently. "If not, I'm prepared to get in the river. Hey." I'd turned away, horrified and ashamed of myself, hiding the tears of mortification in the handkerchief. "It's not your fault. Don't worry. I'm not soluble, you know."

My voice was muffled. "I just *hate* it, that's all. Why can't I be normal?"

Cal gave his lame leg the briefest glance. "Normal isn't everything. Anyway if you were normal, I wouldn't like you. Come on. I'll let you have first dibs on the bath, but don't piss in the water, okay?"

I gave a coughing laugh. "Okay." We'd got to the house before I summoned enough courage to ask the pressing question. "Cal, back there, why did you kiss me?"

"Felt like it. Problem?"

"No, I...but you know I'm engaged."

"Yeah. So? It was only a kiss, not full penetration. You looked a bit sad, that was all, very fragile. I wanted to cheer you up. Sorry if it didn't work."

The weird thing was, I thought later as I lay back in the hot, rusty-coloured water, that it *had* worked. In a kind of sideways, roundabout way. Y'see, despite my undeniably pert chest and my winning way with a *bon mot*, I failed to believe that I had anything much going for me. All right, I was pretty enough in a Miss Average, wouldn't-kick-it-out-of-bed kind of way. But Luke must meet a thousand girls like me in the course of the working day. Cal's kiss had reassured me that there *was* something about me that men found appealing. I grinned to myself and submerged. The enormous freestanding, cast-iron bath was large enough to allow all of me under.

A tap at the door. "You all right?"

"Yes, thanks."

"Do you want a cup of tea in there?"

A pause. "But I'm in the bath. Naked."

"Can't you judiciously pile up some bubbles? I promise not to let my passion be inflamed."

"Oh, go on then."

The door opened cautiously and Cal, pretending to screw his eyes shut, advanced across the floor with a cup held out vaguely in my direction. Since absolutely none of me was visible under the brown water, I chuckled.

"For God's sake open your eyes, man. I know you're peeping anyway, because you avoided that ripped bit of carpet."

"Bugger." He handed me the cup and perched himself on the window seat looking down onto the garden, leg bent up under his chin. "I'm going to have to sell." His voice was almost inaudible under the sloshing of the bathwater. "I've decided. I nearly fell down those bloody stairs, and with the uneven floors, it's just not possible. I mean, it's not the money, but what's the point in keeping it?"

"You could let it out. For holidays?"

"Couldn't bear owning it, but not living in it. This is home. I mean I spent a lot of time here, when I was younger, I...growing up, I...." The words vanished into a shake of the head and he concentrated out of the window very hard for a few moments. When he spoke again his voice was gruff with something he wouldn't let me see. "Better off with a clean break."

I swished water around with my hand, thinking. "I could buy it."

"Nah. You couldn't."

"How much are you going to ask for it?"

"Dunno. State it's in, it's not worth much, but there's the land. Some clever developer could probably get permission to convert the barns, do up the house, two hundred K, probably."

"I could buy it." In my excitement, I nearly stood up.

"What?"

"I could. Oh, not quite yet, but..." And then the story of my grandfather's legacy came tumbling out, mixed-up words and confused sentence structure, but he got the point.

"Wow. Four hundred and fifty thou. You could buy this place, do it up and still have change."

Jane Lovering

"And I want to. Honestly, Cal, not as a favour to you or anything, but I love it here. The atmosphere and the space, the fields. I can grow my herbs and maybe keep the goat. No, I'll get a house cow, plenty of stabling for the kids' ponies. Best of all, you can keep visiting. You needn't feel that you've lost the place forever."

"You'd *do* that?" There was that bright intensity in his eyes again, that tight, concentrated look I'd seen outside.

"Yes, of course. You could even keep your equipment out there in the barn if you wanted."

A sharp glance. "Willow, it would be better if you forget you saw any of that, all right?"

I made a hurt face. "Why? What were you doing, calling the mothership?"

Cal shook his head again slowly, but all he said was "Are you done in that bath yet? I'm beginning to disintegrate here" and left the room, leaving me with the similarly coloured cooling tea and bathwater.

Chapter Fifteen

I didn't tell Luke about the kiss. Hell, I didn't even tell *Katie.* Although I did give Katie and Jazz a highly comically embellished version of events regarding the goat and Katie got a hush-hush outline of my plan to buy the white house once my money came through. The kiss was too casual to mention and might have given rise to some awkward questioning, so I simply pretended it hadn't happened and everything carried on as before. Luke and I continued to date, Clay continued to plague me with his poltergeistular activities around the house and Ash continued not to return from Europe.

Eventually the lack of forward motion got to me.

"Do you think we should set a date for the wedding?" I asked Luke.

"If you like. I thought we were going to wait until the flat was all okay first. But, no, if you want to get the date sorted, that's cool."

We were sitting beside a moorland stream. I was dabbling my feet in the water while Luke watched. He'd taken his shirt off and the sun outlined his muscles, giving his skin a tawny glow. He looked like a young lion with a decidedly predatory gleam in his eye.

"It's not that I'm bothered, as such, just, people are asking. And the sooner we have a target date the easier it will be to organise." That's what it said in the latest edition of *Bride* anyway. It was advice of the month.

Luke shrugged. "You do know that I need to get the business up and running properly, don't you? Before we kick off the married thing?"

"Yes, I know."

"And that the flat is taking time."

I knew that, too. Luke was dealing with all the paperwork and there were, apparently, glitches in the purchase because it was a new building. I wasn't too worried, still hugging the potential of Cal's house to myself. The flat would be an ideal base for us in town, but the white house was where I wanted to *live*.

"So, you want to settle on a date. That's fine with me. It just might have to be a fairly long engagement, until things are definite." Luke took an apple from the basket of food I'd brought and bit into it firmly. I pretended not to notice the lascivious way he licked the juice from his fingers while looking at me.

"Twenty-first of October," I said spontaneously.

"Aw, are you sure you wouldn't rather have a summer wedding? All outdoorsy, you like that sort of thing, don't you? We could have it on the lawn somewhere."

"It's nearly June now. There isn't really time."

"I meant next summer."

"Oh." Now, why on *earth* should that disappoint me? I wanted the whole shebang, the big dress, the big party, hopefully a hen weekend somewhere insalubrious. It was traditional, wasn't it? When he'd said a long engagement, I'd been thinking three months. A year would be much better, give me ages to plan, to go through all the brochures, to pick *just* the right dress and slim into it. I knew he wanted to marry me, so why did I need to hurry things? "All right, next summer. Twenty-first of June. We can have a solstice wedding."

"Very New-Agey." Luke threw the apple core into the stream. "Now, come over here and show me what other New Age tricks you've got."

As we made love, I found my mind wandering. The twenty-first of June. Well, by then I'd have enough cash to make sure things went with a bang. I shivered underneath Luke, who mistook my anticipation of money for sexual frenzy and redoubled his efforts to drive me deeper into the soft peat beneath us.

Afterwards he sat up, panting, and flicked his hair from his eyes. "Bloody hellfire, woman, you are fantastic in the sack, do you know that?"

Gosh. "Am I?"

"Oh, wow, yeah. It's so great to have someone who throws herself into it, not always fussing and nagging. Sorry. Don't mean to compare you with past girlfriends, but..." He gave a whistle. "Yeah. You're hot."

ഇ൦ര

"I'm hot," I announced to Katie and Jazz when we met up the following evening. "It's official."

"Thought I could smell something," Jazz said into his pint.

"Of course you are." Katie handed me my drink. "Never doubted it for a second."

"And I've got something to show you. Got it today."

"Syphilis?"

"Jazz! No, look." Slowly, tauntingly, from my pocket I withdrew the shiny silver object that Luke had driven over to give me that afternoon. "It's the key to our new flat. And anyway, can you *show* someone syphilis? Isn't it sort of invisible?"

"Until your face falls off." Jazz took the key and turned it over on his hand, like an insect. "So. When are you moving in? You and Wonder Boy?"

"Not for a bit. I'm really hoping that this money from Ganda's invention will turn up soon, so that I can get the finances sorted out for the other house and then spend the rest on the flat and the wedding."

"Is Luke not paying for any of this?" Katie asked carefully. I was a bit sensitive to suggestions that Luke's and my financial situation might be a little lopsided.

"Well, *yes*, obviously. He's put the deposit down on the flat and he'll be contributing to the wedding. The house of Cal's, that's private, that's mine."

"I thought you already gave him some money for the deposit on the flat." Jazz was still turning the key over and over. "And for his business."

"Yes, I did. But, come on, what is this? Luke and I will sort it all out between us. At the moment I'm the one with the big cash income and he's still setting up the business, but in the future"—like when I've stopped work to have babies and to wander through orchards in flowery dresses—"then *he'll* be the one with the money. Things work out, Jazz, in relationships. Not that you'd know, of course."

There was a communal in-suck of breath. "Bit near the mark there, Wills," Katie said.

"How come my love life is fair game for the two of you and yet I'm not even allowed to mention Jazz's total lack of success with anything female. Hell, even the cat left him after a week." I rounded on Jazz, jumping to my feet and catching my knees on the underside of the table so that drinks slopped about all over the surface.

"We worry about you. Jazz is quite capable of looking after himself."

"And by implication I'm not?"

"The difference between us is that I know what I want." Jazz mopped at his spilt beer with the sleeve of his jacket.

"Oh, great. So now I'm incapable of looking after myself *and* indecisive?" I gathered my things together. "Thanks very much, guys."

Katie caught my arm. "Will, sit down. We're not having a go at you, we're just telling as we see it. From our perspective things seem to have moved incredibly quickly and, yeah, it's a fantastic coincidence that you met Luke again, and it's wonderful that you've come into this money and everything, but we want you to be sure that you're doing the right thing."

"Bullshit. You think he's after my money. Look, how many times do I have to point out that Luke didn't know I *had* any money when we met. Hell, *I* didn't know I had any money. Luke isn't like that anyway. He's sweet and he loves me and we're going to get married and we've set a date and I was going to tell you, but now I'm not even sure that I'm going to invite either of you because you're horrible to me and I'm going." The three of us eyeballed each other for a moment, or at least Katie and I eyeballed. Jazz raised his eyes ceiling-ward and mouthed "bloody women", then we all burst out laughing.

"You can't not invite me," Katie said. "I have to be the one in the pictures who makes you look all thin and gorgeous."

"What, you mean like I was at your wedding?"

"Yep. I have to wear something so bright that it strobes, and have a fat face with a horrid headpiece which makes me look like a hamster in a wig. 'S obligatory."

Jazz grinned. "And I have to look sensationally shaggable so your new husband gets all jealous and punches me."

"Gosh."

"Yeah. He has to break my nose or it's not a proper wedding, apparently."

"Ooh, ooh!" Katie bounced and squeaked. "And I have to be caught in a compromising position with the best man. So if you could steer Luke to pick someone who's good-looking, or at least doesn't smell, I'll be grateful."

"*I* didn't get caught in a compromising position at your wedding."

"No, but you did get my grandma stuck in the toilet. That counts."

"Oh, yes." I collected my bag and jacket. "I'm glad we got that sorted out. Now I really am off home. Luke and I are going to Cornwall this weekend and I want to pack."

It was a tiny fib, not even that, more a fibbette. I *did* want to get home and pack, but first I wanted to go and investigate the new flat. The key shone virgin in the evening sunshine as I fitted it into the lock and pushed the door open. Inside, the late light sliced in over the balcony and fell just *so* on the spot where I planned to put the intended Italian leather sofa. Mocha, a nice practical colour I could liven up with throws. I wandered around the rooms, much as an artist might walk around a blank canvas—potentially, an iron-framed bedstead just *here* and some light gauzy curtains over *these* windows. Then I went out to stand on the balcony to watch the last of the natural light drain from the sky. Luke was right. It was a fantastically central, wonderfully appointed, fabulous investment. It just didn't feel as though it would ever be my *home*.

හිඟ

As I walked back across the river, I felt a familiar sense of potential hanging over my head. This usually meant the return of my twin—I've explained to you already, haven't I, that Ash and I have the twin-unspoken-communication thing, although neither of us wants it—and, sure enough, there was the red Yamaha slouched in the front garden as though it had never been away. Proving, however, that away had very much been the case, was the rucksack left pointedly by the washing machine. One undone strap gave us a view of grey lycra, like an overweight and grubby stripper flashing her underwear. Farther into the house, Ash was sitting on the kitchen table with his feet on a chair, holding forth to Clay on the beauty of Slovakian architecture, smoking a joint and spinning a beer bottle top in a saucer.

"How long have you been back?"

"Nice to see you, too."

"Sorry. Hello, brother dear. How was your trip and how fucking long have you been back?"

"That's better. Just since this morning. Clay tells me you're going away? With a *man*? God, I can't leave you alone for a moment, can I? Who is he, then? Anyone I know?" He looked at me through a cloud of blue smoke, eyes narrowed, doing Lauren Bacall for all he was worth.

"No. His name's Luke." This was as much information as Clay had and I didn't feel up to giving them any more. "Why did you tell me Cal was gay?"

"And who the hell's he?" Clay asked.

"Friend of Ash's. You met him a couple of weeks ago."

"Oh, yes. Dark guy, awful clothes, ate all the bread and I had to run up to Morrison's in my pyjamas."

"That's him."

"I didn't tell you he was gay." But I could always tell when Ash was toying with the truth. He sort of blushed, although not completely. The tips of his ears went pink and he developed a nervous swallow. He was doing it now.

"You told me you were living with him."

"All right, all right, but look"—Ash lowered his voice—"not here. Come on." Flicking both the joint and the bottle top back into the saucer, he slithered off the table and headed for the stairs. I followed, and we ended up in his old room, sitting on the bed staring at a poster of David Boreanaz peeling off one purple wall. It was just like the old days. "I didn't want Clay to know," Ash explained, draping himself across the bed. "He already thinks I'm a complete wanker."

I shrugged and began picking at the blu-tac remnants on the wall beside the bed, where, until fairly recently, Robbie Williams had resided. "At the moment I'm not far behind him," I said, carefully not mentioning the definitive kiss. "I felt a complete idiot when I found out he was straight."

"Okay." Ash took a deep breath. "Here it goes. I met Cal."

"Three years ago when you were both in therapy, yeah, I know. Can we cut to *why you lied*?"

"Shut up, bitch. Let me tell it. So, I was...well, I was having some problems. So I went for help and met up with Cal. We hit it off. Used to hang out together on and off. I got the feeling he didn't see too many people. Not a social guy if you know what I mean." Ash's idea of social was someone who went clubbing six nights out of seven, who slept with at least four different men a week and had a black leather organiser with more addresses and phone numbers in it than the Yellow Pages. "I never hit on him and he never hit on me, but, you know, I always got the *feeling*. Right, so, hadn't seen him for a year or so. Suddenly ran into him again about six months back when I had a PDA giving me problems. He sorted it out for me and we got talking. He was pretty low, he'd got very isolated, you know about the leg? He doesn't put himself about much. I was looking for somewhere to stay and he said he had a spare couch I could sleep on. Think he was lonely to tell the truth. You started going on about not meeting people, and I thought, 'hey, I could introduce Will to Cal'. Thought he was straight enough, at least for you."

"Oy!"

"Come off it, Will. You know you like 'em a bit fey. You're not a girl for a big guy who wants his ironing done and some little woman waiting at home for him, are you? Anyhow. By now I'm thinking he's not as straight as he makes out. He...we...okay, I reckon I fancied him. In fact, I'd started to wonder if he could be *the One*, if you see what I mean. Looking back, Christ, Will, I was fucking stupid. He was obviously interested in you, but I couldn't see it, and then..." Ash stopped and developed a sudden and intense interest in a loose piece of thread hanging from the underside of the mattress.

"Then, what?"

"Then, when I took your laptop for fixing, I dunno what happened. It was..."

"Oh, spit it out, man."

"That's not what they usually say." Ash gave me one of his mischievous grins.

"You are *such* a tart." But I grinned too and a spark of the old twin thing flipped between us again.

"Cal was really, really uptight. Totally wired. I thought he'd got hold of some bad stuff. Guy says he doesn't do drugs but, huh, I mean, who is he kidding, anyhow. He's sitting there, strung out to hell, kind of crying. It was more than I could stand. I mean, Jesus but that boy is *ripped*. Something about the eyes, I reckon, just flips me out. So I sit down beside him, ask him what's happening. He says something about not standing a chance with anyone. Next thing I've got my arms round him, he's not fighting, not saying anything much so..."

"You kissed him." God, if only it hadn't been my brother, this would have been funny.

"Yeah."

"And?"

"And he kissed me back. Honest to God, full-on. So I go to take it a bit further, if you know what I mean, and he stands up, very quietly, and says, 'sorry, Ash, but I think you misunderstand'. Something like that anyway. Then he says that I'm a good friend, all that kind of shit, but, basically, he doesn't go for guys. And I'm really screwed. Guy broke my heart, right, so I fucked off to Europe. Tried to ring you a couple of times and explain but never seemed to catch you in. That's it. End of story."

A long pause during which we both stared at different parts of the room without saying anything.

Ash broke first. "All right, I'm sorry."

"It doesn't matter."

"*What*? Way you were carrying on, I thought it was some major fuck-up cause."

"No. I just like to make you sweat, oh, and apologise. God, it feels good."

"You bitch." Ash got up off the bed. "So, you and Cal?"

"No. Like I said, I'm going out with Luke. Cal, he's a friend. Kind of. He's bloody weird though, isn't he?"

"Oh, *yeah.*" Ash and I gave each other a slightly ashamed smile. "Fucking sex-on-legs though. Wasted on girls." He stretched himself out in the doorway. "Right. I'm off out."

"Slapper."

"Hey, I could be digging old ladies' gardens, all you know."

"That's what you call it now, is it? Well, don't forget to put your Marigolds on before you plant anything."

"I never forget." Ash began to make his exit, but turned back. "Oh. FYI."

"Mmmm?"

"Cal. Hung like a fucking donkey. Even bigger than Plastic Dave." Plastic Dave was a silicon-enhanced beauty who ran a bar down one of the seediest sidestreets York had to offer and was reputed throughout the gay community to be A Big Man.

"And how would you know?"

Ash just tapped the side of his nose and winked, then spiral-jumped down the stairs. Seconds later I heard the bike engine fire up, a few moments of door-slamming as he came in and out, fetching helmets and gear, then the punctuating roar of the 750cc engine being kept, more or less, to the speed limit as far as the end of the road. I went to my own room to start packing, hoping that my eyebrows would begin to come down to their normal level before I had to leave for Cornwall.

Chapter Sixteen

Cornwall in late May, and the tourists were starting to pack into the tiny county, filling the beaches with flabby bellies. Bodmin Moor, isolated and, despite the general sunshine everywhere else, draped in torn shrouds of mist, was where we ended up, in a gothic hotel. The place looked not so much built as extruded, a huge pile of grey granite, towered, turreted and moated. The rooms were all high-ceilinged with room for half the Addams family under the beds.

But, on the upside, I got to see more of the great outdoors than I had in the Lakes. Luke had brought his laptop, needing apparently to catch up on some paperwork and also to drop a bunch of emails to prospective clients, so I booked myself on a day trek to Dozemary Pool. Riding a thoroughbred at the gallop across heather rid me of any tetchiness I'd been harbouring. And, since we also managed to fit in more than our quota of sex (more than the sex quota of a small Catholic country actually), I didn't really feel cheated.

Even better, when we arrived back on Sunday evening, there was no sign of either Clay or Ash. Luke kissed me goodbye, promised to pick me up the following evening in time to catch a film at the City Screen, with drinks beforehand, and hurled off in a slightly alarming puff of black smoke. The big black car had clocked up nearly a thousand miles that weekend, and it looked as though the distance was telling on significant valves.

The phone rang as I carried my bag upstairs. I ignored it, but it rang again as I was showering, and then again when I was making myself some tea. Figuring that anyone *that* desperate to reach one of us would probably be glad to get answered, I picked it up.

"Oh, Willow. Thank God it's you."

"Hey, OC." There was a breathy pause. "It's not the baby, is it?" I asked. OC still had a couple of months to go and I didn't like the sound of the silences coming down the line at me.

"Can you come?"

"What, now? Have you rung Paddy?"

"*Please*, Will, just come." My sister's voice broke up and the line went dead. I stood and stared into the receiver for a moment, then started to panic properly.

Clay was out and besides he didn't have a car. Ash was God knows where, and anyway, if OC was in labour, being slung across a throbbing saddle would probably obviate any need for obstetric intervention.

I called Cal, but his answerphone was on, I didn't have his mobile number and the farm wasn't on the phone. So that was Cal out of the white charger rescuer league. Who else did I know with a car?

"Moat House Hotel, how may I help you?" The receptionist had a strong accent, French or Spanish.

"Um, I need to speak to one of your guests, Mr. Luke Fry. Could you tell me which room he's in, please?"

"A Mr. Fry, is that correct?"

"Yes. I mean, if it's a matter of security you don't have to tell me his room number, just get him to pick up the phone.... Tell him...tell him his fiancée needs to speak to him. Urgently."

"Mr. Fry." I could hear the girl accessing the computer, the sound of a mouse clicking and a keyboard being tapped. "I'm sorry, there doesn't seem to be anyone of that name staying with us at the moment."

"Luke Fry. Tall bloke, longish blondish hair."

"I'm sorry, Miss...?"

"Cayton. Willow Cayton. He must be there somewhere?"

"Then I'm sorry, Miss Cayton. There is no one of that name resident in the Moat House Hotel at this moment. Was there any other matter I could help you with?"

"I don't know. Can you drive or deliver a baby?"

"I am sorry." Obviously labelling me a complete nutter, she hung up.

So, *where the hell was he?*

I tried his mobile, but he'd still got it switched off. He often left it turned off, or sometimes even back at the hotel. Where *was* he? He'd been staying at the Moat House ever since he came back to York. *Why* didn't they recognise his name?

Now I was worrying on several fronts. Luke had disappeared, Cal was out of contact, my brothers were God knows where and, although I had a driving licence, I had no access to any vehicles. In desperation I called Katie, who doesn't drive, but has a husband who does. She told me that Dan was up in Newcastle, at some kind of literary do, but why not try Jazz?

"I didn't know Jazz could drive."

"Yes, you did. He passed his test before you, remember? You said that if you failed you'd have to go and live on the Orkneys until he forgot about it."

"Oh, yes. Has he got a car?"

"Yeah, Skoda. Pretend to think it's a BMW, he likes that. Oh, and tell OC good luck and remind her to put ice on her stitches when she pees."

Please, remind me never to have children. In fact, strike me infertile now.

Upshot of said discussions—Jazz, gingerly driving his pristine white Skoda ("First time I've had her out this year.") with me alongside, not full of confidence, heading for the old rectory. We didn't speak. Jazz was almost as bad a driver as Cal, hunching over the wheel like an elderly spinster, hands ten-to-two-ing like fury. I was too busy worrying about OC and Luke to say much more than "turn right here" and "mind that *bus!*"

When we pulled up at the end of the rectory drive, I was encouraged by the sight of my sister at the front door, not bent double and biting through her own knees. (I'd been an avid reader of Catherine Cookson's more lurid fiction as a teenager.) In fact she looked poised in a navy maternity top and jeans, and her makeup was immaculate.

"Willow, how nice to see you. Do come and have some tea. Jasper, you look amazing. Come through."

But as she walked us through the house to the kitchen, I could tell things weren't right. For a start, the dogs weren't confined to the garden room but loose, running up to greet our ankles with whiskery sniffs and lurking by OC's side when she eventually lowered herself into a chair in the glass-roofed kitchen extension. For another thing, although her makeup was all in place, I could see traces of redness around her eyes, puffiness of the lids. OC had been crying. She had also been baking. Fresh scones were lined up on the granite worksurface, and buns and muffins cluttered the scrubbed refectory table. OC bakes when under stress.

Jazz looked intimidated by the conspicuous wealth around him and took the dogs into the garden. "So?" I poured boiling water into mugs. "What's up?"

"Mmmm?" She was pretending to read a *Mother and Baby* magazine, one hand on her rapidly emerging bump, but she hadn't turned a page since she'd sat down. "Oh, you know." But she didn't meet my eye. "Jasper's looking very trendy these days, isn't he?"

"If you like that sort of thing. Personally I'd rather take fashion advice from a squirrel. OC..."

I could see the tears now, dripping onto the pages she held, falling with a sad little popping sound. Her hands were shaking. "Willow." Her voice was tiny. "I don't know what to do. He's left me."

"Fuck me." I sat suddenly. My worries about Luke's unfindability folded into insignificance. "Paddy? He's gone?"

Still without looking up, she nodded. "He sent me an email. Says that he's found somebody else. Somebody who..." The words clotted in her throat and she dropped her head farther onto her chest, fingers caressing her bump. "Somebody who makes him feel 'alive', apparently."

"Shit."

"Oh, I can keep the house. And he'll make an allowance to pay for the baby, but he doesn't want to see it." Now she met my eye and the glint of misery made my own heart shrivel. "He called the baby 'it', Willow. Last week we were thinking of names, now this"—she stroked her navel possessively—"is just 'it'."

"The bastard." But words couldn't do justice to the way I felt. My dear, mellow, house-proud sister deserved way better than this. And her baby deserved a better father.

I sat with her in her spotless steel-and-chrome kitchen and watched her break her heart over the worthless spunk-machine that she had married. Jazz came in later. The spaniels ran to OC and put their doggy heads in her lap as if they, too, knew how miserable she was, and she played with their ears while Jazz and I made her something to eat and then forced her to eat it. Gone was the hostess face she showed to everyone else. Instead, for once, the real OC was on display. I'd forgotten what my sister was like. Underneath the Cath Kidson aprons and the Barbour jackets, she was far more like me than I'd remembered. Jazz, too, showed another side of himself, rather than the hard-drinking cynic. He was softer, kinder, more touchy-feely. He hugged OC frequently, told her that Paddy had never deserved her, until I began to think that there might be something in Katie's suspicions about where his true feelings lay.

When we came to leave, OC started to panic. "Take me home with you, Wills," she pleaded. "Don't leave me here on my own." Then, when I agreed, she had to rush around packing things, and I hadn't realised that the deal would involve Booter and Snag, because she had to pack things for them, too, and take her hospital bag and all her maternity records "in case", until I was nearly screaming. But I could see that all this activity was distracting her, and maybe getting away from this place for a while wasn't such a bad idea. For a start, if Paddy came creeping back to say that it had all been a terrible mistake, she wouldn't be here, which Jazz and I, probably for wildly different reasons, both agreed would be a good thing.

So, variously tear-streaked, shell-shocked, exhausted and, in the case of the dogs, wildly overexcited, we arrived back in York where OC was greeted by her eldest and youngest

135

brothers, who provided a new audience for her tale, while Jazz and I hid in the living room with the gin. I dug my mobile out of my bag and sent Luke a text saying, "where r u? I called hotel, they sd u rn't there?"

"I'm going home, Will." Jazz got to his feet, rubbing his eyes. "Oceana needs to be with her family right now. But if she needs anything else, or if anything happens, you know, with the baby, for fuck's sake, call me."

"I will. Thanks, Jazz."

But he'd already gone into the kitchen to drop a kiss of farewell on my sister's tear-ridden cheek. There, you see? I told you I read too many Catherine Cookson novels. Deserted wives bring me out in clichés. He did no such thing. He just ruffled her hair, grunted "see you" and disappeared.

We all went to bed. I was shattered but couldn't sleep. From the sound of crying in the next room, OC felt the same. I kept checking my mobile in case Luke texted back, but his phone must still have been switched off because there was nothing. In between paranoically snatching at my Nokia and lying in the dark listening to my sister cry, I worried. Could he have checked out of the Moat House because of the cost, not wanting to say anything to me for fear that I might offer him more money? But surely if cost was that much of an issue, he'd have chosen to come and live here with me, rather than move on? And there was always the flat, if he was desperate. All right, so there was no furniture in it. But he could have borrowed some, at least a sleeping bag and a microwave. And if money was such an issue, where had he got the cash to take me to Cornwall? Places like that didn't come cheap.

But then I thought of Luke's obvious concern for my happiness and wellbeing. He'd encouraged me to go off riding while he was stuck in our room with his laptop, so that I could "enjoy the countryside instead of being cooped up". I thought of his complete abandonment when we slept together, the wild (and even slightly exotic) sex. He wouldn't hide anything from me, I was sure of it. This whole Moat House thing was a simple misunderstanding, being blown out of proportion by my tiredness and my concern for my sister.

Tomorrow it would be resolved.

Chapter Seventeen

Funny, isn't it, how a simple question can make itself so hard to ask? I sat there in the dark, eyes front, while my mouth became drier and drier and my brain churned the words into meaningless syllables inside my head. The French film playing on the screen, the feel of Luke's arm behind me, even the taste of the reckless brandy cocktails that I'd drunk, none of it seemed real. It should have been easy—all I needed to do was to ask Luke outright. But the more time that elapsed between his picking me up and my framing the sentence, the more difficult it became to form those flittering, elusive words into the required order, and the more nervous I became.

"Are you all right?" Luke whispered as I shifted and fidgeted about in my seat. "Aren't you enjoying the film?"

"It's fine," I hissed back, my stomach pure acid.

"What's the matter then?" He had his mouth almost against my ear, the feel of his breath on my neck made little goose pimples break out all down one side of my body. "You've been quiet all evening."

"It's nothing."

On screen, a dishevelled yet sexy Frenchman was berating his girlfriend for some imaginary misdemeanour while she yelled and slammed plates into the wall. I wished I had her guts.

"Are you sure?"

Luke's hand stroked down my bare arm and more goose pimples joined the ranks. My heartbeat was thundering and my brain was playing chicken with the phrases passing through it. "I"—swallow, swallow, wipe sweaty hands along seat—"I was just wondering." Okay, still not too late to back out, pretend confusion at the plot of the film.

"Mmmmm?" His attention had wandered back to the screen, not surprisingly, because the girlfriend had now taken most of her clothes off and was being consoled by another woman, who was also wearing very little.

I felt sick. "Just wondering...where are you staying, at the moment?" There. Done it. The words were out, everything in the open, said. No longer my responsibility.

"Oh? Why do you ask?" Suddenly Luke's attention was on me, fully. His eyes, black in the gloom, searched my face.

"I tried to get in touch with you last night and I rang the Moat House. Your mobile was off, you see, and I couldn't think of any other way." I spoke quickly, the words running into each other like panicked sheep. "The receptionist told me there was no Luke Fry staying there."

He smiled. "Haven't switched my phone on all day. Yeah, I moved out a week or so ago." His attention floated back towards the film, his voice offhand. "Work was a bit slow on the showroom because the builders weren't always turning up on time, so I thought I'd go and stay on site for a bit to chase them up." A hesitant glance my way, and I felt stupid, as though I'd been caught out being the paranoid fiancée. "You're not upset, are you? I didn't say anything, but it was really important that I was on site, particularly first thing in the mornings when the bloody men sometimes don't get started until ten, eleven o'clock. Being there, I can chivvy them along as soon as they arrive."

Oh, pure, pant-wetting relief. My whole body leaped with joy at this simple, straightforward explanation. "But the hotel? What was the problem there?"

"I bet it was a new receptionist. They change over every couple of weeks. The one you spoke to probably hadn't ever seen or heard of me." A few more moments of Gallic passion elapsed before our eyes. There's something about a twenty-foot-high threesome that's a bit off-putting. "Were you worried? What did you do?"

"When the Moat House refused to acknowledge that you existed, yes. But it's fine. I got Jazz to give me a lift in the end, so that was fine."

"Jazz? Isn't that your ex?"

"Um. Well." I tried to remember how much detail I'd gone into about my imaginary bad breakup, whether I'd actually said that Jazz had been the other party.

"You haven't been... I mean, he's not back in your life, is he?" Luke watched me earnestly now, raking his hair away from his face, looking vulnerable and scared. A hand grasped my arm, almost pulling me from my seat. "Promise me, Willow, you're not seeing him again?"

"There's nothing going on between me and Jazz, I promise," I said as sincerely as I could. After all, it was true. "I wouldn't do that to you, Luke."

"Okay. I believe you. I know you wouldn't fool around behind my back." Another glance, flicking between the screen and me. "Look, I dunno about you, but this is making me horny as hell. What about getting out of here, shooting across the river and christening those new wooden floors?"

I let him pull me to my feet giggling and we ran out of the cinema and all the way to the flat, where the laminate flooring received a baptism of fire. Relief made me passionate and his minor insecurity seemed to provoke Luke to ferocity. In the event, there wasn't a room in our home-to-be that didn't witness sex of flame-thrower intensity.

"Take me to the showroom." I was emboldened by our lovemaking. "I've never even been there."

"It's an old building site. Honestly, nothing to see." Luke propped himself up against the wall where we'd planned our bed would go. "Bulldozers and holes in the ground."

"There must be a bit of a building though, if you're living there. Go on, show me. Take me over there now."

"Now?" He looked a bit flustered. "But, really, Willow, there isn't anything interesting going on."

"I still want to see. After all," I played my minor trump card, "if I'm putting money into the business, I at least want to see where it's going to be."

"Weeellll, okay. But it's a bit late now, isn't it? Won't you be wanting to get back and find out how your sister is getting on?"

"Oh, sod, yes, I'd better." I thought of OC, up at five this morning, walking the dogs in the park. Her misery and confusion had translated into furious overactivity. I worried she'd do herself some kind of homemaking mischief.

This time the Morgan was back in evidence, and Luke left me soundly kissed on the doorstep. I felt seven stone lighter than I had when I'd gone out. Relief made me bountiful, understanding, blissed out—capable, even, of dealing with Ash.

"Hello, everyone, I'm home!" I trilled like the bird of happiness soaring over the pink pastures of pleasure. "How are we all?"

141

Ash, who was the only visible recipient of my delight, just grunted and carried on reading, sprawled skankily on the leather sofa.

"How's OC?" I lowered my voice to ask.

"Cleaning Clay's bathroom, last I heard."

"Do you think we should let her do all this? I mean, it might be bad for her, or the baby."

Ash raised his head and made a sweep of the living room with one hand. It was immaculately tidy. Even a pile of old newspapers I'd been meaning to take to the recycling bin for the last few weeks was gone. "Look," he drawled, "the carpet has a pattern. Who'd have thought?"

"All right, point taken."

"So, we ought to make her rest more, but just let her finish cleaning the place first, yeah?" Ash moved his feet to let me sit down. "Besides, you know what she's like for jumping up and down over bits and pieces. Oh, and Cal was asking how your laptop's been performing since he had his wicked way with it."

"It's been fine."

"Give him a call, will you? He's driving me crazy. I think he gets off on thinking about you." A pleasant, warm feeling crept through my stomach, like a delayed-action vodka. All right, I was spoken for in the firmest way possible. But even so, it was encouraging to know that men still found me attractive. "But then," Ash went on, "he doesn't get much action. He'd fancy anything that talks to him nicely. Even a scraggy bitch like you."

The bird of happiness mutated into the vulture of viciousness. "Yeah, and I notice *you've* been home a lot more since you came back from Prague. Waiting for the antibiotics to start working, are you?"

"Cunt."

"Prick."

"Ah, the joy of family life," Clay remarked, walking in on our bickering session carrying a huge stack of files. "I'll bet OC decides to stick at one child."

"Well, Paddy's not going to help her out if she decides she wants another, is he?" I rummaged around in my bag for my mobile, then put it down on the table in order to have another rummage for Cal's number.

"No, thank God," Ash said. "If this one turns out to be anything like him, can we stuff it back in again?"

"Excuse me, you are not stuffing my child back in anywhere." OC came into the room on the tail end of Ash's remark, with her hair tied up and wearing a neat *circa* 1950 apron tied around the bulge at her front. I hoped she hadn't heard my observation about Paddy. "Will, could you give me a hand to untie this please?" She turned and presented the strings of the apron. "I can't reach around the back."

As I scrabbled at the too-tight knot, Clay dumped his pile of files onto the table. "Let me do it."

"Clay." I looked up.

"What?"

"Have you put all that stuff down on top of my phone?"

"Um. Whoo, sorry, Will." A tentative sideways movement of the files, like clearing the rubble from an earthquake victim. "Oh dear." The cracked casing revealed the battery and we all peered through the gap at it. "Can you tape it up?"

"I'll tape *you* up." I sighed. There would be no more saucy nighttime texts to or from Luke. "I'm going to bed."

"I'm going to give the dogs their last walk." OC stretched her back. "Either of you two coming?"

Ash just sniffed flamboyantly and spread himself farther along the sofa. "I'll come," Clay said. "If we can go up to the allotment."

I left them quarrelling quietly about how far two elderly spaniels should be expected to walk in a day, and hastened upstairs. This was my best opportunity to get an undisturbed bath, and I intended to make the most of it.

Chapter Eighteen

"That's it. So, what do you think?"

Luke had parked on the deserted tarmac and was pointing over at a large warehouse undergoing beautification. Scaffolding surrounded it. Huge plate windows gleamed between poles and girders. The whole thing was contained behind a rigid chain link fence which drooped in places like a slut's fishnets.

"Gosh. It's huge." I got out of the car, Luke hesitantly following. An enormous digger stood framed on the skyline, arrested by nightfall in the act of scooping a bucket of gravel. A mini-crane and two cement mixers hugged the shadows. "It's like a *Twilight Zone* episode of *Bob the Builder.*"

"You can't go on site." Luke stopped me climbing the fence by grasping my hand. "Health and Safety."

"But it's *your* site. You own it."

"It means I get sued if you fall down a hole. Come on, we can walk round outside the fence. This is the back. Round the front is where all the cars will be parked, and where the offices will be."

I skipped to keep up with his fast walk. "Why are you allowed to stay here then?"

"Who's going to get sued if *I* fall down a hole? I just have to take my chances. Besides, I know where all the holes are." He

Jane Lovering

pointed again. "Over there, where the roof's on, that's where I've got my meagre bedroll, my microwave and my kettle."

We arrived around the front of the building, which must have covered at least the floor area of a football pitch, not counting the space outside, which was hard standing for the cars. "Oh."

"What?"

"Well." I indicated the sign, newly painted and erected, still with the chains attached which had been used to lift it into position. "Why the name?"

"Sampsons? What's wrong with that?"

"I thought it'd be called after you."

Luke laughed. "If I put up an enormous sign saying Fry's, I'd be inundated with people wanting to buy chips. Sampsons is the name of the place in Boston. We decided to keep it for this one, too. Sort of a tradition, I suppose."

"Oh, I see." I shivered to myself. The night was chilly under clear skies. Although it wasn't late, the streets were already empty of cars and this hulk of a building was atmospherically scary. I felt better for having seen it at last. Concrete proof, ha ha, of how my money was being spent. Enough proof to shut Katie and Jazz up anyway. Enough to stop them moaning on about how much investment, physical, emotional and financial, I was putting into my relationship with Luke. In reality they were just pissed off that our drinking sessions had dwindled and I hadn't rehearsed with the band for weeks. Katie was also annoyed that I'd turned down an invitation to spend this evening at her place whilst Dan was out of town, so that I could go and stand around outside what she called "a garage".

Luke put his arm around me and started leading me back towards the car. "Come on, let's get out of here. I told you there was nothing to see."

146

"Ah, but now I've seen for myself." I smiled up at him. He was extraordinarily good-looking tonight. A new razored haircut gave him an edge of bad-boy glamour, the stubbled I-don't-careness mitigated by a soft blue sweater which made his eyes look purple. I hoped he'd wear blue for the wedding.

"Your brother's got one of those old allotments, hasn't he?" The Morgan roared away from the pavement and out into the curiously traffic-free street. "Out along Sowerby Road?"

"Yes. He wanders down there most days with his pencil and sketchbook. Bless."

"Does he know that they're up for sale as building land?" My eyes went news-to-me wide. "Yeah, apparently there's only a couple still in use, so the council's selling them off. Worth a bit, I should think."

"I'll mention it to Clay."

"Good idea. He might be able to drive the price up."

"I don't think Clay will be bothered about that, but he might get worked up about losing his allotment."

We'd reached my front door, and the Morgan was idling throatily. I could feel the eyes of my siblings boring through the brickwork. Upstairs, a curtain twitched. "Well, thanks then, Luke. See you tomorrow?"

"Of course."

I think Luke was a bit disconcerted by the abrupt way I pecked him on the cheek before I got out of the car, but I couldn't bear the thought of one of our more involved kisses being witnessed. Particularly by Ash, who would then spend the next ten days criticising my technique. To mitigate any annoyance, I stood and waved until Luke was out of sight at the road junction, before I turned to put my key in the front door. It opened before I had chance.

"Good. Glad you're back." Clay stood inside, like the father of a post-curfew teenager.

"Why? What have I done now?" As I stepped over the threshold, I became aware that both OC and Ash were sitting on the living room couch.

"You might want to sit down," Clay went on.

I sat beside OC, who flashed me a completely unreadable look.

"Right. I've asked the others, now I'll ask you. Do you know anything"—a dramatic pause—"about *this*?"

An outstretched hand proved to contain a crumpled-up ball of paper which had obviously been flattened out and screwed up again. The original "you don't deserve it" letter.

"Oh."

"Fuck." Ash turned to me. "Is it me or did it just get all *Amityville Horror* in here?"

I explained about receiving the letters, about how I'd been shocked and hurt at first, but since nothing seemed to come of it, and the letters had stopped arriving a few days ago, I'd decided the whole thing had been a mistake.

"Thing is, Will," Clay said awkwardly, "the letters *didn't* stop coming. I've had a couple. So has Ash."

"I picked one up this morning," OC added helpfully.

"We all thought we were the one they were aimed at, you see."

"Why?" I was suddenly prurient. "What have you done?"

Clay shuffled his feet. "Speaking for myself." The room hushed. Even the birds singing outside sounded as though they were listening in. "I can't think of anything exactly *specific*, but there's a few people with a bit of a grudge. Some of my coworkers out in China might have taken offence at the way I terminated my contract and left them with higher caseloads."

"Wow, crime of the century," Ash said dryly. "I can think of at least half a dozen people who'd be happy to see my bollocks on a plate. 'Sides, Clay, these were delivered in person. Surely no one's *that* destroyed about you leaving that they'd follow you over?"

"I thought," OC spoke quietly, "that it might be from Paddy. The one I got this morning. That he might be meaning the baby. Maybe he's decided to go for custody once it's born."

"So we've all been picking up these letters and thinking they were meant for us?" I started to giggle. "How egocentric can you get?"

"Balance of probability though, Will." Ash stood up. "You've lived here while we've all been elsewhere. They're gonna be aimed at you. Oh, and can you *please* ring Cal. Guy's been on my case all evening, something about a *goat*?"

"Why would anybody want to send you anonymous letters, Will?" OC asked. "You don't have any enemies, do you?"

"Could it be anything to do with this Luke guy?" Clay looked slightly ashamed of himself for asking.

"What do you mean? Luke wouldn't do anything like this."

"I didn't mean that he'd write the letters, but might he have some pissed off ex in the background? Or some business rival?"

"They'd go for Luke then, surely, not me."

"Since they aren't exactly threatening, I vote that we bin them as they arrive and say nothing." OC shifted her weight onto her other hip. "It will only gratify the sender if they think that their target is getting upset."

I left them to their discussion and took the phone upstairs. "Hey, Cal."

"Ah. It is you, my fair, goat-moving maiden. How're you doing?"

The wine-scent of his breath, the firm touch of his lips on mine... "Just a sec." Not even time to make the bathroom. My stomach lurched and dived without warning, as though I stood on the deck of a temperamental ship, bucking and kicking its way through a force ten. I glanced around in dismay and finally *in extremis* seized on my red dress, emptying the best part of an evening's entertainment into its skirts.

"You okay?"

Horrified, I realised that I'd been holding the telephone to my ear during the performance and that Cal had been treated to a virtuoso rendition of Retching, in E Minor.

"Better now. It was something I ate."

"If you say so. Anyway, to business. Do you fancy a bit more livestock-wrangling? Winnie's run away."

"Run *away*? She's a frigging *goat*. What did she do, pack her hay net and thumb a lift to Doncaster?"

"Goats don't have thumbs." Cal's surrealism was infectious.

"Precisely my point."

"She's up on the hill, but it's a steep walk and I can't do it with my stick. I mean, let's face it, she only has to walk briskly in the other direction. So I threatened her with you."

"What happened?"

"She peed on me. Well, not so much *on* me, more *at* me. So, would you? Tomorrow evening? I could pick you up."

"Tomorrow I'm out with Luke."

"Bring him. I'd like to meet him. If you're serious about buying the place, that is. Once you're married he's going to have to know, isn't he? So maybe you could kind of introduce the idea? Show him how lovely it is out there and, trust me, this is a good time of year to do it. You do *not* want to be giving him the guided tour in February, always supposing you can get down there. Lane freezes solid for months at a time and we've usually two foot of snow lying until March."

"You silver-tongued salesman, you," I said.

"What, the idea of being snowed in with nothing but the sound of the wind in the hills, stoking up the Aga to keep the place warm, bottles of whisky in bed waiting for the snow plough to get through, that puts you off, does it? Then you're not the woman I think you are."

"It sounds..." I gave a little shiver, but more at the tone of his voice than the thought of snow drifts to my waist. It might have been my imagination. In fact, it almost certainly *was* my imagination, but it sounded to me as though Cal was flirting, ever so slightly. I wondered if Ash had been right, if Cal really *was* so lonely that he fell for every woman who was nice to him. "It sounds wonderful, actually."

"Okay then. I'll be at the place about seven. I'll see you both down there." And he was gone, giving me no chance to stammer about taking Luke being a bad idea.

Chapter Nineteen

"And it would make the most *sensational* weekend place." I was half-full of informative animation, and half-full of vodka and Red Bull. "You could take clients up there." *Sell it to him, Willow.*

"No harm in having a look, I suppose."

That had been easier than I'd expected. "I'll have more than enough money to buy it in my own right, so you don't need to have anything to do with it if you don't want to. I thought I could start up a business, maybe growing herbs or something. In the meantime, maybe I could let it out to OC. She's selling the rectory, and she's going to need somewhere for her and the baby." I didn't say that, if this was the case, I'd have to get a move on. OC had woken up today swearing she was having contractions, but by lunchtime she'd decided it had probably been a dodgy prawn sandwich.

"Steady on, Willow." Luke laughed. "If we buy anything, and we really should do it in both names, then it will have to be suitable for both of us."

"There're some barns around the back. You could keep cars there."

"And land, you said? How would it be for planning permission?"

"You'll see. We're nearly there. Pull in over here, in this lay-by." I was a bit shocked by Luke's immediate desire to change everything, but then he hadn't had time to fall in love with the place as it stood yet.

"There's no access? Willow, how could you run a business with no road access?"

"It can be sorted. Come on, down here."

As we approached the end of the narrow lane, I covered Luke's eyes with my hand. "You can look in a minute." And led him by the wrist until we arrived at the top of the meadow. "Now look." I uncovered Luke's eyes and waited, heart pounding, for his verdict.

"It's very pretty."

Was that all he could *say*? The sun and clouds were playing chase me across the fields, giving rise to an interesting stipple effect of light and shade. The breeze softly wafted the smell of flowers across to us and there was no noise, apart from the cry of a sheep. It really couldn't be any more bucolic if it had the Wurzels in it.

"Those are the barns I told you about."

"Very nice." Luke turned to me earnestly. "Actually, Willow, I think you might be on to something here. The potential is just..." A wide-armed gesture said it all. "It really is fabulously sited. Look at the little river there." We walked towards the house. Cal was still in the yard watching us approach. "Oh my God, these are genuine cruck-framed buildings. How old *is* this place? It's fantastic!"

I introduced Cal to Luke. There was a moment of stiff-legged confrontation as they shook hands, then Luke smiled. "I really like your place, Cal. Fantastic opportunities here, yeah? Be worth a fortune to a developer. Can I look round?"

153

"Help yourself. I'll borrow Will to give me a hand with the goat." Limping, in what I considered to be an excessive fashion, Cal led the way out of the yard and down the lane which led up onto the hill. "He seems all right."

"He is. He's *so* good for me, Cal. I never thought I'd meet anyone who'd actually want to *marry* me, you know? I'm not the easiest person to be around. Not just with the, well, you know, but, with my family and everything. I kind of got used to being me-ish, I suppose."

We reached Winnie's hideout on the hillside. Cal found the going increasingly difficult because the ground was uneven, pock-marked with hoof-holes and rabbit dugouts, like a micro-scale battlefield. "There's nothing wrong with you." Cal sounded angry. "I don't know why you think there is."

"I puke on blokes."

"Your system doesn't cope well with emotional overload, that's all. It's not something so abnormal, so *perverted* that you have to marry the first man who asks."

"I'm thirty-two, Cal," I said slowly, wanting the words to sink in. "I know that's not old in men-years, but in terms of woman-time it's pretty nearly over the edge into Botox and suck-it-all-in underwear."

"You don't have to get married, though, do you?"

"Luke wants to."

"And you? What do *you* want, Willow Cayton? Hmmm?"

Banks burst. "I want to live *here* and have babies that grow up being able to ride before they can walk, and milk cows and weave, and know what plants they can eat and what they can't. I want to grow things and make perfume and medicines out of them, and cheese with plants in and candles with dried flowers and...stuff."

"Let me guess, *The Good Life*?"

"Maybe. Maybe I'm just a hippy who missed the boat." By now Winnie had got fed up with eyeballing us from a quarter of a mile away and was sidling up, curiously.

"You've got a very pastoral image of life, haven't you?"

"I know the realities." I felt somehow that I was being got-at.

"And Luke? Does he know? Does he have any idea what it's like to have to get up at four to milk the cow, fight to get the Aga lit, chip the ice off the water trough before work, bring animals in, fetch animals out, all up to your thighs in mud? Nothing ever clean, nothing ever dry, everything full of bits of hay and mouse shit in the larder? Because *that* is winter up here. *I* know and I love it. Will you? Will *he*?"

"I thought you only spent your summer holidays here?"

Cal sat down like a folding deckchair, dropped his head forward and let his hair hide his face. Winnie was fascinated. "Yeah. I lied about that," he said, as though challenging me to say anything. "I grew up here. My great-aunt adopted me when I was five, when..." Shaky territory, obviously, because he suddenly pushed his hair back and grinned up at me. "If you reach out now, you can grab her collar."

Without looking, I stretched my hand sideways and closed it around the leather belt. Winnie curled her lip in contempt and took off at a trot. Fortunately our joint inertia forced us gradually to the bottom of the hillside until we reached the lane. Winnie was puffing at the exertion of dragging me, size ten of pure muscle and thirty years of chocolate, and I was glad that I'd kept my footing. I was sure she'd deliberately headed through every cowpat and gorse bush she could see. Farther up the slope I could see Cal edging his way down, using his stick as a brake, anchor and occasional flail on the thistle-strewn pasture. It seemed somehow demeaning to watch so, taking advantage of Winnie's momentary breathlessness, I hauled on her collar until she moved into the gateway to the paddock, then wrestled the gate open and shoved her through. My previous experience with ponies had taught me once out— always out, until the escape hatch was firmly closed with wire, preferably in Winnie's case, electric and running off the mains.

"What did she do, jump?" I asked, completing my circuit of the small field to find Cal leaning on the gate, trying to look as though he wasn't gasping for breath. "I can't find a hole anywhere big enough for her to have got through. Although I wouldn't put it past her to have tunnelled."

"She got out through the gate."

I looked disbelievingly at the solid, five-bar gate he was resting against. It was a good five-foot tall, conventionally built with no gaps big enough for a solidly constructed Toggenburg to have squeezed through. "What, with a crowbar?"

"No." Cal pulled open the gate, standing aside. Winnie, on the other side of the field, raised her head and I barely managed to drag the gate shut before she hit it at a dead run.

"You let her out? Why?"

"Firstly because she's a total cow and I hoped the local foxes would form some sort of association to bring her down, and secondly, would you have come, otherwise?"

"*What*? Yes, of course I would!"

"If you say so. Shall we go back? Your other half will be wondering what we're up to."

We wandered slowly through the yard and into the house, to find that Luke was up in the loft, tapping at timbers with a Swiss army knife and muttering about woodworm. He barely noticed me appear in the hatchway and disappear just as quickly.

"He's happy," I reported. "Can I borrow your mobile? I want to ring home to check that my sister hasn't popped her infant out without due regard for the seventy-eight-hour labour she's been warning us she's got in store. Mind you, if she had, I think Ash's hysterical shrieking would have been audible from here."

"I didn't bring my mobile. There's no signal in the valley." Cal put the kettle on the Aga plate to boil and leaned his back against the stove. "Where's yours?"

"Clay broke it."

"Oh. Can't you use…" A gesture towards the ceiling.

"I never use his phone. Anyway, you said there's no signal."

"If you walk up to the road, you can get two bars, apparently. I've got satellite broadband out in the barn, if it helps."

We were both trying to avoid looking at Luke's jacket (pure wool, impeccably tailored) hanging on the back of one of the spindle-legged chairs.

"I could email, but it might take ages for anyone to pick up." Another sliding glance. Cal grinned.

"Sod it, no one's going to die if you borrow it for one quick call, are they?"

The tiny sliver of phone was tucked into an inside pocket, with Luke's credit card. It felt warm, the jacket smelled of him. I stroked the sleeves back into place as I removed the mobile, feeling comforted by the softness under my fingers.

"Come on. I'll come with you up the hill. He's going to be ages yet. What was he doing, exactly?"

"Prodding the beams."

"He's not one of these mild-mannered sales assistant by day, *Super Surveyor* by night types, is he? What's wrong with the beams?"

"Just woodworm, I think. They look sound enough."

Cal muttered something and hauled away up across the meadow, outdistancing me. "What?" I asked, catching up.

"I said, I've never been up there. Can't. Ladders, d'you see."

"Oh. Oh, you mean your..."

"War wound, yes. Can't do ladders. Great excuse never to have to paint window ledges. Or fit bird boxes."

"Or groom giraffes." I slowed down to walk beside him. "But, it's not that bad, is it? I mean, you get about all right. It's not like you're..."

"What? Not like I'm disabled? But I am, Willow. That's precisely what I am. Disabled, special needs, a cripple, call it what you like. That's me." His voice was so bitter that I was surprised the words didn't drop, blackened, to the ground. "A *spastic.*"

"Cal."

"Go up to the cars. There'll be a signal there." Cal stopped walking and turned around, looking out over the house.

"Cal..."

"Just *go.*"

I left him, clenching his jaw and staring ferociously into the distance, and walked up the lane to the road, where the two cars were parked. I leaned against Cal's (didn't dare lean against Luke's, might have smeared the paintwork), working hard not to notice the used condom lying on the backseat. So Cal wasn't quite as unlucky in love as Ash made it sound? I tried to conjure the image of him making love to a girl in the back of the Metro, and failed. Not because I couldn't imagine him naked, oh no, that bit was worryingly easy, but because I couldn't imagine any woman getting down and dirty amid the cast-off sweet wrappers, crisp packets and changes of clothing. I wondered who she'd been. Lucky bitch.

Luke's phone was fairly straightforward. The power button was under the flip-top. After a few stabs at random icons, I found it and, miracle of miracles, it showed two and a half bars of signal. I'd just tapped in the area code for home, when the phone started vibrating in my hand and I dropped it into the long grass with a girly little shriek. "Stupid bloody thing." I had to grovel about in the damp tussocks to retrieve it, still buzzing away its receipt of calls or messages. Finally my fingers closed around the now-slippery casing and I hauled it up to eyelevel, seeing the screen flashing an envelope signal on-off-on-off. I ignored it and dialled home.

"Hello. Are you all right? Nothing happening?" I asked of my dear sister, when she finally deigned to answer.

"That depends what you mean by nothing, I suppose," she said. "Jazz is here and he and Ash are comparing gig scars."

"Who's winning?"

"Jazz, at the moment, with a nasty gash under the ribs from a, what was it? Oh yes, a Compounded gig in Manchester. I'm only hoping Ash doesn't bring out the big guns and start showing everyone the scar he got when that roadie bit him in the bollocks."

"That was at an after-gig party. That doesn't count. Anyway, just called to make sure you were okay. Better go. I'm on someone else's phone." And I rang off, before I got any more details. The envelope was still flashing. I'm sure it was accidental. Yes, I'm *sure* it was, but in my attempts to switch the phone off, I ended up accessing the messages inbox and opening the most recent of the messages he'd received.

"C u l8r. X." I felt the world stop spinning, judder to a halt beneath me and flex. Previous message: "We cud go wlking on th beach.;)" And before that: "Srry bout last nite. I no it will b alrite."

"It will be all right," I repeated, like an idiot. The earth under me was still holding its breath, unsure how to start moving again. I held on to the Metro for support, my heart booming in my ears, a sour taste beginning in my mouth. What could...I mean, who would...he...*Luke*...

"Has something happened?" The voice made me jump, nerveless fingers let the phone fall again. "Your sister? What *is* it?" Cal was beside me now, picking up the phone from where it had fallen, trying to hand it to me. But I squealed and backed away as though it were infected. "Willow? Willow, take it easy. Do you need me to do something? Take you somewhere? Come on, talk to me, girl."

As though remote-controlled I pointed to the phone. "M-m-messages," I stammered. "Luke. Messages."

Cal found the inbox immediately, scrolled through, opening messages. Certainly the three I'd read, maybe he went past those. He just looked up eventually and said, "Shit."

The shock was beginning to fade, passing over me to be replaced by rationalism. "It's nothing incriminating though, is it? I mean, there's a perfectly reasonable explanation, obviously. I mean, that X doesn't have to be a kiss, that semicolon might not be a winking smiley. It might be that the messages are from somebody who can't punctuate, called..."

"Xanthe? Xavier?"

"Yes. Or short for Alexander."

"'I'm sorry about last night.' 'See you later.' He must be very good friends with this Alexander."

I snatched the phone away, shoving it into my pocket. "Yes, well, we don't know anything. It could be business."

Cal opened the Metro and pushed me into the passenger seat, where I sat and shivered. He didn't say anything, for which I was grateful, but stood outside the car looking over its roof towards the house, a lost expression on his face. I tried not to think of the condom behind me. The sun was beginning to sink behind the hills, the sky turning a chalky red, the clouds as pink as conjunctivitis and away to the east I could see night boiling up, insinuating its way in under the daylight. Cal swung into the driving seat beside me and rested his arms on the wheel.

"Right. Bedtime story, to take your mind off things," he said. "Once upon a time, there was a little boy—that's me, by the way—whose parents had waited a long, long time to have him. And then, when he was born, he arrived much too early and had to spend a long time in hospital, in a special cot. His parents didn't mind. Because they'd waited such a time for him to arrive, they were happy simply to have him. Then he grew up, and he wasn't the lovely, perfect child that they'd thought. Instead he was weak and ungainly and clumsy and couldn't walk properly or run at all. And these parents said 'we don't want a little boy who isn't perfect', so they gave him away. Gave him to an old lady, who loved him, and did her best for him, but who wasn't his mother or father. That little boy grew up to be someone who didn't trust the perfect people and kept out of their way, and only mixed with his own kind, the damaged and the weak. But then, do you know what? This boy grew into a man who realised that nobody was perfect. Oh, some of them pretended to be, and they were the worst ones. The ones that looked like they'd been sent from heaven, all shiny and bright and lovely, because underneath they were rotten and black, the sort of people who'd lie and cheat and steal and...anyway. My point, if I've got one, is that, well, nobody's perfect. Not really. We're the lucky ones, because our imperfections are there for everyone to see. I can't walk straight and you can't keep your lunch in place. Apart from that, we're perfect. *You're* perfect. And that Luke case, he doesn't deserve you."

"That's...what happened to you, it was...wrong!" Cal's story had distracted me, but the feelings were a paper-thickness away.

"I know. Took a lot of therapy for me to deal with it, to come to terms with the fact that my parents weren't perfect. Hadn't been perfect. That they'd had no right to demand perfection of me. I was a *child*, their child, and they should have faced their responsibilities, not given up on me as though I was an untrainable dog. But they didn't. End of story. Sorry. I didn't mean to encroach on your feelings there but I just thought you should know. Me. All of it. Well, most of it, anyway."

"Are you saying that Luke isn't what he appears to be? That he's *too* perfect?"

"Hey, put your own interpretation on it, why don't you?" He faced me and gently flicked my nose with a fingertip. "You have to make up your own mind here, Willow. These messages, yeah, I agree they aren't exactly hanging evidence, but there's somebody out there. You might want to find out who that is, before you let this go any further."

I picked up the phone. "It could be his brother?"

"Could be. If they take"—Cal winked—"*that* kind of beach walk together."

"Or a friend?"

"Again, yes."

I flipped to the Messages Inbox. Called up the first message and found the sender. The world stuttered. *Oh, Luke. My beautiful Luke.* "It says 'Home'."

We walked down to the farm, slowly and without speaking. Back at the yard, Luke was waiting for us. "Hey, Will, where've you been? It's time we were getting back. Y'know, we've both got work in the morning. Are you okay? You look a bit pale."

"Just feeling a bit faint." Cal rescued me, saving me from having to speak. "Look, if you're in a hurry, I can run Willow back later. We wanted to have a chat about some damp-proofing that needs doing." As he spoke he'd gone into the house. By the time we got in, he was digging around in a cupboard clearly standing absolutely nowhere near Luke's jacket, although one of the sleeves had been slightly disarranged.

I wanted to grab Luke, to reduce the physical and emotional space, wanted to hold him close, *so close*, to feel his heartbeat and his arms around me, telling me that everything was fine, would be fine, that I was the only person he loved. I wanted to trust him.

From being my gorgeous husband-to-be, dress picked out, bridesmaids selected, he'd become a stranger, with secrets. God, I wanted comfort right now. A hug, that would do—although Luke didn't hug, didn't do that kind of closeness. Why did I want it from him now, when I unquestioningly accepted his remoteness? I felt so exposed, as though I wore all my nerves on the outside.

"I'll go back with Cal. You go on, Luke, I'll..." I swallowed. "I'll see you tomorrow."

I saw Luke look from me to Cal, then he beckoned me outside into the yard. "Are you sure you'll be all right?" he asked, pulling his jacket on. I was pleased, sort of, to see that the phone was back in the right pocket. "I mean, can he drive?"

"Yes, of course. That's his Metro up on the road." I realised I was clipping my words and managed to stretch a fake smile over my lips.

"Oh right, he's got one of those specially adapted things, has he? Okay then, if you want to stay here, I'd better go."

Yeah, I thought, *you head "home"*. "Tomorrow then." And I ducked my head as he went to kiss me, so the kiss missed my mouth and landed on my forehead.

"Yeah. I thought we could go over to Leeds, maybe check out some of the clubs?"

"Sounds great." Just go. Please, just go away.

"Hey, then maybe we could go over to the flat? It seemed to suit you last time."

I was nearly sick on the spot. I'd opened myself up to this man, given myself completely, done things I would never have done with anyone else. And all the time he'd... "Maybe." Tight smile, cover the heartbreak.

"Later, then." And with a blown kiss he was on his way up the hill towards the car.

Thank God for night. The dark hid me safely, hunched in against the wall of the barn, as I turned my face to the wooden door and sobbed myself senseless. Cal left me until I'd cried myself to a shell, then came over and stood beside me as I blew my nose repeatedly and mopped my eyes on my sleeves.

"What happens now?" he asked.

"It's really strange, you know. I can't think. I feel like my head's been stuffed."

"Living taxidermy. Good hobby for a growing boy." A flash of smile, as though he worried I might burst into tears again at his levity, but I was glad of it. Nothing had changed. I was still the woman Luke wanted.

"After all, if he *did* have someone else, someone waiting for him at home, then how come he's never been the least bit worried about us being seen together? You'd think if he was..." Come on, say it, Willow. Face the fear, at least to yourself. "If he was *married* or something, he'd be a bit cautious about going out. Anyway why propose? He could have carried on dating me. I wasn't going to press him for anything more committed."

Cal gave a sideways shrug. "It doesn't add up, does it?"

I seized on his doubt. "No. Exactly. Did he look to *you* like a man who was being unfaithful?"

"How would I know? Do they grow a second head or something? All I know is that he doesn't seem to touch you very often." Cal bit his lip. "I'm surprised he can keep his hands off you."

"We both like our own space, that's all." I took a deep breath. All my insides felt achy from crying. "It's nothing, I'm sure. Maybe someone sent him messages to wind him up."

"You need to talk to someone who knows him. Have you met any of his friends or family? Anyone who might be able to put you in the picture?" Cal leaned companionably beside me against the barn door.

"No. Not really. I mean, there's only his dad in Wales. Oh, and his brother James in Boston. But I've never met or spoken to either of them. And I don't think he's made many friends back in York yet. He's only been over here for six months, and most of that time he's spent with me. What are you doing?"

"Making notes." From a pocket Cal had fetched a tiny electronic notepad. "What do you know about the brother?"

"James? Not much. Runs the franchise in Boston, a couple of years older than Luke, that's about it."

"American citizen?"

"I don't think so. No, I'm sure not."

"Do you know his date of birth?"

"What? No, of course not. Oh, wait a minute, we were talking about star signs and horoscopes and, yes, Luke is a Gemini and his brother was born two days before Bree. That's right, I remember now."

Cal tapped in the date. "Leave it with me. I can probably get a phone number. Then maybe you could call, have a chat. He'll know if Luke has any particular friends, won't he?"

Despite the balmy night, I found myself shivering again. "I don't know if he'd tell me anything though."

Again, the sideways shrug. "You've got nothing to lose by talking to him."

I felt the weight in my heart, my stomach. A leaden grey feeling as though my soul was punctured. "No, I suppose not."

"Although it's Luke you should be talking to. You know that."

"And what do I say? 'I was sneaking through your phone messages'?"

"Whatever *you* did"—Cal faced me—"*he* has no right to put doubts in your head." He laid a casual hand on my cheek and wiped away a tear. "No one has any right to hurt you, Willow."

His fingers were very warm. I closed my eyes. "It might not be what it seems. Maybe I shouldn't be doubting."

"You certainly shouldn't be suffering. Come on, let me take you home." The hand was still resting on my cheek. I leaned into the pressure and felt the ponderous slowing of time, drugged by proximity, as his fingers cupped under my chin and moved my head. "Oh Christ. Bad idea, Cal, bad idea," he whispered, then our mouths made contact, and that was that.

Moons passed. Ice ages came and went.

At last, he moved away. Neither of us spoke. There was nothing to say. Together we crossed the moonlit field, picked our way carefully up the muddy pathway and arrived at the car, the only sound our breathing, eerily visible in the chilled air, rising like prayers. I sat in the passenger seat and broke the silence. "Cal."

"Yeah, I know, I know. It shouldn't have happened. I took advantage of a bad situation. If it's any consolation, it wasn't intentional. I only wanted to make you feel better." He started the engine, but wouldn't meet my eye. "I can't...I wanted to show you that I...that you are worth something. I'm sorry."

We drove about twenty miles without another word being spoken. Even my stomach was still, whereas normally in this sort of situation it would have been undulating and the lining of my nose would be stinging with acid. Eventually, when we were almost at my door, I said, "There really wasn't anything to apologise for, Cal. It's okay. I don't feel 'taken advantage of'."

"But you were and I should have known better." But he still slipped me one of those gorgeous, shy smiles. "Won't happen again. If it does, you have my permission to slap my face and Moulinex my groin, all right?"

"All right." The car pulled up at the kerb, behind Jazz's Skoda. "Thanks for the lift." I started to get out. "You don't have to hang around, you know."

Cal was getting out, too. "A gentleman always shows a lady to her door," he said, following me up the path. "Door, lady—lady, door."

"Oh, very funny." I turned awkwardly on the step. "I'm back now. So. You can, you know, go."

"Right. I'm sure everything is going to be fine. Luke, I mean, why would he?"

"Thank you, Mr. Erudite and his amazing Clarity Orchestra, for that thought." We stood and stared at the night for a bit. "It's a long drive back, would you like some coffee?" I looked at him sternly. "I really *do* mean coffee."

It was only when I'd opened the door and led him through to the kitchen that I put a lot of thoughts together. Cal, the used condom, the kiss. Some poor girl, somewhere, who liked Cal enough to perform some high-level gymnastics on the shelf-like Metro seat with him, was walking about unaware whilst he was snogging me against a barn wall.

The kitchen was empty. I boiled the kettle and nearly slammed the mug of coffee down in front of Cal. "So, what's your girlfriend's name?" I asked, trying for nonchalance, but only getting as far as shrill.

"Um. Jessica?"

"Don't you *know*?"

"Sorry, I thought I was being Luke there. Thought maybe you were rehearsing what you'd say when you saw him next?"

"*No.* I meant *your* girlfriend."

"I don't have one. There was somebody a while back, couple of years now, but she...she took off with someone else."

"I think," I hissed, between gritted teeth, "that is a lie, Cal."

His face blanked. It was as though somebody had taken a sponge and wiped every trace of emotion away from the inside, except the expression in his eyes. Hurt, and trying to hide.

Today couldn't get any worse, could it?

The kitchen door flew open and Clay shot in as though he'd been shoved from behind.

"Oh, bloody hell, Will! OC's doubled over on the living room floor, we can't move her and she says her waters have gone."

Cal was already out of his chair, but I was panic-propelled, and made it to the living room while he was still circumventing the dresser. "OC?"

Sure enough, there she was, bump pressed into an accommodating beanbag chair, rocking gently and moaning. "Will? My bag is upstairs, my records are all in there, we need...oooooooooh...we need to get to the hospital."

Jazz looked at me over her head. "She was carrying on about it being a false alarm until a second ago." I looked at where he and Clay were trying to avoid looking, a big wet patch on the carpet, half the bean bag and OC's shoes.

"I just thought she'd pissed herself." Ash was on the other side of the room, mobile to his ear.

"Any luck with the hospital?" Clay asked.

"Still engaged."

"We have to go." I hardly dared to look at Cal. I'd just accused him of being as bad as we suspected Luke of being and now I needed his help. "Cal can drive one car. I'll go in the back with OC. Jazz can bring the boys in his car."

"Ooooooooooooooooooaaaaaaarrrrrrrrrgggghhhhh!"

"And hurry!"

Everyone was electrified. Clay, Ash and Jazz got into the Skoda, and I helped OC to her feet, despite her protests that she couldn't stand.

"You wanted an active birth, girl." I hauled on her arm until she rested her entire bodyweight against me. "Looks like you've got one."

"This...isn't *active*...it's bloody...*torture!*"

Cal had a look of concentration on his face that didn't quite cover up the darker stuff underneath. Even with a pregnant woman clutching at his shoulder there was a splintered quality about him, as though the black-eyed jokily abstracted personality overlaid the real, fractured man underneath, like a metal casing over a broken watch. Gently, tenderly, he helped OC through the door, her other hand clenched in mine, driving her nails into the back of my wrist, and together we eased her down the steps and into the back of his Metro.

"Oh God," she said in a sudden moment of pain-free clarity. "Please don't let my baby be born in here. Please get me to a nice, clean hospital."

"Doing my best."

So, with Cal in front and Jazz following, we drove slowly and carefully through the streets towards the hospital, both of them with their noses nearly touching the windscreens, shuffling the wheels through their hands and checking the rearview mirrors every ten seconds, even though the roads were almost deserted. It was like a Mr. Magoo procession. On the backseat, still gripping my hand, arm, and anything else she could reach, OC huffed and puffed and groaned like an airlocked boiler.

"Every two minutes," I said, from the back, in a slightly high-pitched voice since OC had her nails currently embedded in my thigh.

"What?" Cal glanced at me in the mirror.

"Her contractions. Every two minutes."

"Is that bad?"

"Not for the baby, no, but it might be for us. Can you go any faster?"

"I can do my best."

We arrived at the hospital and, in something of an anticlimax, OC was wheeled away out of sight. Bree joined us, and I and the five men sat along the maternity ward corridor listening to the shrieks. We were lined up like students waiting to see a particularly punitive Head.

A midwife popped her head out of a room farther down. "Are you with Oceana?" she asked, and when we all nodded, went on, "So which one of you is the father?"

The lads all exchanged looks.

"Oh, come on. I need someone in here to hold her hand and give some encouragement. I'm not asking you to deliver the baby."

"Um, none of us are the father," Clay said hesitantly.

"What, five men and not one of you the expectant dad?"

There was much shaking of heads among the boys and muttering like a Greek chorus. "I'll do it." Jazz eventually stood up. "As long as it really *is* just holding her hand. I don't want to have to look at anything nasty."

"Don't worry, that's my job." The thankful midwife whisked Jazz in through the doorway. I hoped that OC was too far gone in labour to protest. Jazz had never even so much as seen her in a bikini.

Cal sidled over to me and held out a coffee. "Peace offering. Although I'm not *quite* sure why, but I got the feeling back at the house that maybe we'd declared hostilities?"

I swallowed a scalding mouthful. "I've seen the condom."

"As far as statements go, I usually prefer 'I've seen the light'. But, anyway, go on, tell me about this"—he lowered his voice, conscious of the fact that, in a maternity ward the word condom is probably not to be spoken—"item. Where have you seen it and what is it to do with me?"

"Backseat of your car. Which, unless you're in the habit of picking up ladies who charge by the hour, puts you firmly in Infidelity Land."

Cal stared at me. "Just a minute. You're accusing me of shagging some girl, then leaving a used Durex on the backseat of my *car*? How big a slut do you think I am? No, don't answer that. I already know I'm not exactly *Good Housekeeping*'s Bachelor of the Year, but, urrrggghh, Willow."

I dropped my eyes and drank more coffee to cover my confusion. "Well, what was I supposed to think? I mean, it *looks* used and everything."

"It *is* used, you bloody stupid woman." But his voice was softly amused. "I put components into condoms to transport them. Water can wreak havoc with computer bits, and the small ones get lost so easily. I tuck them inside a Durex and they're waterproof, easy to find and"—confidentially—"they can't get you pregnant. Right, you finish your coffee. I must have a word with Ash. I think we might have a bit of ground to make up, him and me."

And he left me standing, plastic cup melting into my fingers, feeling a complete tit.

Chapter Twenty

"A little girl, six-pounds-ten," I announced to Katie on my slightly late arrival at work next morning. "Born at twenty to two, six weeks early, but mother and baby doing well, although Jazz has got a big bruise on his forehead from where he fainted onto the gas-and-air machine."

"Jazz?" Katie hesitated her fingers over her keyboard like a stop-frame animation. "What was Jazz doing there?"

"Long story." I threw my coat at the back of the chair. Today, I was determined to be bright and breezy, to push any thoughts of those mobile messages to the back of my mind. To concentrate not on *possibilities*, but on *actualities*. "Have you still got that furniture catalogue you brought in when you were buying a new wardrobe?"

"I think I filed it."

"Good. I want to start choosing stuff for the flat."

"Yes." Katie grinned at me. "Nice big bed with handcuff-compliant headboard, two-seater sofa and a champagne bucket. What more do you need?"

"It'll do for now." Besides, with those few necessary items installed, perhaps Luke and I could think of moving in. Together.

"So, give me all the details about last night." Katie tapped a final key and swivelled her chair around to face me. "Was it fantastic?"

"I don't know about *fantastic*." I thought back to last night. To the lightness of the Cal's touch on my face, the intense, breath-holding elasticity of the kiss. "It was a bit confusing. I mean, half the time he treats me as if I'm a slightly amusing diversion, and the other half, he makes me feel like I'm the sexiest woman alive."

"*What?*"

"Cal. He...oh. You meant OC's baby. That was...um...yes, very Madonna. I mean, mother-and-baby Madonna, not pointy-bra and 'Like a Virgin'. Well, obviously not like a virgin. Otherwise we wouldn't have been there and..."

"Willow. Shut up. Now, tell me about this making you feel like the sexiest woman alive, and what Cal has got to do with it."

A quick check to make sure that Neil and Clive weren't knuckling their way around the outer office picking fleas off each other, and then I gave Katie the whole story, or at least the edited highlights thereof. I cut out the misunderstanding about the condom, obviously, and any mention of odd messages on Luke's mobile. I'd just got to the bit about getting home to find OC in labour, when the phone, on what is laughingly described as my desk, rang.

"Willow?" It was Luke, sounding breathless and disturbed. "I've been trying to get you all morning."

"I was out with the dogs, then I dropped in at the hospital. Sorry." Then I wondered why I was apologising. After all, wasn't this man two-timing me? "My sister was having a baby."

"Only it occurred to me that you might ummmm..." Still disturbed, very nervous. Not at all Luke-like, in fact. "Is there any chance that you...yesterday, might you have borrowed my phone?"

My mouth opened and closed a few times like a guppy feeding-frenzy. "Ummm."

"Only I noticed some messages had been accessed, and I was worried that you might have, that you could have got a wrong impression."

My heart entered freefall. "Mmmm?"

"It, oh, this is all very difficult. I'm afraid that I have to tell you something. I...God this is hard. I lied to you. Please forgive me."

Shit. In fact, *shitty* shit. This was precisely what I did not want to hear. Tell me it's a mistake, Luke. Tell me it's all a misunderstanding. But please, oh God, please *don't tell me you lied. Tell me you love me.* I almost spoke across him. "It's all right. It doesn't matter. I don't mind, whatever it is. Please, I don't mind."

"No, Willow, I want, no, I *need* to explain. You see, I lied when I told you my mother was dead. In reality, she left my father. It was, everything was confused. But she...she and I have been in contact. She's the one who sent me the messages, you see. But I didn't tell you because, well, I didn't, and I'm sorry, and when I realised that you might have misinterpreted what you saw, then, forgive me, Willow."

Katie raised her eyebrows at the way I kissed the receiver. "Nothing to apologise for. Luke, honestly, I quite understand."

"Oh, but."

"No. It's fine. Everything is fine." And it was. The sun, which had probably been shining since about five o'clock this morning, had just broken through the cloud in my own personal sunrise. The erstwhile grey, sunken mass which had been my hope for the future was now leaping about in a pink tutu, singing a million Broadway songs, tap-dancing like a pro. "You don't need to explain any more, Luke. I'll see you tonight." Oh, and prepare for the shagging of your life, I didn't add, but only because Katie was listening.

"You really are the most fantastic woman I've ever known." Luke's voice was quiet now, the relief in it almost oozing down the line. "Have you ever thought about entering the Church, because you make confession soooooooo sexy."

I giggled. I couldn't help myself. "Luke, you are shocking."

"Yeah. And that's not all I am right now. God, woman, you make me horny. Any chance of getting away at lunchtime and meeting me in the flat?"

I was supposed to be going to the hospital to see OC and the baby, but, "I'll see what I can do." The release of the tension that I'd been holding since I'd turned his phone on was bubbling through my blood. That and Cal's incredibly sexy kiss, which had revved my whole system and left it ticking on standby all night.

"Luke?" Katie was waiting when I put the phone down, her scandalometer clearly reading into the red. "What's happened?"

"Nothing, nothing," I trilled. "Well, not exactly, we just had a bit of a misunderstanding, that's all."

"Oh, right, about him moving out of the hotel and stopping at the showroom instead?"

"Ah, no. This was another misunderstanding. A different one." Buoyed up and riding on the tide of goodwill that Luke's admission had brought, I told Katie the full background to last night's little, ahem, indiscretion on the lip frontage. When I'd finished, she frowned.

"Do you and Luke ever actually, y'know, *talk*, Wills? Or do you spend all your off-duty time shagging and communicating in mime?"

"What?"

"You do seem to have an extraordinary number of *misunderstandings*, don't you? For a couple who are supposed to be so deeply in love that they're planning to get *married*, there's a lot he doesn't seem to tell you about. And, please God, if you're going around kissing strange men, the reverse is also true."

"Cal...it wasn't...it wasn't *that* sort of kiss." I said indignantly. "And of course Luke and I talk, don't be stupid. It's just, you know how prone I am to grabbing the wrong end of the stick and using it to beat myself."

"Yes, but the stick does have to be held out for you to grasp in the first place." Katie put her hands on my shoulders and looked me deep in the eyes. "I'm worried about you, Will. Okay, so Luke might have good reasons for all the misconstructions that have gone on, but it's more that they've happened than what they've been about that worries me."

"Well, my dear, worry no more." I twirled around on my chair. "I'm going to suggest to Luke that we move into the flat next week and start living together properly. It can't be comfortable for him camped out in the showroom, and we might as well start getting it all together. How do you feel about wearing peach for the wedding?"

"Will, if it makes you happy I shall wear a whole fruit salad," she said solemnly.

"Willow." The door opened and Neil came in. "Bloke for you in the front."

"Good Lord, it speaks. Evolution in action."

"Shut it, frosty knickers."

"What, Clive not with you? Was the separation a success?"

"And you can shut up an' all." Neil grinned. "Dunno 'oo he is. Some weirdo. Bit of luck, he's a mad axe murderer."

He wasn't. It was Cal, loitering about in the front office, looking at the photographs on the walls. (Man Rescues Tortoise—Pictures Inside.) "Hi."

"Hello." Katie was hanging around by my left shoulder like a conscience-devil. "How are you?"

"Fine. I came to..." Cal clocked Katie and began to stammer. "I...I...you, yesterday...quite...upset."

"Everything's sorted now, just another misunderstanding," I said smoothly. Well, I could have belched every word and next to Cal's delivery it would have sounded smooth. "Cal, Katie."

"Oh, so *this* is the guy with the lip action. Pleased to meet you, Cal." And Katie turned round to face me and half-whispered, "Fuck me, Willow, you didn't tell me he was such a *ride*. I mean, look at him."

"Forgive my friend, Cal, she has a form of Tourette's. We normally keep her locked up for her own good."

Cal smiled broadly and Katie went "phwooooarrrr" in my ear. "Chuffin' hell, will you look at the eyes on your man?"

"And she's Irish. Happily married. Quite respectable."

Katie leaned over the desk towards Cal. "But prepared to be unrespectable, if the offer's right." She pursed her lips and Cal's smile grew slightly broader.

"Are you any good with goats?"

"Um."

"So, that's a 'no' then." I hustled Katie to one side with my elbows. "It's fine, Cal. I've spoken to Luke, he's explained. It was something personal."

"Anyway. The brother in Boston? I've got the phone number, if you wanted to ring and introduce yourself."

"What a great idea." Katie derailed the nearest elbow and slotted herself in beside me again.

"Have you got something in your eye?" I asked her suspiciously.

"No, I'm fluttering my eyelashes, can't you tell?"

"I don't think Cal's impressed by fluttering eyelashes, Katie."

"No, but I'm mightily impressed by anyone who can move my goat."

Katie's appraising stare narrowed. "Is that some sort of code, Willow? Is he chatting you up in code? Because if he is, that's really unfair. No one chats me up in code, not even Dan— not that he chats me up anymore. Doesn't even chat much, if you want to know the truth. He sort of grunts and points. I think he learned it off the twins."

Cal and I shared a baffled shrug. "So, do you want to call him now? You can borrow my mobile."

"Well, not right this second. I mean, I'm at work and everything and it'll be the middle of the night in Boston, won't it? Tonight. I'll do it tonight."

"Why are you putting it off?" He tipped his head on one side. "Are you worried about what he might say?"

"No! I told you, Luke and I have sorted everything out. If I ring James and he tells Luke that I called, then it looks as if I've gone behind his back and don't trust him."

"But you *don't*, do you?" The words dropped into a clanging silence. I stared at Katie who didn't even look ashamed of herself. "Come on, Willow. If you trusted him, he wouldn't need to explain himself to you because the situations would never arise in the first place. I mean"—her voice became gentler—"you know I love you, Wills, but you can be a complete and utter zombo where men are concerned."

"Is that a real word?" Cal asked.

"It is on Planet Katie," I answered, a little bitterly. "Kate, you're warping things again. Luke and I are fine. We...oh, sod the pair of you. Give me the number, Cal. I'll call after lunch when it's a civilised time in Boston. Katie can earwig all she likes to make sure I ask the right questions. There. Are you both happy now?"

The two of them agreed that, yes, in this instance they were fairly satisfied with my reply, and Cal left the office, Katie watching his every move. When she noticed his limp, her eyebrows almost twanged.

"Christ Jesus, he even manages to make *that* look sexy. Aw, do an old married woman a favour. Before you marry Luke, shag Cal just the once"—a libidinous look—"and tell me *all* about it."

"*Katie!* I will do no such thing. Anyway, Luke's sexy too, isn't he?"

She stopped boiling over and switched down to simmer. "Yeah, he's sexy, too. But it's different with Luke. He's macho sexy, all swagger and cock-first into a room. Your man there, you can tell he's the kind who'll make you wait, then lick you till you're screaming."

A pause while we thought about this.

"You really do need to get out more, don't you?"

"Tell me about it," she sighed.

℣ℤ

At lunchtime, I paid a quick visit to OC, delivered a pile of magazines, and had a trepidatious first cuddle with my new niece. ("I'm thinking of calling her Grace. What do you think?" Actually that's the quickest way to ensure you have the clumsiest child in the county, but never argue with a post-natal woman.) Then I tied up with Luke (and I use the term advisedly) in our new flat.

"Why don't we move in? Properly? I mean, this would all be far more comfortable if we had, say, a bed," I suggested from a section of floor by the balcony doors, a moisturising film of sweat being all that was between me and the beech laminate.

Luke was outside, on the balcony. His shirt was unbuttoned and hanging loose over his tan, trousers undone. He didn't seem to mind that he was giving all of York a prime opportunity to ogle the contents of his underpants. (Lycra shorts, if you must know. Those ones that hug it all close to the body.) "Sorry? Wasn't listening there." I repeated my question and he turned slowly away from the view to face me. "Well, yes, obviously that would be great. Unfortunately"—and he stepped through the double doors to stand in front of me, a wayward breeze lifting his hair and tugging at his shirt—"although the sale has gone through, we can't actually move *in* for a few more weeks."

"But why not? We own the place. Surely we can move in when we like?"

"Oh, I don't know. Don't ask me." He crouched down beside me and rubbed a finger over my bare shoulder. "Some kind of estate-agent thing. But, I was going to tell you, I've met a bloke. He's something to do with custom-built furniture. If you like, and if we can shell out a few grand upfront, he'll come and measure the place, and start making some bits and pieces for us ready for when we can move in. How does that sound?"

"What 'bits and pieces'?" I rolled beneath the pressure of his hand, like a puppy wanting its tummy tickled.

"Well, I've seen some designs he's done for beds." Luke lowered his head and nibbled at my skin. "Very modern, all curves and arches. Erotic. Is that what you'd like? Oh, I *know* what you like."

"The people opposite..." I started.

"They're across the river. What can they see? Anyway, let them look. We're worth watching, aren't we? Don't you think? I think they should *pay* to see this."

They would have got their money's worth, that's all I'll say.

ෂංෲ

Back at the office, some time later. Who am I kidding—I was severely late, bursting in through the doors with my jumper on backwards and a pink, postcoital glow that was probably visible from the moon. I looked like someone had tried to fry my face.

Katie was waiting. "Here's the number. You promised Cal you'd ring, and you wouldn't want to disappoint a man like that, would you?"

"I swear you're a witch, Katie Gardner."

"Yeah, of course. By the way, Will, how did Cal get the phone number? You don't know anything about this James."

"I dunno. He just did. Where's the number?" There were more digits than in the amount I owed my credit card company.

"But, it's not like you can, say, ring Directory Enquiries, is it? Excuse me, I'm looking for the number for a James Fry, just *a* James Fry."

"I said, I don't know. Why don't you ask him yourself? Oh. Sshh." The telephone rang in the distant United States and I held my breath. "What am I going to *say*?" I whispered.

"Hello?" The voice was definitely British.

"Is that James? James Fry? Luke's brother?"

"Uh, yeah. I guess. Who's that?" American phraseology, a slight accent.

"Look, this is going to be a surprise but, I'm engaged to your brother. We're getting married next summer and I wanted to introduce myself. That's all."

"Oh, yeah, hi there. Yeah, Luke's told me all about you. How is he, the old bastard?"

Katie tapped me on the shoulder and mouthed, "What's he like?"

I mouthed back, "Sounds really nice," and listened to James going on about Luke and how he'd done nothing but talk about "the fantastic girl he's going with" and how Luke was going to make his millions. James clearly liked the sound of his own voice bouncing off a satellite, so I let him jabber away, interjecting every now and then with an "is that so?" and "sounds great". I heard that the weather in Boston right now was hot and humid, the air conditioning was bust yet again, that Luke had promised to visit sometime soon, did I know when, and that James had met a gorgeous New England girl and he hoped to be settling down, maybe just after Luke and I. "So you'll be sure to fly over for the wedding."

"It will be lovely to meet you."

"Yeah, you too. Luke's been real different since he met you, you know. I know he's had his problems, but this past year he's less restless than he was before."

"I'm sorry?"

"Well, since he met up with you, what, last fall, he's been like a different guy."

"James, Luke and I have only been together since March." Behind me, Katie moved closer, put a hand on my arm.

"Nah, gotta have been in the fall. I remember him talking about you on Thanksgiving, when he flew over."

My heart felt uncomfortably too large for my chest. "Right. Yes, sorry my mistake. Fall, autumn, yes." My mouth was dry and my tongue stuck to my teeth. "Um, James, can I ask you, when he talks about me, what does Luke call me?" I manufactured a deathly chuckle. "Only we're having a bit of an argument about him using my nickname."

"Oh, right. Yeah, I guess Dee-Dee does come over a bit childish."

"Dee-Dee." I sounded hoarse. "Yes. I wish he'd use my proper name."

"D'you know, I don't know if I've ever heard it?" James sounded distracted now. "Look, it's been great shooting the breeze with you, but I've gotta get moving, I'm at work and..."

"Work. Yes." My lips were scything against my teeth as my chin trembled. "How is business at Sampsons these days?"

A half-embarrassed chortle. "Sorry, I must be missing something? Company I work for, they're called Pearson Brothers. Pearson Brothers Electrical, we do components for hot air driers."

I put the phone down while he was still explaining the tricky nature of hand-drier manufacture. Very, very carefully and softly, as though this was snow country in avalanche season. "Well," I said, surprised that my voice still worked, "at least I know her name now." It was my own stupidity that was overwhelming me, rising to my nose, my eyes, until I thought I might drown in it. Stupidity and humiliation. I was so full of it, there wasn't even room for tears. "I'm going to the loo."

"You're not going to do anything stupid." Katie watched me with anxious eyes.

"What, you mean more stupid than I've already done? I don't think that's possible. And anyway, in the *toilet*? I do have some dignity left." I went into the women's cloakroom and surrendered most of my dignity to a snotty weep.

When I came back into the office, Neil and Clive, bless them, were handling my workload and Katie was waiting with an avenging angel face on. "Right. Time to talk. Clive, Neil, hold the fort."

"Rightcha are love." Uncomplainingly they went back to thumping my keyboard and frowning into my telephone.

"They'll probably produce the works of Shakespeare while we're gone." My voice was tremblingly close to hysteria.

"Those two wouldn't recognise Shakespeare if he had a walk-on in *EastEnders*." Katie hustled me out of the office and down the road to the Grape and Sprout, where Jazz was keeping a bottle of vodka company at a corner table. The two of them pressed me into a seat and Jazz poured me a drink. I noticed his hand was still shaking.

"I..." I began, but Katie shook her head.

"We're just waiting for the others."

Others? "Are you okay, Jazz?" I asked. He looked different today, less, well, less. No platform-soled boots for a start, and no enormous black coat. It was as though someone had taken him and whittled.

"I, Willow," he pronounced so carefully that I wondered if he was already drunk, "am *incredibly* okay."

He'd shaved off the goatee, too, and there was a thin, pale line around his face where it had been protecting his skin from the sun. Katie caught sight of this and began to giggle.

"You look like you're being haunted by your own beard."

"I've turned over a new leaf. No more dark Goth. I am cleaning up my act."

Katie and I looked at each other dubiously. "Last time you said that, it was because you'd found the Church," she reminded him. "I hope we're not going to have any of *that* kind of thing again. It took me ages to get the smell out of the curtains after you'd practiced with the incense."

"Yeah, but on the plus side I've got a great outfit. I'm just waiting for the first Tarts and Vicars of the season."

Jazz had taken the Church as seriously as he took everything else, i.e., extremely, for a week. It was the celibacy that got him in the end.

"Who're we waiting for?" I asked, as another tiny ripple of miserable self-pity rolled its way onto my shores.

"I asked...oh, here they are. Over here, guys."

To my slightly startled horror, Ash and Cal came through the doors, laughing together as though there had never been an awkward moment between them. "Oh God, *Katie*! I thought we were going to have a consoling drink and you two were going to tell me what an idiot I am."

"Yeah, and then you were going to go right out, rationalise everything, and carry on as if nothing had ever happened, weren't you?"

"No. Well, yes, probably. But still, why did you ring those two?"

"Ash is really good in a relationship crisis. He tells it as it is, cuts the crap," Jazz said, pouring two more drinks for the newcomers as they made their way over.

"And you invited Cal because you fancy him." I turned fierce eyes to Katie.

"I invited Cal because he likes you and we could really do with an alternative perspective on things here, Will. This guy, *Luke*, he's got another girlfriend, definite. He's lied about it to you, definite."

"He's a cheese face, definite," put in Jazz.

"Er, yes. But you know all this. And look how miserable it's making you, trying to pretend you're not seeing what's right in front of you." Katie poured me a drink but avoided my eye.

"But I didn't *know*."

"Bull. You knew as soon as you read those messages. What else has he lied about?"

"Nothing."

"Willow."

"All right, so he moved out of the hotel without telling me. Big bloody deal. He had a perfectly valid reason for that."

"And his brother? What the hell is *that* all about?"

"*I don't know!*" I stood up and shouted. Everyone else in the Grape and Sprout stopped talking and turned to look. Luckily they were all midafternoon wine drinkers, so their opinions didn't count. "I don't know," I went on more quietly, once the chatter had resumed. "Maybe Luke's ashamed of James, maybe James is a gambler and lost the business on the wrong card. I don't know, but I won't condemn Luke without evidence."

"Well, *duh*, darling, but how much *evidence* is it going to take to convince you?" Ash slouched in the seat next to me. "If you're determined to take his side, you could catch the boy *in flagrante* and still believe him when he said he was getting a splinter out of her tush with his tongue." He downed his vodka in one and waved a hand. "Just dump him. Plenty more fish in the sea, if the holes in your net aren't too big."

"Thank you, Oscar fucking Wilde," I snapped.

"Oh, come on, you're not exactly choosy, are you? I mean, most of the guys you dredge up I wouldn't poke if my knob was on fire and they had Lake Windermere up there."

There was a momentary silence as we digested this particular Ash-ism.

"But surely," Jazz began, "if your knob *was* on fire—"

The conversation which broke out was overloud and overanimated. "Drop the man, Will. No excuses. He's *lied* to you."

"Don't give him a reason. Or you could hint that he's fuck-useless in bed, that always gets them."

"But we're getting married, we've bought a flat. Why would he do all that if there's someone else? And, I mean, *Dee-Dee*, what kind of a crap name is *that*, sounds like a bloody poodle."

"Is he into animals then?" That, of course, was Ash.

"Not like you mean."

"I might be able to help," Cal interrupted for the first time and we all stopped talking to look at him. "I...I mean I could...there's ways..." he stammered his way through being the centre of attention.

"What ways?"

"Oh, Cal's into all the arcane practices."

"Ash," I said, warningly.

"I don't want to go into it, but there are things I could do, to find out." Cal talked to me directly, into my eyes as though we were the only people in the room. The concentration stopped the stammer. "Only if you want me to." And he held my gaze after he'd stopped speaking, which made my stomach tremble in an all-too-familiar way.

"'Scuse." I dashed for the doorway and the lovely, convenient drain outside.

Chapter Twenty-one

I lay my aching head on the pillow and thought about what a stupid idea it was to try to get over emotional traumas by drinking. I'd stopped analysing whether my raving stomach was down to the effect Cal's eyes had on my psyche or the more prosaic effects of eight vodka shots per hour.

It was, predictably, three in the morning. A time at which all souls are at their lowest and thoughts immediately turn to picking at the biggest scab on the psychological knee. Me, I didn't even know where to stick the metaphorical fingernail. My mind felt like one huge raw wound now that Jazz, Katie and Ash had all had a good poke around in it. Even Cal had stuck his oar in, although admittedly only to offer his assistance.

Why was it that they all thought they had a say in my life? Did I advise Katie on how to bring up the twins? Give Ash the benefit of my experience of club-drug culture regarding sex and promiscuity? I don't think so. And yet they'd all given me their own versions of the ditch-the-bastard speech. Okay, so I knew that Luke wasn't the faithful type, much too good-looking and aware of it, but fidelity wasn't everything in a relationship, was it? There was trust, and respect and yes, right, I know that trust and respect are difficult if your partner is shagging the length of the street but, there's affection, too. Luke had explained that as a deserted child he had problems with physical affection, but he could still do sex. And sex is a very important part of any healthy relationship. Just ask someone who isn't getting any. Katie, come forward.

So, all in all, Luke and I had a lot going for us.

I rolled my head onto a cool part of the pillow—big mistake, because the whole room started rolling, too, and I had to close my eyes to stop it. But, on the plus side, I fell asleep again and woke up at eight feeling only slightly nauseous. Someone was pounding on my bedroom door.

It was Clay. "That bloke's back," he said without preamble, sitting on the end of my bed and effectively pinning me down under the covers. At least he wasn't trying to fart on my head, the intervening twenty-five years having smoothed his social edges somewhat.

"What bloke?"

"And I've got a letter from the council. Apparently they're selling off Ganda's allotment. For building, if you please."

"Yes, I did hear something."

But Clay was off on one. "So I thought, what I might do, what I'd really *like* to do. I've been looking for some land to build my own house on, but I didn't want to go too far out of town. I want to design Modern Urban, do you see?"

I refrained from mentioning that his land was York allotments, not derelict warehouse in inner-city Birmingham, but it was obviously Clay's idea of urban. "Sounds like you've really thought about it. Excellent. Brilliant idea. Now, for the love of God, *what bloke?*"

Clay jumped up, his mind once more on steel and chrome. "Er. You know. The one that ate all the bread and I had to—"

"Go to Morrison's in your pyjamas. Yes, I remember. It's Cal. Where is he 'back'?"

"Downstairs." A look of horror crossed Clay's face. "God, I left him alone with the loaf!" He fled the room while I tried to fix my appearance so that I didn't look like a vampire porcupine.

ℰℐℭℛ

"Morning."

I don't know why it annoyed me that Cal sounded bright and breezy, but it did.

"Why are you here?"

He raised one eyebrow. "Don't you remember? Last night?"

I decided to try for comedy. "What, I didn't sleep with you, did I?"

"No," he said into my eyes. "You *would* remember."

Whoa, where did *that* come from? To cover what was quite a large confusion, I started "business with kettle and mugs". Actually, my memories of last night were a bit scattered rather than being absent altogether. I knew I'd rung Luke and called off our date, pleading a sudden onset of flu. I knew that I'd carried on drinking with Cal and Ash after leaving Katie in the bar, that Jazz had gone off to visit OC, carrying a ridiculous number of fluffy toys (where had he hidden *those* when we'd been in the Grape and Sprout?) and, er. "Humour me."

"You're having the day off and we're going digging."

Oh, great. Here I was, feeling as though I'd stubbed my brain, and I was going *what*? "Digging?"

"You'll see. Come on."

An hour later we were up on the moors, parking in the lay-by. The last time I'd been here Luke had parked on *this* spot and I'd been happy. No thoughts about other women. "Look, I'm wasting both our times here. Let's go back to town. I really should be at work anyway. It's not fair on Katie." But Cal was ignoring me completely, swearing under his breath as he negotiated the trackway down to the house. The mud had dried in the brief hot spell we were enjoying, but this seemed to make things even harder for him. Instead of slipping and losing his balance, he had to contend with ruts and unexpectedly deep potholes. "Cal? Did you hear? I said I ought to be going back."

Cal turned round, resting against one of the old oak trees that lined the path. "They said you'd do this. Katie and Ash and Jazz, they told me you'd try to deny anything was wrong. I'm looking on this as saving you from yourself, and I'm rather looking forward to it, if you want the truth. So you might as well shut up and go along with it. Right?" He crouched down suddenly and pushed aside some undergrowth until the trunk of the tree was revealed. Without its accustomed blanket of brambles and nettles, the bark looked nakedly pale. "Here. See?"

Intrigued, despite my misery, I bent down next to him. "What is it?"

"I carved this when I was ten. The tree was a bit smaller then. See, those are my initials, CM. Callum Moore. Bloody nearly cut my finger off doing the M and Mary slapped me sideways when she found out I'd used one of her good silver knives."

"I didn't know your name was Callum Moore."

"You do now. I was a miserable little guy back then, loner, reckoned no one understood me—hey, look at me now, nothing lasts forever. Right, that's you distracted, shall we go on?"

"God, you really are weird, aren't you?"

"They told me you'd do that, too." Cal turned away and led the way farther on, out into the field.

"What?"

"Be rude. It's what you do, apparently. To keep people at a distance. One thing though, Willow." He reached the gate and pushed it open, stood waiting for me to follow him through. "It's a bit too late."

There were sheep in the field today, cropping down the overlong grasses and watching us in baa-filled distress. They'd eaten all the little white flowers and for some reason this made tears bubble up in my eyes. I scratched them away with a ferocious sleeve and followed Cal down into the yard. Instead of heading into the house, he produced a key and went straight to the locked barn, fiddling about with the padlock for a second. The air was suddenly overflowing with screaming siren noise. I clamped my hands over my ears but, unconcerned, Cal released the lock and went inside. Two seconds later the noise died.

"Sorry. Forgot I left the alarm enabled. Come on in."

Cautiously I crept over the threshold. Inside the barn was all the equipment I'd remembered, plus a few extra pieces that I'd either not noticed, or were new. Cal wandered around throwing random switches, flicking the lights on and generally looking like A Man in Charge. He'd looped his hair back again, too, and tied it up, acquired the focussed and deliberate movements I'd noticed in him before when he'd been working.

"Let's roll." As before, I sat behind him on the bale of straw, watching as he flicked the tiny headset on, clicked a couple more switches, then settled himself into the oddly shaped chair in front of the keyboard. He looked over at me once and winked. "All *right*," he said, into the headset. "Come on, bitches, talk to me."

From somewhere a voice rattled out. "Hey, Sandman!"

"Hey, Fortune. Who else we got?"

"Dix."

"Ratboy."

"Zakalwe."

Different voices, different accents. I could feel the flesh down my spine prickle. "Who *are* they?"

Cal stood up and came over. "Boys, I've got someone to introduce here. She needs a bit of help and we're going to give it to her, yeah?" Dropping his voice, he whispered, "Say something. Tell them who you are. It's okay, they can hear you. Just speak into my mike here."

"Oh. Er." Like anyone, anywhere, told to "say something", I clammed up completely. "What shall I say?"

"Try, hello."

"Um. Hello." I had to lean up against him to talk into his headpiece. "My name's Willow."

"Hi, Willow."

"Yeah, hi there. Glad Sandman's got some female company at last."

"Nice handle."

"Why are they calling you Sandman?" I whispered.

"It's my... Look, I'll explain it all later, all right? Just let me get this underway," Cal whispered back. "Okay, guys. Dix, can you get me records on that guy, James Fry? Background specific. Business."

"On it now, Sandman."

"Zakalwe. Another name. Luke Fry. Car imports. Check him out?"

"On it."

"Fortune, Ratboy. Warehouse flats in York, UK. Riverside, Number six. Agents called Cambridge and Simpson." A query glanced my way and I nodded. "Yeah. Check out the sales records. Find out what glitches there are. Friend of mine's bought in but can't move. Need to know what the deal is."

"On it."

"Stars, all of them." Cal whipped off the headset, shut down the computer and whirled out of the barn, sticking his head back through the door a second later to ask, "Are you coming then?" I was still sitting, dazed enough not to notice the straw particles sticking into my bum through my best jeans.

In the fusty kitchen, Cal made a huge pot of coffee, still riding that peculiarly tight-focussed energy beam. I sat at the scrubbed table in silence, sipping and occasionally shaking my head. The film of my life had suddenly stopped being a sedate rom-com and switched to hi-tech thriller. The casting director must be having kittens. "All right. I give in. What the hell was that all about?"

Cal refilled his mug. "I could tell you," he said, watching me over the rim, "but then I'd have to kill you."

I laughed. "Oh, come on. Just tell me."

"Willow." Cal put down his mug. "I'm being serious. The stuff you saw in there, what you heard, you *must not* repeat to anyone. Do you understand?"

The laugh died. "What do you mean?"

"Look. It's work, all right? It's what I do. And it's all stuff that... I'm covered by the Official Secrets Act. Do you know what that means?"

"Yes, but, God, Cal, you *are* serious, aren't you?"

"Never more so."

"Official Secrets. That means you can't talk about it, even if you want to?"

Cal stared down at the pitted and worn tabletop. "I can, if I trust you."

"And do you?" My heart thumped hard against my ribs.

He looked up and his eyes met mine. "I want to." His voice was so quiet, so soft, that it seemed to hang in the air. "I've never trusted anyone before. Not with this, not with anything that mattered."

"Cal—"

"But I'm afraid. Always afraid, always losing..." The words were gently spoken, almost inaudible.

"Well, I promise not to tell. Anyone. Ever. And I'm good at keeping secrets, just ask Katie. Or, don't ask her because she won't tell you because it's a secret. But I know things about her that even *Dan* doesn't." I was blabbing, trying to break the suddenly sombre mood.

I was worried that I might have gone too far, been too light-hearted about something that was obviously very important to Cal, when he grinned at me. "I can tell you some of what I do, but don't repeat it. I'm part of something called a Tiger Team. Huh, listen to me, Mr. False Modesty. I'm team leader. We're what you'd probably call hackers, if you didn't know anything about it."

"Hackers? You mean, breaking into people's security systems?"

"Er, no. We're what's known in the trade as 'white hats', the good guys. We check out people's systems. They pay us to try to break through their security set-ups. Means companies can make sure they're watertight. If we break in, we get to sell them our security system. All right?" He poured me another coffee. "Infodump over."

"But, why are you telling me? I thought it was all Official Secrets stuff?"

He shrugged, his face hidden for a second by his hair. "Too much time on my own?"

197

"I thought you were a computer consultant."

"Men can multitask, too, you know." Cal brought the coffeepot over again, accidentally brushing against my hip as he refilled his mug. I felt myself shrink into my skin. "What I do here, this is what keeps me going. The stuff back at the flat is cover. Yes, I enjoy fixing people's machines, diagnostic work and troubleshooting and stuff but"—he looked out of the window over the yard, unconsciously fiddling his hair back into its ponytail—"this is *me*. Fortune and I write the software. The guys all have their own areas of expertise. Together...let's say we're the best in the business."

"And you're using all that just to help me?"

A ray of sunlight shot into the kitchen, freezing the moment. "Any friend of mine is a friend of theirs," Cal said easily, ignoring the atmosphere. "Besides, I'm the Sandman. They do as they're told."

"No wonder you don't want to leave here."

Cal shook his head. "I can set up somewhere else. I like it to be away from the flat. Keeps things separate, if you know what I mean. Compartmentalised. But I'd still like you to buy the house. If you're sure you're interested. It'll be nice to know it's gone to someone who'll appreciate the place."

"Oh yes, Luke's got lots of plans," I said eagerly.

"Fine," Cal snapped, and we drank the rest of the coffee in silence.

"Why Sandman?" I asked, when the distraction factor of watching dust motes whirl in the sunbeam had faded, and I hoped that enough time had elapsed since my mention of Luke for Cal not to start nagging me again.

"Oh. Graphic novels. By Neil Gaiman. Sandman is the name of his character Dream—coolest thing alive. Or, well, not alive, as such, but, ah, you know what I mean."

I nodded. "Yes. You are pretty cool."

Suddenly the beam of sunlight was nothing. Cal had smiled. "You think? Really? Hey, no one's ever called me cool! Geeky, yes, spazz, certainly, but not that."

"It suits you. You act kind of dreamy, but you're not really, are you?" This was the closest thing that I'd ever made to a personal remark about Cal, apart from my foot-in-mouth moments regarding his limp. "You just think a lot."

There was a flicker in his eyes, which could have been a wince. Too close, Willow, back off. But he didn't say it. "Yeah, live in my head, me. Amazing, isn't it? Brain the size of a planet and here I am worrying about rising damp. There's a wall on the landing that's going to need replastering. You'd better come and take a look, since it might be you that ends up having to do it." He got to his feet.

Subject changed. I followed him upstairs and pretended to pay attention to the dampness of the plaster. "How long do you think it's going to take for your team to find the information?" I crouched next to him on the bare floorboards, smelling the dust, noticing how darkly stubbled his cheeks were, trying not to feel his hand occasionally brush against me in the confined space of the landing as he poked at the skirting-board-level plaster.

"Not long. They're good, and I've put Ratboy and Fortune together on the estate agents. They'll be trying to outdo each other, so they should be fast."

My heart was swirling the blood in my ears. "It seems a bit underhand." I took a half-step away from the wall and there was a crunching sound as a floorboard gave way, splitting into two under my feet, sending my leg down towards the joists of the kitchen ceiling. I staggered and lurched off balance. Cal reached forward and grabbed me by the arms, pulling me towards him so fast that I cannoned into him, driving him against the wall. "Ow."

"You all right?" Cal hadn't moved, still had his back flat against the plaster.

"Yes, just a bit scraped."

He had hold of my arms, above my elbows, so I couldn't move away. His hands were very warm. His whole *body* was warm. Leaning full-length against him, I was perfectly positioned to know that, yes, he was warm. And hard. No, I don't mean *hard* hard, although, all right, yes, I did notice that as well. Slowly I eased myself forward, trying not to put my foot down the significant hole. "Um."

Cal elbowed himself away from the wall and put his arms around me before I could get any farther. Not that I tried, once I felt his embrace. In fact, I took another tiny step forward and, in an instant, our mouths were on each other and the heat was flooding from him to me so fast that I could feel my cheeks glowing with it.

As he kissed me, deep, exploratory kisses that I could feel in my toes, I let my hands run over him. From his shoulders, down over his chest to his waist, and then I was inside his T-shirt and passing my fingers over a coil of hair in the centre of his chest, sliding down, down... Smooth skin and ridges of bone, a slick trail of hairs leading the way to his belt where he caught my hands and held them. "No."

I didn't get it. "Cal?" I thought maybe he was playing some game, some delayed-gratification thing, until I met his eyes, where such sadness looked out that it made me catch my breath and pull away.

"No. I'm sorry." And from the way he was panting, I knew he meant it. "I know what's going on and I can't...I can't be part of it."

Ah, rejection. Well, *this* is familiar territory. "Right," I said tightly, but trying not to show how hurt I was. "So what *is* going on? I thought we were...we were...that it was all fine."

Again, that pain, that shattered expression in his eyes. "Luke's being unfaithful to you. You have sex with someone else, with me and you're equal. He's done it to you, you've done it to him. I can't do that, Willow. I can't be your revenge."

"You felt keen to me. You *acted* keen enough."

"Yes, I'm sorry. I let myself get carried away. Willow, do you have any idea of how lovely you are? I'd have to be stone not to feel something. But *not like this.*"

I shook my head. "I'm not lovely. I'm what I've always been—just me."

"Yes, I've wondered about that." In the semidarkness of the landing, it was hard to see any expression on his face, only in his eyes. "You've never moved away from the house you were born in, you've got the same friends, the same job you've always had—even though you are patently qualified for something much better—and now you're going to be set to marry a man you've held a torch for, for over a decade. What's it all about, Willow, you wanting to keep everything the same?"

"I don't."

"You do! Look at yourself. You've got your life planned out—marry Luke, do as he says. Hello, there's a big wide world out there. There's...there are other people who'll care about you. It doesn't have to be him."

"Stop it." Anger was fighting with misery now, and just about winning. "You've got no right. I mean, what have you ever done with *your* life?"

I saw the slow, beautiful smile build on his face. "*I* went from being an adopted cripple boy to running the most successful anti-hacking software business in the country,

201

Willow." He spoke very softly, so I had to lean forward to hear. "And now I've made you face up to your life. I think I'm doing pretty well so far, don't you?" I slapped him. Hard. Caught him on one cheek and he staggered sideways, unbalanced. "Yes! Come on. Hit me again. Let it out, finally. Stop being Miss Goody-Two-Shoes."

The bastard was laughing at me. I swung my arm back to take another shot at him, bashed my hand against the opposite wall with such force that my knuckles grazed and I let out what can only be described as a bellow of rage. "You complete *fuck*."

Cal was still laughing. "I know, I know *exactly* what I am. And now, are you beginning to see what *you* are? That you don't have to marry some guy you've had stuck in your head for years, and work in the same grotty little office selling ad space in a paper no one reads? Think, Willow, think about what you *want* to do, not what you *have* to do."

"Someone has to keep the house together," I yelled at him. "Someone has to have a sense of responsibility! Do you have any idea what it was like, growing up with Sophie and Iain? When we could wake up one morning and find that they'd buggered off to sell shell-models on a Greek beach, or joined some travellers to go to Stonehenge for the solstice? And then Bree or Clay would have to go and fetch Granddad to come over and look after us and...and one time when he was in hospital and we all had to go to foster homes for a week and we all got split up and I was terrified! And I promised, then, that we'd never get split up like that again."

"But you don't have to take that responsibility." Cal looked as though he was enjoying himself, apart from the splinter of pain in his eyes. "They're all adults now, Willow. OC is a solicitor, for God's sake. *It doesn't have to be you.*" He smiled again. "Well, that was all very cathartic. Now, shall we go and see if any of the team has had a hit?"

Chapter Twenty-two

I sat on the sofa and shivered. It gave the whole flu story an added veracity, although Luke had clearly already fallen for it. The house was full of flowers and get-well cards and fluffy little teddies wearing "get better soon" T-shirts.

To his credit, Cal hadn't been going to leave me. He'd offered to stay, to call Katie, to do anything I wanted, but all I wanted was to be left alone right now, in my own home, wrapped in this blanket and my misery. I think he was scared of what he'd done to me. Frightened of the way that my heart seemed to have turned to ice, my soul frozen over, my body flinching and curling over on itself like a frosted plant, blasted and withered and brown. "Christ, Willow," he'd said, as Dix, Fortune, Ratboy and Zakalwe reported in, rattling their words over his headphones almost too fast to take in. "If I'd known, if only I'd *known*."

But how could he? How could any of us have known the extent of Luke's duplicity?

It had started with Ratboy and Fortune, as Cal had predicted, working fast, feeding off each other. Checking the estate agents, finding out that our flat, our home-to-be, the place for which I'd given Luke sixteen-thousand-pounds deposit, wasn't ours at all. It was rented for the next three months, in Luke's name. At a cost of only two thousand pounds, total. While my jaw was still recovering from this dropping piece of information, Dix had come back from checking up on James. Who, best information suggested, had gone out to Boston to work for US Electrical, having qualified from Manchester University with a degree in Electrical Engineering. He'd worked there for four years, and then moved on to become vice president in charge of research and development at Pearson Brothers Electrical. No mention or trace of any Sampsons or car trade. Full stop.

And then, finally. Zakalwe. Who sounded really nice, a genuine, decent guy, who wasn't to know that what he'd found was going to blow my world open.

"Hey, Sandman. You wanted the inside on Luke Fry, yeah? Okay, not much to find. No trace of the guy doing car imports, 'less he's working without a licence and that's impossible if you're dealing with the States. He's been in Wales, yeah. There's a paper trail a hundred klicks long from there, unpaid credit card stuff mostly, few loans going critical, named in two applications for child support, both still open. All goes quiet for a few years and then he's showing again from last September, drawing benefits in York. Guy looks like a major-league loser."

"Cheers, Zak. Owe you one."

"He's been lying to me." I'd whispered it then, carried on whispering under my breath until Cal had brought me home, shocked and chilled. Not so much by the fact that Luke had lied, but by the fact that I'd believed him. Believed everything, all of it. Cal had even double-checked the Sampsons warehouse being built in York. Turned out—oh, you're not going to believe this—the place was owned by a *toilet manufacturer* who was going to open a bathroom equipment wholesaler there. How stupid is that! How stupid am *I*?

"Hey, Willow? Hey there, are you okay?"

Dreaming. Surely. Bright, blistering sunlight squeezing in through a gap in the curtains. Me, hunched in a most untenable position on the sofa like a preying mantis on the verge of breakfast, blanket draped over my head. Room, full of people—no, not full, a squinty glance reassured me—only Cal and Katie and Ash. Oh and Jazz as well, over there, flopped in the armchair with Booter on his lap and Snag nudging at his laces. So, not really people, either.

"Whaeerrr?" God, I must look scary. I've been lying here for two days straight. I'm sure I've been getting up to go to the toilet, but the inside of my mouth doesn't think so and my clothes are showing evidence of this not being the case. But then, I haven't showered for two days, so things might not be as bad as they look. "Blurhurgh?"

Cal. Last time I saw him I kissed him, slapped him, then went catatonic. No wonder he's looking a bit confused, crouching down beside me and stroking my hair. Uurrrgh, it really *is* stuck to my face, isn't it? Wonder what with? No, best not wonder.

And then a snapping, zipping sound as life reasserts. Normality is restored and I sit up.

"Thank Christ." Ash, smeared along the chesterfield, lit a joint and passed it to Jazz. "Thought I was going to have to rattle a gin bottle to get you awake."

"Why are you all here?" I yawned and went to run a hand through my hair and then remembered that most of it was stuck to my chin. "What's happening?"

"We're waiting for you to tell us, darling," Ash drawled.

"We were worried." Katie bent down to come into view. My eyes still weren't too clever at rotating in their sockets. "You've been down for days."

"*You* were worried, you mean. *I* said she'd be fine. Men come, men go."

"Well, you'd know, Ash." Katie examined her nails.

"Quelle fucking *drag.*"

She was restraining herself from hitting him now. "And stop being camp, it's not impressing anyone."

"Cal." I moved so that I could see him. He was perched on the arm of the sofa next to me, still stroking my hair. "What's going on?"

"We want to know what you want us to do." He was looking at me out of Sandman's eyes, bright, sharp and concentrated. So I knew he wasn't only meaning those there present, but the team as well.

"Okay," I said slowly. Everyone looked at everyone else. It was clear they expected me to prevaricate, possibly even expected a few moments of insanity. But they forgot, I'd had two days lying on this sofa, thinking. "No one tells Luke anything, right? As far as he's concerned I've had the flu. I need more time to think." My heart was still, despite everything, wondering if, at the bottom of all this, there might not be a good old-fashioned love story. Luke, seeing me again, falling for me, not able to confess that he was now a penniless, attached man and concocting an involved fantasy simply to gain the object of his heart's desire. *Could* it be? "Maybe he wanted to impress me."

"Surely honesty would impress you more." Cal said, and I wondered if he was really thinking about his own secrets. Maybe regretting telling me.

"How *could* he be honest and still keep me? I need to *know.*"

"We'll all do what we can, Willow, but none of us want to see you get hurt." Katie handed the joint back to Jazz. "Or, any more hurt than you already are."

"But it *can't* be about the money," I burst out. "That's what you're all thinking, isn't it? That Luke's been using me to get money. I keep telling you that *he didn't know!*"

"Maybe it *is* just coincidence." I felt a sudden rush of gratitude for Katie. "He can't have known about the inheritance, so..."

"Exactly." I made a kissing face at her.

"So maybe he is just a bastard, two-timing you with someone else."

ৰುম

Two-timing. Sounds rather picturesque really, doesn't it? Makes me think of antique clocks, the ones with the seasons painted round the faces and the big keys to wind them, or an old music-hall dance done by girls in frilly crinolines with parasols. I couldn't associate the phrase with Luke in any shape or form. Particularly now, sitting side-by-side on an overstuffed sofa in the Blue Monkey bar, polished little cocktails in front of us, poring over a menu and laughing (me, rather overheartily) at a group of drunken twentysomethings falling off their chairs at the table opposite.

"So?"

"Mmmm?"

"Willow." He took the menu from my hands and laid it down on the sofa. "You're hardly here at all, are you? Sure you're okay?"

"I'm fine."

How *could* he be a liar? His behaviour was so *normal*. "You wanted to talk? You said when you rang, something was bothering you?"

Yes, it had been less of a phone call and more of a controlled blurt, I'm afraid. I'd wanted to admit everything, acknowledge that I'd checked up on him, but couldn't without bringing Cal and his team into things, and I couldn't do *that* because I'd promised Cal not to say anything. So I'd ended up saying that we needed to talk and leaving it at that. Trouble was, now I had to think of something to talk *about*, without giving away my uncertainty.

"I'm not sure that getting married would be such a good thing."

His eyes didn't even flicker. "If that's how you feel, then sure. But, what brought this on? You seemed to be quite happy, last time we spoke."

"I...I don't know. Cold feet, I suppose. Things being all right as they are."

A long arm curled around me. "Whatever you want, that's fine by me. Honestly, Willow." He showed no sign of being a man suddenly let off a hook or, conversely, a man suddenly disappointed. *But then, if he had married me, he'd have been entitled to half of everything.*

"I...I wasn't sure how you'd react. What with the flat and everything."

"Ah. The flat." The arm uncoiled and he picked up his drink, sipped it slowly through the corkscrew straw. I watched in hypnotised fascination as the blue liquid rose and fell through the roller-coaster bends. "There's a bit of a glitch with the flat. I didn't tell you because I didn't want you to worry."

Over the glass he was watching my face. *He thinks I suspect something.* "Really?" My heart was thumping. Two-time.

"Yes. I'm really sorry. We've got the place, for a while, but someone else put in a higher bid. I kind of misled you. I know how much you loved it and I was kind of hoping that these other people would pull out, or the sale would fall through and we'd get it anyway, so I didn't say anything." Another flash from those purple eyes, half-amused, assessing me, watching my reaction. "I didn't want you to be disappointed."

I felt relief just for a second. Then I swallowed it before it made me careless. *Not just the flat. Everything else. He's lied about everything else.* "Oh, I see. Never mind." Did I hate him? Love him? Why didn't I *know*?

"Are you *sure* you're all right? You really do seem very off, tonight."

God, he was attractive. Almost as though he was trying extra hard, stone-washed jeans tight over firm thighs, blue shirt which echoed his eyes like the sea echoes the sky, hair curling onto his collar in the same fashion it had ten years ago, long, strong fingers closing around mine and the smell of a spicy cologne sharp in my nostrils. "It's the flu. Still feeling a bit rocky." Couldn't I just pretend? For a little while longer?

"Of course." We chatted, generally, about OC and the baby, my family, the weather, all safe, neutral topics which didn't make my skin prick with anxiety. We ate, although my appetite was gone. ("The flu, taking a terrible long time to shake off.") And drove up to a nearby beauty spot to sit and watch the sun go down. Luke was all concern, didn't press me to have sex, just carried on the gentle conversation. Asked if Clay had decided what to do about his allotment and how sad it was that, if he didn't buy the land, his inheritance from Ganda would be wiped out, and had I heard any more about Ganda's road-surfacing invention?

"No. Maybe I ought to chase them up."

"Good idea. Look, let's get the picnic rug out of the boot and sit on the grass. It's a bit soulless, sitting in the car on an evening like this. Reminds me of all those holidaymakers."

"Yes. That sounds nice."

"You won't get too cold? I've got a jacket in the back."

"I'm fine."

"I'll get it anyway. Will you fetch the rug?"

He buzzed open the boot and I found the rug, neatly folded in the corner. Lying on top of it was Luke's laptop, his inseparable companion. I looked at it and had the first faint glimmerings of an idea, one which might not work, or even be of any use, but it was an idea. Mine. My chance.

I did nothing for a while, lay on the rug next to Luke and relaxed as much as I could. It was, I had to admit, easy to relax with Luke. He was Mr. Urbane, with his carefully general remarks about last night's TV and the beauty of the view spread out before us like a visual episode of *The Archers*. He made no move to seduce me, apart from taking my hand and holding it while we lay, stroking my palm with his fingers in a way which, had I been feeling a little more sure of him, would have had me writhing in pleasure and begging him to use my body in any way he saw fit.

Finally the sun sank. It had, from my perspective, been taking its own sweet time about it. Night gradually closed down around us, the birds putting up the shutters, the heat draining from the air. I gave a rather over-the-top shiver.

"Would you like my jacket now?" Luke offered.

"No, it's all right. We really ought to be getting home. I've told them I'll be back at work tomorrow and I still need a lot of sleep. Recuperation, you see." As I spoke, I got to my feet. Luke duly followed, and I folded the rug over my arm. "I'll put this away."

Again Luke popped the boot for me. This time, whilst he was putting the jacket into the car, I managed to shuffle his laptop onto the rubber edge of the boot, balancing it against me while I put the rug into the recess.

"Ready?" Luke came behind the car and I pretended to jump.

"Oh, you startled me! Oh, *bugger!*" As I'd hoped, the laptop had fallen with a rather nasty cracking sound, onto the stony ground underneath the boot. "God, I'm sorry, Luke. Is it all right?"

Luke, a little grim-faced, retrieved the machine. "Fuck. Looks like the battery might be damaged. Shit, these things cost an arm and a leg to fix."

"I'm really sorry." Contrition came easily to me. I was always sorry for something.

"Ah, not your fault really. Stupid place to keep a laptop, but I like to have it on me."

We surveyed the dented black casing for a moment. "Expensive to fix, you said?"

Luke's head came up. "Fairly. More ready cash than I was looking to lay out right now, why?"

He'd bitten. I was almost ashamed of myself. "Well, you remember Cal? The guy who owns the farm up on the moors? He fixed my laptop. He's absolutely brilliant. I'll pay, of course. It's my fault it's broken. But he doesn't charge too much."

Luke thought for a moment. "If you're sure. And he's good, you say?"

"Fantastic." But I wasn't necessarily thinking of his winning ways with a computer.

"Here you are then. Could you get it back as soon as possible? Only I need it, for business."

Yeah, sure you do.

Chapter Twenty-three

The following evening I went round to Cal's flat and caught him leaving for the farm. "I need a favour."

"Oh?" He stuck his head out through the window of the Metro. "You'd better jump in then and tell me about it on the way. It's good timing, actually. I need to shift that bloody goat again."

"Why don't you employ someone to do it?"

"Because I've got you, and you need a favour." I climbed into the Metro and sat on a pile of magazines. Cal looked at me sideways. "So. How are you?"

I had the lie lined up on my lips ready. The "oh, I'm fine" that was working so well for Katie, but once his cool gaze landed on me, the lie failed. "Pretty shitty, actually."

"Uh-huh? Feel like talking about it?"

"I'm *angry*, Cal." Until now I hadn't even been sure *how* I felt, but now I knew. "I'm angry that I've been duped and that I fell for it. I should have *known*."

"Why?"

"What?"

"Why 'should' you have known? Did he approach you wearing an I'm-a-fraud badge and covered in lipstick marks?"

I laughed. "Of course not."

212

"Well then. Stop beating yourself up about it. He's clever, he's good looking and he thinks on his feet. There's no way you could have sussed him."

"Maybe, but I still should have known. Good-looking men don't exactly fall for me, you know."

"Perhaps they do, but you're so worried about throwing up on them that you step over and make a beeline for the boring ones. Now, what's this favour you need?"

"It's this." I held up Luke's laptop. "I want you to hack it for me."

"Ssshhhhh. Willow!"

"Who's going to overhear—a traffic warden hell-bent on industrial espionage?"

"Even so. Whose is it? His?"

I smiled. "Hack it and you'll find out."

Cal rubbed a hand over his unshaven cheeks and then grinned. "Go on then, I could do with the practice. Been a long time since I had a personal. What are we looking for?"

"I don't know."

"Even better, a full-file job. It'll be just like old times."

"I don't want to know what you used to get up to."

Again the sideways look. "Ah, you do really. You want to know everything about me. And even if you don't, I'm going to tell you anyway."

"Shut up and drive."

The white house had a kind of dejected air about it when we arrived, like a puppy tied to railings. The fields looked unkempt and there was a corner of guttering coming away from one edge of the roof. Cal sighed as we went into the kitchen, and opened the windows to let out the overcooked air. "It's going to kill me to sell, but... Since Great-Aunt Mary died, there's so much stuff I can't do around the place."

"You could pay someone to do things like the guttering though." I looked out of the window to the paddock. "And look after Winnie."

"I can't have anyone stomping around. Not with the tech I've got going on out in the barn. Too risky. Besides it's a lonely old house, especially in the winter. I don't want to be camped out here. Shit, I've just thought, you're not going to want it now, are you? Now that...I mean, sorry, I'll shut up now."

My fingers gripped around the edge of the kitchen table and I felt the solidity, the permanence of it, the safe security of the four walls. "I want to live here." I dug my nails into the wood. "I've still got my dreams, Cal. They weren't all dependent on marrying Luke. With the money from the council I'll have enough to live on for a while until I get some sort of business up and running, even after I've bought the place. So, I'll be poor, but I'll have my own roof and my own land and I can always grow food and if the electricity gets cut off, I'll go to bed early."

"And the loneliness?"

"I'll get a cat."

Cal nodded slowly. "That should deal with the mouse shit in the larder problem. Good call."

"And besides, you'd still be around, wouldn't you? With the barn and all."

Cal turned away from me, fiddling with the Aga plates. "I don't know. I might have to shift somewhere else. Security."

The bruise that was my heart gave a little twitch. "Oh," I said, damply. "Oh."

"Okay then." I knew Cal was getting into work mode when he fixed his hair back away from his face like this. "Pass me the laptop. Let me see what I'm doing."

I handed the case over without speaking. As he took it, our fingers brushed and I felt it, as though he was wearing acid gloves. "I'll go and see to Winnie then, shall I?"

"Mmm." I'd lost him. Everything about Cal changed when he had a computer on his mind. Even his face became different, his eyes unblinking, his mouth a tight line of concentration. I watched him for a moment, the way his flexible fingers removed the black casing from the laptop as matter-of-factly as if he were peeling a banana, the shifting of the machine so that his less-strong arm didn't take all the weight. There it was again, flittering across the back of my mind, the flash of acknowledgement that he really was a very sexy man—and then he looked up and caught me looking. "Go on. Bugger off and see to that goat."

He'd seen me watching. Seen the desire and longing spread across my face and dismissed it. I took a deep breath and left the room, holding the feeling until I cleared the yard, when I had to spit it into a gorse bush while Winnie watched and sneered.

But at least her close attention made her easy to catch. I moved her into the field by the house and let her loose. By the time this manoeuvre was completed, and I'd finished the swearing and cussing and my face had returned to a colour not associated with emergency situations, Cal was in the barn with the laptop connected to the big computer.

"Any ideas?" he asked as I poked my head cautiously through the door. "About passwords? Anything he might use? I've tried your name and got nothing. Sorry," he added.

"What about Dee-Dee?" My teeth were so clenched when I said her name that I could hear my jaw cracking.

Cal tapped away at his keyboard. "Hey, yeah. That's got one file. Hmmm, nothing much there, few letters. What kind of guy *types* his love letters, hey? Oh. Sorry. Again. Keep forgetting."

"I don't care if he's been writing erotic letters to an entire women's prison."

"But there's nothing in there we could use, it's all"—his attention passed from me for a second—"pretty hot, actually. Quite heavy. Is he really into all that bondage and repression stuff? Sorry, sorry, any other password potentials?"

I couldn't think of any.

"I'll have to bring up the big guns then. He's working behind a firewall, so I can't piggyback a virus in to rewrite the passwords. Besides, he'd know then that someone had got at his files. So..." He tapped away. "I'll run a decryption program. That should break it. He's not exactly security conscious, our man."

"I don't suppose he's ever thought anyone would want to break in."

"Everyone should have security systems. You never know. There. We'll leave that to run a while. Do you fancy a glass of wine?" One of the boxes in the barn turned out to be a chiller unit, stacked with everything one might want, from Coke to champagne. Cal pulled a bottle of white wine out without even looking.

"Very smooth." I accepted a glass.

"It's regular party time in here sometimes. The team and I, when we finish a job, we often have a drink together."

"Together?"

"Figuratively speaking. Like the dress, by the way. Did it not come in your size?"

Had I dressed up to go and see Cal? What do you think? The dress in question was turquoise, halter backed and short skirted. It showed off my brown legs and arms and made my shoulders look slim and elegant. "What's wrong with it?"

A long glance. "Nothing. What there is of it, is fine. And, just for the record, what there is of you is fine, too." He raised his glass to me and smiled, but I could no more tell what he was thinking than I could read Greek. His eyes said he wanted me. But hadn't he told me, in no uncertain terms, that he *didn't*? Was I reading things wrong here? And a little voice inside my brain said, "Don't forget. Ash read him wrong, too."

"Do you ever get lonely, Cal? You seem quite happy on your own, but sometimes you look as if..." *Where the hell had that come from?* I looked at the glass of wine in surprise, almost as if *it* had spoken. "Blimey, this is strong."

"No."

"Oh, I think it is. Bloody hell, I've only had one, all right, one and three quarters of a glass and I'm already talking bollocks."

"I meant, I'm lonely all the time, Willow. Goes with the territory, really. I can't talk to people properly in case it comes out what I do, which would mean gangs might try to get at me. I always have to be on my guard. I never know who I can trust. Are you ready for another story?"

He refilled my glass and led me out of the barn and through the yard to the house, where the air was cooler now. "Three years ago I met Hannah. Oddly enough, it wasn't the palindromic nature of her name which attracted me. She was bright, funny, pretty—not, in fact, unlike yourself in a lot of ways, with the same sparky kind of personality. Quick, you

217

know the sort of thing I mean? Anyway, I'd got a job writing software, she worked with kids at a play scheme, after-school clubs and such and we were happy, I thought. She didn't seem to mind the war wound. At least she never said."

There was a deliberately bland expression on his face, and he avoided meeting my eye. He carried on speaking as though talking to his glass.

"She moved in with me. I lived up on Petergate then. Nice flat, but too many stairs. I loved her. Loved her, but couldn't talk to her. She didn't...she wouldn't have understood the implications, thought that the computers were just... She loved me anyway, even if I was a bit secretive."

Now he did look at me. It was a look that dared me to pity him.

"One day I got in and she'd gone. Left to go and live with someone she'd met at work. I thought the only people she met at work were under the age of fifteen but apparently not. I never found out. We'd lasted a year, she and I. After that I threw myself into running the team, setting up my own business, so I've been on my own. And strangely, women don't seem all that interested in a guy with a dud arm and leg, funny that."

"Ash thought you were gay." Blaaaaaaahhhhhhhhhh. Perhaps if I held my mouth shut these things couldn't come out. I pinched my lips together but had to let go to drink.

"Yes, I felt really bad about that, thought I might have led him on. I was *so* lonely, Willow, you cannot imagine. I'd go to therapy and talk to my counsellor then go home, knowing that I'd probably not speak to another soul for the rest of the week, and when Ash and I got on so well, d'you know, I even considered going to bed with him? To feel someone hold me, arms around me. I didn't push him away, you know that? I let him kiss me, until... It took me a moment to realise that I couldn't do it, couldn't sleep with Ash. It wouldn't be fair to either of us."

"I think you're gorgeous."

A half-laugh. "Thanks for that."

"Katie thinks you're gorgeous, too. And Ash. We can't all be wrong, can we?"

"Unfortunately. I'm a geeky guy with a weak arm and a leg that won't do as it's told. No social graces. I'm shy, I'm awkward and I stutter when I don't know people."

"And you're funny and kind, and you have the most fabulous eyes I've ever seen."

"I'm nothing like Luke, you know. The only six pack I possess is out there, in the cooler."

"Luke is a first-class *bastard*."

"But one you've fancied for ten years. You're only finding me attractive because I'm skinny and dark and introverted, and he's hurt you so badly that you don't want anyone who reminds you of him, even obliquely."

"That's therapy talk. I'm not thinking of Luke at all." I let Cal refill my glass again, feeling our knees bump against each other as he carelessly leaned across the table. It was true, Luke and all his treacherous deceits were far, far away. From horizon to horizon all I could see was Cal's huge, dark eyes and sculpted face, pencilled with stubble and lined with remembered pain.

"Do you know something?" He lowered his gaze to stare at the cracks in the flagstone floor. "Right now, right *now* I don't care why you want me. *I* want *you, so much*, and, Christ, I haven't been with anyone for two years and if you don't stop looking at me like that, then it's all going to be over in the next five seconds."

"I thought you didn't."

"Willow, I want you so much I can hardly move."

"Cal."

"But if you and Luke decide, despite everything, to get it together, if you decide you can live with what he's done, then where does that leave me? Wanting more of what I can't have, can't *ever* have. But you're damaged and hurting and I can make it stop for however long, and I would do *anything* to stop you hurting." Eyes met mine and locked on.

"I won't. I want you."

"For now. As for the rest, I'm used to losing people." He held his hand out to me, I took it and his fingers closed around mine, pulling me to my feet. Still without speaking, he led me up the wonky staircase, slowly, hesitantly, across the landing and into the beamed bedroom, where the sun arched onto the bare boards, painting the walls a dying scarlet and flame. For a moment we stood in the middle of the room, hand in hand, staring at each other, waiting, both of us trying to ride the moment and not spoil anything by moving too fast.

At last, when the tension between us was stretched so tight that I could hardly breathe, he reached out and touched my face. Time exploded into crazy freeze-frame moments, his lips against my neck, my fingers tangled in his hair, hands beneath clothes. That second when we'd undressed each other and stood naked as the sun slipped beneath the eaves and put a blanket of shadow on the floor. We lay, whispering in the ghostlight, wondering at one another's bodies, touching, exploring, mouths and hands and eyes and then, finally, locking together, rocking and sliding and eventually cascading into lip-biting chaos until we both fell, satisfied.

And, oh yes, for once Ash had hardly exaggerated at all.

Chapter Twenty-four

I don't know how I managed it, but I slept. When I woke up to a draught poking at me from between the floorboards, I found I'd been covered with Cal's shirt and my dress and I was lying spread-eagled and alone on the dusty ground. A shape, which could either have been a small mouse or a huge spider, scuttled into a shadowed corner opposite and I crouched to my feet. There was no sign of Cal, apart from the shirt. Stiff and chilly and blurry with sex, I dressed and went downstairs. Darkness had fallen, silvered by the moon, and I could see the barn door standing open. There was an overspill of green glow on the yard cobbles and the silhouetted figure of someone walking up and down inside. Either Cal was working oi ET had phoned home.

"What's going on?" Adjusting my dress for length and coverage, I went in. Cal was pacing the hay-strewn floor, barefoot and shirtless, talking urgently and quietly into his headset, the laptop screen was displaying an entire menu of icons in front of him.

"It... I've been... Hold on a second. Someone just came in."

"Who, Willow? You get laid, Sandman?" Cal's flick of the button was too late to prevent me hearing the voice from the speaker. His grimace of embarrassment made me laugh.

"Sorry."

"It's okay. They must know you pretty well."

"I really meant, sorry about everything. Earlier. I...it wasn't how I wanted it to be, that's all. You deserved better."

"Wow, you can do better than *that*?"

He smiled. "There should at least have been a bed. Sex on the floor is a bit..."

"It was fantastic, Cal. Really, really, amazing."

Now he laughed. "Not bad for a lame geek, eh?"

"Not bad at all." It was still happening. Undiluted by the earlier passion, his eyes had the same fascination for me. I'd supposed so far that it was the mystery, the unfathomability of Cal that I found attractive. Now I knew it was so much more than that. "Have you found anything else on Luke's machine?"

"You are changing the subject."

"Well, we could stand here all night and talk about how fabulously sexy you are, but you're insufferable enough already, so?"

"No, let's stand here all night and talk about how fabulously sexy I am. Honestly, you'll like it far more as a topic."

"Why, what did you find?"

"Letters and emails, all to women. I've only just got started, seems like he's been shagging all over the country." Cal tilted the screen towards me. "Oh yeah, and he's got a file on you, too."

"Show me."

Cal nudged me aside and typed in a password. "Sickgirl? His password for my files is *Sickgirl*? I didn't even think he knew." I scanned down the page. Luke had my address, my family members' names and jobs, all kinds of things about what I liked and disliked. I blushed to read some of it, but Cal had already found out for himself. "The bastard."

The other women predated my meeting Luke. "I wondered how he managed to shake off the credit card people and repay the loans. Companies like that don't just forget about you, after all." Cal was reading over my shoulder. "Looks like he found women to pay them off for him. Oh, and before you ask, I've copied all these files onto my hard drive."

"We have to stop him." I didn't realise I'd spoken aloud. "He's *used* all these women. Somewhere out there there's women feeling like I do, and he doesn't even care. He's just kept paying off his debts, dumping the women and leaving." I met Cal's eyes. "We *have* to stop him."

"How? He's got away with it so far, and I'm sure most of these women"—Cal flicked the screen—"felt exactly the same when they found that he'd skipped out with their wallets. No one's managed to bring him down yet."

"But they didn't have *proof,*" I said. "They didn't have *this.*" I copied Cal and flicked the screen. "I bet every one of these women thought they were the only one and felt stupid when they found out they'd been fooled. Or maybe they never did. Maybe he got the cash and then broke up with them, like here. 'I need some space, some time to myself, so I'm going to work in Africa. I'll call you when I get back from the Missionary Hospital.' Yeah right. He can't even cope with the missionary position, never mind the hospital."

"Oh, badmouth him again. It makes me feel good."

"Good? In comparison, you're a bloody saint."

Cal raised an eyebrow and thrust his pelvis forward in a very unsaintly gesture. Unfortunately he spoiled the effect by having to grab at the wall so as not to fall. "Wonder if Patron Saint of Nerds is still vacant?"

"Not sure, but I think Patron Saint of Cocky Bastards might be available." As I looked up at him, he grinned and, if his smiles before had lit up his surroundings, this one illuminated several acres.

"Can you blame me? I mean, really, Willow, can you? Look at yourself. You're beautiful, you're any man's idea of sexy and you've slept with *me*. I can hardly get my head around it."

"Cal. You and I—"

"Please, don't." The smile died and the pain crept back, inching onto his face. "Don't say it. Just let me have these dreams. Don't let real life come into it, not yet." One hand reached out, fingers traced down the side of my cheek. "Let me pretend," he whispered.

A whistling noise made both of us flinch. High-pitched, it couldn't fail to attract attention and his hand fell away from my face. "What is it?" My voice came out small, uncertain.

"The guys. Sorry, Willow, I'm on something right now I've got to finish. I'll run you home when I'm done, okay?" As he spoke he picked up the headset, slid it on. "Do you want to take the laptop inside and read through everything?"

What else was there to do?

How many others had there been? The emails and laptop dated back about two years. But from what I remembered of Zakalwe's research, Luke had vanished off the bad-debt radar several years ago. That meant that all these women, and so far I'd counted nine, were only the tip of the iceberg. Presumably he was keeping their details so that he never found himself backtracking—there must be whole areas of Britain he could never go to again in case someone recognised him.

Things came back to me. Our first date, in the restaurant, when his mobile had rung and he'd turned it off after he'd checked the number, then been called on the restaurant phone. And he'd told me it was James. *How would James have known where Luke was?* It had been the other woman, the one I'd started to think of as Luke's real girlfriend, hadn't it? Calling from home. He must have spun her some line about entertaining a client, covering himself in case someone saw us and reported back. Was that what he'd always told her? Was that why he'd never worried about us being seen together? No wonder then that he'd taken so long to get around to sex with me. I bet he'd been scared shitless she'd find out. Then there was the flat. He'd rented it. Never intended to buy. I was sure I'd never been meant to find that out. All that stuff about a friend who made designer furniture. Had Luke been about to take more money from me? To "buy furniture"? The careful, concealed questions about the progress of Ganda's invention. The texts from his alleged mother. Now that I knew about Luke, everything began to slot into place. It had all been about the money. Somehow he'd known about the money. All that garbage about fancying me at uni... *It had all been about the money.*

I was crying again. I thought I'd done all my crying over Luke Fry by now, but it couldn't be helped. Not only had he lied about his life, but he'd lied about *me*. How attractive had he found me, *really*? Okay, he'd managed sex with me, but I'd yet to meet any man who'd turn down a willing partner. All the time I'd been building a relationship with him, planning for our future, he'd known we didn't have one. What a bastard. And now I wasn't crying for myself, I was crying for all of us, with our ruined dreams and unused wedding dresses, for all the broken promises and shattered hearts, and I knew that I owed it not just to myself, but to all the lonely, deserted women out there, to nail the fucker to the *wall*.

Chapter Twenty-five

"Call for you, Willow." Katie shouted through from the front office. "It's Luke!" Then, screwing up her face, she covered the mouthpiece of the phone and made stabbing motions at it.

"Oh." My heart started pounding. "I suppose I'd better... Hell, Katie, what shall I say?"

"Tell him to go rot his carcass in acid, the double-crossing liar."

"That might be a bit prejudicial. Anyway, we don't want him to know we're on to him."

"True." Katie did the *Psycho* stab a few more times. "Can I blow the dirty-caller whistle at him though? Oh, please, Will, just once."

"Go on then," I said, indulgent as a parent, and Katie fetched the ear-blaster of a whistle which we kept for deafening phone pests, dealing Luke a drum-splitting blast. "Sorry about that, Luke," I said, retrieving the phone from her. "We've got a fault on the line."

I was afraid that the tremble in my voice would give everything away, but Luke really didn't listen to me. "Hey, Willow, have you got over that flu bug yet? Only I thought we might go somewhere this weekend?"

"Oh, that sounds lovely." I tried to ignore Katie doing hanging man faces and pretending to throw up. "But I've got an appointment at the council offices on Friday afternoon to go and see Ganda's invention being tested."

"Oh, right." As I'd thought, he didn't want to come between me and a potential half a million pounds, or at least he did, but only in a purely open wallet way. "Never mind, only a thought. We don't seem to have seen much of each other lately and I'm missing you."

Yeah, and I'm missing you, too. But my aim is improving all the time. "I'm sorry. I've been really busy at work, what with the flu, and now OC's home from hospital, it's hell on earth. I don't like to leave her alone with the boys. Clay's too absent-minded and Ash tries to amuse Grace by sitting her in front of WWF. I'm sure she's going to grow up with a fixation on men in leopard-skin trunks." I found that, if I kept talking, it didn't feel so bad. When he turned on the treacle-charm, it was hard. He did it now.

"Only, I'm *really* missing you, if you know what I mean. I keep thinking of you, naked on the floor in the flat, the way you stroke my—"

"I'll give you a ring and let you know how Friday goes." I hurriedly put the phone down and let out a long breath. "I wouldn't put it past him to turn up in the office next. If he does, will you say I've gone out?"

"I'll do better than that, I'll set Clive on him. He can tell Luke you've gone lesbian. He tells people that anyway, every time you've turned him down."

"Now that Luke's got the smell of money, I think it would take more to put him off. Oh, has Cal rung back yet?"

Katie looked at me pityingly. "You've got it bad, haven't you? No, Willow, he hasn't rung. I would tell you if he did." Cal, since dropping me off at my front door, hadn't been seen or heard from. I'd left so many messages that his answerphone tape was full, but he hadn't replied. "Why are you so uptight?"

"Because I had fantastic sex with him the other night."

"You *what?*" Katie sank back into her chair. "You lucky, lucky cow. Can I have a turn with him next?"

"You've got Dan."

"Your point is? No, I don't mean that. Dan's lovely. It's just, jeezus, woman, if you were any more jammy, you'd be a pudding. Cal, eh?" She got up and shouldered her filing pile, heading out of the office, but sprang back through the door a moment later. "No, it's no good. I've tried, but I've got to know. *What was it like?*"

For the sake of sparing Cal's blushes, should I ever get to see him again, I only gave her the edited highlights. But even those were enough to make her shake her head and mutter things about lucky, lucky bitches. She made me go over and over it. Spellbound, she insisted, by the romance of it all.

"There's nothing romantic about cold floorboards under your bum."

"Listen, Willow, with a man like that, it would be romantic shagging in the freezer section in Sainsbury's. He was born romantic, you can tell. Why else would he grow his hair and wear all that black?"

"Jazz wears black."

"That's only so the dirt doesn't show. Jazz has all the romance of a bin liner. Come on, Willow, admit it. Your man is the ride of the century."

Katie was so determined to make Cal and I a couple in her head, she neglected to acknowledge that he hadn't even returned my calls. Hadn't been in touch at all. Not as much as an email, in fact. So, all in all, I was rather shocked, when I reached home, to turn the corner, enter my own kitchen and walk into the man in question holding forth to Ash, whilst wearing a tea towel round his middle and carrying a wooden spoon. There was a wonderful smell of cooking and something bumped and spluttered on the stove.

I stared and walked out. "I'm coming in again," I announced, from the hallway. "So if either of you is a mirage, this is your chance to leave." When I looked again, they'd stopped talking. Ash was leaning against the wall supervising a saucepan and Cal was retrieving something which smelled of garlic from the oven.

"Ah, you're back. Just in time."

"What are you doing here?"

"Cooking garlic chicken. In a minute I shall be *serving* garlic chicken, so would you like to give the others a shout?"

Feeling like a visitor in my own home, I rounded up the remaining brother and fetched OC from the garden where she was reclining in a hammock whilst Grace slept in her car seat. "How long has he been here?" I asked her, as she clambered dozily out of the swinging canvas.

"Since this morning, I think. Turned up on the step with a chicken and a laptop, not long after you'd gone."

"Sounds like Cal. He'd never turn up with a bottle of wine, would he?"

"What?"

"Sorry. Nothing. Thinking aloud."

We sat around the kitchen table and ate Cal's delectable roast garlic chicken, although I noticed Cal himself didn't seem to have much appetite. Whenever our eyes met, he'd hold my gaze for a second or two and then look away. He was fiddling with his cutlery or turning his attention to Ash, until I began to feel awkward and concentrated on the food on my plate. I found myself grateful for the interludes when Grace cried and needed fetching from her chair, or when the water jug needed refilling.

Eventually we'd all finished. Ash leaned back in his chair and lit a joint, blowing the smoke carelessly, which made OC huff and remove Grace to the living room. Clay made some excuse about "finishing a drawing" and left for his attic, and I started clearing the table.

"I got your messages." It was the first remark Cal had directed at me since we'd sat down. "You said you wanted to talk?"

Ash, demonstrating the first ounce of tact in thirty-two years, stood up. "Right. I'm off. Enjoy yourselves, children." Pressing the remains of the joint into Cal's hand, he swept off, trailing his wrists dramatically.

Being alone with Cal made me nervous. "Perhaps we should…" I indicated the living room.

"No. We need to… Look, I'm sorry, Willow. I never meant to compromise anything. Our doing what we did, it wasn't…it just happened. If you never want to mention it again, then say so, and as far as everyone else is concerned then nothing went on between us. Ever."

"Why the hell should I want to deny it?" To cover the heart-pounding confusion, I began stacking plates into the dishwasher.

"Because, you and I, come on, Will, you know it would never work out."

"Why not?" I kept my back to him. There was a feeling in my throat as though my adrenal glands were trying to climb over my larynx, fizzing and burning and filling me with light-headedness.

"Because you're...you can be with anyone you want. Why the fuck would you want to shackle yourself to a limping tech-head?"

Noises off. Grace had begun an extended wailing session in the next room, upstairs a thumping beat indicated that Ash was playing music, and the pipes were gurgling as Clay, in his nest under the eaves, began one of his four-hour baths. After Cal's remark, these sounds fell into the quiet like stones into a pond.

"Because"—I raised my voice slightly—"I think I'm in love with you."

Of course, the second I started to speak, all the sounds died away. Even Grace stuttered to a standstill and I yelled the end of the sentence into near-silence. An embarrassed pause followed, then Grace started up again. I suspect OC might have scared her on purpose.

"Oh."

"Is that all you can say? 'Oh'?"

"I'm thinking. You haven't, possibly, been beaten with a stupid stick today? Or, maybe, eaten some hallucinogenic sandwiches?"

"No, Cal. I'm well aware of what I'm saying." I turned around and faced him and my heart did a quick waltz around my chest at the way he was looking at me.

"To use Ash's vernacular, no shit." He tried to get to his feet, but tangled his bad leg around the chair as he stood, sending himself lurching against the table. "Willow, are you sure you're not just rebounding? I'm the last person to want to investigate your reasons for this really quite astounding statement, but I want you to be sure."

"Oh, I'm sure," I said, into the grave-deep eyes. "But do you know the really crazy thing?"

"What, apart from the fact that this joint burned my fingers?"

"This isn't what I wanted to talk to you about. All the messages asking you to call me, I've thought of a way to get even with Luke."

"Again, with the *no shit.*" Cal shook the smouldering roach from his hand. "Hell, I'm becoming dangerously predictable here."

"The day you become predictable is the day I hand over my badge as Sheriff Strange of Weirdsville, Arizona. Population: you and me."

"Look, shall we go over to my place and talk? I've brought his laptop back for you, but, like I said, all the files are copied onto my computer at the farm."

"I think we might need some of them." I led the way to the front door. "And maybe the help of your boys."

"You really have got plans, haven't you?"

"You'd better believe it."

On the way over to Cal's flat, I outlined Plan Revenge. Cal whistled once or twice, nodding slowly most of the time, apart from when he was pulling out to overtake woodlice and tree sloths, which were the only things in the known universe to be moving slower than us. When I'd finished, we'd arrived.

"Whew, some plan. Can you carry it off?"

"If everyone helps out. If it all comes together. I know it's going to take some organising, but I think we owe it to everyone he's ever shafted."

"Going to take guts, Willow. Can you pretend like that?"

I stood very still. *Could I?* Could I really do it? Then I thought about all the wedding magazines under my bed, about the plans I'd had, about the life I'd envisaged. "Oh, yes. I can do it."

"Good."

In the flat I flopped down on the big sofa overlooking the window. "Coffee?" Cal stood nervously in the kitchen. "Or something else? Or, shall I cook?"

"We've just eaten garlic chicken," I reminded him. "Coffee is fine."

"Or tea? Or there's some hot chocolate."

"Cal. Coffee is fine."

But he didn't move, simply stood, staring at me. "God, you must be mad." He ran fingers through his hair. "Wanting to be here, with me. I mean, look at the place, look at *me*. Not exactly Johnny Depp, am I?"

"You really don't have any ego at all, do you?"

"I think there's a jar in the cupboard somewhere."

"Cal, shut up."

"It's the fact I'm... You women, always with the willy thing."

"Cal, shut up."

"I keep looking at you, waiting for you to disappear in a puff of smoke."

"Callum Moore, if you don't shut up and come over here I bloody *will* disappear."

"Ooh, I like a woman who knows her own mind." He sank down onto the sofa beside me.

"And if you don't kiss me properly within the next ten seconds, I'm going."

"I like a woman who knows *my* mind even better."

"It's like living in a fridge magnet factory, being with you." But his lips were cool on mine, his fingers gentle on my face, the slight scratch of stubble against my cheek and his hair in my eyes, and I could forgive him anything.

Apart from eating all the bread. I was still working on forgiving that.

ઈଔ

Cal's bedroom was pale green and terracotta, poster-sized blow-ups of computer innards framed and hung around the walls. Windows racked with blinds against the night. A fan, circling, blowing streamers of tape which made tricksy little shadows. A drenched oasis in a cracked-earth reality.

"Hey."

"Hey yourself." Cal lay tangled in the sheets, a cunning fold of bedding covering his groin and leg but leaving his chest bare.

"Did you arrange yourself like that before I woke up, just so you'd look debauched?"

"Give me a break. My bauch is without question." Cal sat up, still trailing sheets artfully.

I gave a little shiver, remembering the shameless sex that had carried us through the night. Exciting, edgy, nothing like the sex that I had with Luke. "You were incredible, Cal."

Instead of the self-deprecating remark I was expecting, Cal smiled, slowly. It was like watching a cat grin, enigmatic, poised and very slightly smug. "Yeah," he said. "Wasn't I just."

I'd even dared, last night, to look at Cal naked and uncovered. I'd averted my eyes before, scared that he might be twisted or deformed, but to my relief the leg looked almost normal, slightly less muscle tone than his right as we'd worked up a sweat between us—but nothing scary.

A sudden thought struck me. "What's it going to be like for you, if I have to keep pretending to Luke that he and I are still an item? I don't want to sleep with him again, *urgh*, but I'm going to have to keep you in the background."

Cal still had that lazy smile stuck to his face. You could have taken his picture and used him to illustrate the statement self-congratulatory. "I'll live with it. It'll be worth it in the end. And besides." He rearranged my hair as it fell on my shoulders. "Why should I worry? I'm a much better fuck."

"Ah, the return of the ego."

"Can you blame me? You've made me feel like *this* doesn't matter anymore." He twitched the covers aside and slapped at his weak leg. "Like I could conquer mountains, swim the Atlantic. Anyway. Enough about you, now let's talk about me. I'm thirty-four, Sagittarius, I like cooking, photography, reading..."

"Shut up." I laughed. "I don't want to know."

"You don't want to know *all about* me? Good God, woman, what kind of girlfriend are you? Next you'll be saying that you don't want to know how much I earn."

"Listen, I knew *everything* about Luke Fry. Back in the old days, I could probably have given you a chart showing how often he crapped! Didn't help me, did it? So, yes, I do want to know about you, but let it come in its own good time, Cal." I climbed out of the bed and began searching for my erotically discarded clothes. "And I'm really not bothered about the size of your salary."

"That's not what you said last night."

"That wasn't your salary."

"Oh, yeah."

"Cal, you are absolutely *insufferable.*" I giggled, hauling my knickers off the trendy bent-poled lamp in the corner. He looked at me with suddenly hooded eyes.

"I've done with suffering," he said quietly. For a breathless moment we stared at each other. I could see his chest twitch with his heartbeat. He was so thin that each pulse trembled his skin. He moved slightly in the bed and the covers slid lower, revealing the dark hairs ringing his navel and running down in a pencil line. His body was perfectly shaded, the hollows deep and his flesh pale, his face highlighted with stubble and the twitch of his untidy hair. "Willow." It was a whisper, a plea, gently, unbearably sexy.

"Oh, bugger." I pulled off what clothes I'd managed to put on and fell back into him again.

Chapter Twenty-six

"Oh, and here's your laptop. Cal's fixed it, done it for nothing in fact, as a favour. He said he'd got all the bits in his workshop."

"Willow, what's the matter? You're talking fit to bust here. Is something upsetting you?"

I paused, fork halfway to my lips. Was it my paranoid imagination or did he think I'd been checking up on him? What kind of person did he think I *was*? Apart from blindingly stupid and gullible, obviously. "No, everything's fine." I swallowed a mouthful of venison. "Just a bit jittery. I can't make my mind up about getting married. I mean it's *so* expensive. I looked at dresses yesterday with Katie, some of them were over a thousand pounds."

Luke clicked his tongue. "That does seem a bit steep."

"And I thought, what's the point in wasting Ganda's inheritance on stuff I'll only wear once. I'd rather save it for, you know, investing."

I watched his face carefully, but he was good. Bloody good—he never so much as twitched a muscle. "At least investing it will get you a return."

Not if I invest in you, sunshine, I thought, suddenly vicious. *You only proposed to me so that you could talk me into putting everything in joint names, then sue me through the courts for your half.* I forced down another venison sausage, but couldn't resist a quick stab. "And if we get married I wouldn't put up with any bad behaviour from you, you know."

Luke gave me a cheeky grin. "You quite like my bad behaviour."

I pretended to laugh. "Not *that* sort." *And anyway, Cal's 'bad behaviour' knocks yours out of the window. Now there's a man who knows how to be BAD.* "I meant, if you were unfaithful or anything."

Luke poured more wine, clinked glasses with me. All without a flicker of guilt. "Willow, married to you, why *would* I stray?"

"Excuse me a second, Luke, I need to...powder my nose." I almost ran from the restaurant, clutching my napkin to my mouth and only just making the Ladies before dinner returned in an unsightly rush. How dare he? How *could* he? How was it possible for anyone to lie so convincingly? It had strained every facial muscle I had to tell him that I'd got a "slight infection *down there*" and the doctor had recommended no sex until it cleared up. His disappointment had been obvious, but then I supposed it must be a perk of the job, having rampant sex to convince me of his honest intentions.

"So. How's the business?" was my bright opener when I returned.

"Not too bad. Showroom's getting there, I sold the Morgan yesterday, hence." He indicated, with a wave of his knife, the undoubtedly expensive restaurant we were eating at. Equally undoubtedly paid for with part of the twenty-six grand he'd had out of me so far. "I've had a few other leads on cars that might be up my street. One in Michigan, if I can afford to fly out for a look." No movement, not even his eyelashes stirred my way.

"Oh? Well, if it's a sure thing, maybe I could give you the cash to get out there?"

"I'm not committing until I know it's a really good deal. But thanks, I'll let you know."

I bet you will. "Um, Luke." My hands started to sweat under the table and I surreptitiously wiped them on the linen tablecloth. "I'm going tomorrow to see Ganda's invention?" Why did I phrase it as a question? Duh. Come *on*, Willow. "So I'm hoping that they'll give me at least part of the money soon."

"Oh." Affecting total nonchalance.

"Only, I was thinking." I hoped he didn't hear the sudden intake of air. "I'd really like to invest some of it in your business. And, I was thinking, what about if the following weekend we go away somewhere? I thought, kind of, a hotel somewhere really special. I'd book it and everything, as a celebration." Tinkly little laugh. Was I going too far?

"I think that sounds very nice." Maybe there was no too far where Luke was concerned. "Next weekend, you said?" A dip into his pocket and he drew out a brand new, very expensive, palm-top computer, pressed a few keys. "Yeah, that all looks pretty free. Um, just so I can let the bank manager know, how much were you thinking of investing? Sort of? I mean, you don't have to be precise, obviously. It won't matter one way or another, but, ball-park figure?"

"I was thinking about a quarter of a million. Would that do?"

A double blink. That was the only sign he gave that he was impressed. "Two hundred and fifty thousand? That sounds very generous. You should get a nice little return on that, depending on sales, but James is doing well with the cars in Boston, so..."

I let out a small breath of relief. James obviously hadn't told Luke about the phone call, which was just as well. I'd had to work out a cover story rivalling *The Da Vinci Code* in its impenetrable complexities to prevent Luke from finding out exactly how much I knew about his activities, and I wasn't one hundred percent sure of being able to remember it without cue cards.

Oooh, and that was a big, filthy *lie* there, Mr. Fry.

"Great. Anyway, I'll always hold a share of the cars, as security. So I know you won't rip me off, ha ha." Ha bloody ha, indeed.

Luke and I finished dinner and I pretended annoyance at not being able to take up his offer of "going back to the flat for a bottle of champagne". I told him to put it on ice for me. With any luck it would get frostbite and drop off.

"Goodnight then, Willow." He dropped me at my front door, his attempted vigorous kiss being narrowly averted by my pretended interest in next-door's cat on the wall. "See you in a couple of days?"

"Not tomorrow?" More pretended annoyance.

"Well, I'm a bit busy. Got some architect coming round with plans for the showroom interiors. Several companies are pitching for it, so I like to be there in person to see what they're offering. Anyway, you're off to the council tomorrow, aren't you? And then it's the weekend and I'm going to Wales to visit Da."

"Maybe we should save ourselves for next weekend then. And," I dropped my voice flirtatiously, "by then I should have the all clear from the doctor. I'm rather hoping to give you an absolutely unforgettable time."

"Sounds good to me. I'll pop in and see you, to make sure it's all okay." He revved the engine of the big black car (I wondered who it *really* belonged to) and set off.

I did a little pavement dance of glee and hopped into the Metro, which Luke had failed to notice parked at the end of the road. Cal was sitting inside reading Jasper Fforde and wearing a huge Panama hat as a disguise.

"He's gone for it. Weekend after this. Will that give us long enough? How are the boys getting on?"

Cal pulled the hat off and shook his hair free. "Pretty bloody well, since you ask. I know how to pick a team and I think they're impressed with you. Firstly, the deviousness of your mind, and secondly I told them about the thing with the melon."

"It wasn't a melon, it was a tangerine, and kindly don't bandy details of my private life about with your mates."

"Aw, go on."

"Well, all right, but only the stuff that makes me sound good."

Chapter Twenty-seven

I was kept waiting at the council office. One of the people concerned hadn't turned up, so instead of being met in reception and taken to my destination, I found myself kicking my heels and engaging Vivienne Parry in conversation. Which wasn't difficult. I had the feeling that the woman could chat equally well to a delegation of nuclear physicists or a round of tuna sandwiches. (Although what either of these would be doing hanging around the York Council Roads Department, I couldn't imagine.)

I learned that she'd worked at the council for ten years, four of them in the Roads department, that Mr. Parry was a teacher of English, and that she'd been extremely overworked lately. "What with Nadine taking so long off sick and one of the other girls on maternity leave, it's been busy, busy, busy."

I took a sip of the coffee she'd made me. It was highly sugared and not really to my taste, but better than nothing. "I was at university with Nadine, you know."

"Yes, she mentioned, when you were first here. That was about the last time she was at work, actually, now I come to think about it, poor girl. Practically had a nervous breakdown in the Ladies that day, sobbing her heart out, she was. I told her, no man's worth putting yourself through that much pain, but she wouldn't have it. Apparently he's the love of her life, although quite why she thinks that of a man who's treated her so appallingly, I don't know."

"It's surprising what you'll put up with when you're in love," I said, thinking of Luke. "Or, at least, when you *imagine* you're in love."

"I think"—Vivienne lowered her voice and I bent in close— "that he might have got her pregnant and that's why she's been off so long. Apparently, *them upstairs* have given her indefinite leave, which is what often happens when there's an *unfortunate event.*" She threw a significant look at the ceiling. I supposed she meant the collective council bosses, rather than a pantheon of gods.

"Fancy getting pregnant by someone who's that unreliable." At least that was one mistake I hadn't had to tick off in my Eye Spy Book of Terrible Misfortunes.

"Yes, from all accounts he's a real smoothy. Had all the chat, took her to expensive restaurants, spent a fortune on her, and then gave her a real runaround."

"They're always the worst."

"Yes." Vivienne sighed wistfully, and I got the impression that Mr. Parry could never have been accused of being a real smoothy. "Poor Nadine."

There was just something in her inflexion. Na*dine.* "What was his name, did you say?"

Vivienne shook her head. It took several moments for her chins to stop moving, but when they did, she said, "I'm sure she mentioned it, but I can't say I was really paying attention. You know how things are. Although, hold on a moment." A hatch in the desk opened and I was beckoned through, and ushered into an inner office. "There's a photo, there, on her desk. She may have written his name on it."

It *had* to be Nadine's desk. No one else, outside of Barbie's fan club, would have had such an arrangement of pink, fluffy items of dubious provenance. There was even a pink *pony*, for heaven's sake. And a little troll. Had this woman no shame? The picture had been taken on a cheap camera, with the resulting grainy effect, and it didn't look as though he'd even known she was taking it. Nevertheless, there he was, wearing the blue shirt I liked so much and those lovely chinos that hugged his bottom so tightly. "Luke."

"You know him?" Vivienne shoved the picture back. Obviously a surge of loyalty to Nadine was wading its way to her surface. "Then, could you *please* ask him to sort things out with Nadine?"

"I'm not sure how I'd go about that," I muttered to myself. "So, Nadine's been having a bad time with him since I turned up here?"

"Oh, a little before that, I think it started. A couple of weeks or so. She was quite quiet about it at first, but then one day I found her in the kitchen in tears, and she told me that her boyfriend was seeing another woman. But apparently it was all right because this other woman was going to invest some money in his business. He's a designer, clothes or some such, and he was sweet-talking around her, taking her out, wining and dining her until she handed over the money. But poor Nadine was convinced there was more to it than that, and you can't reason with someone when they're in that state, can you?"

A few more pieces of the puzzle slotted together. Nadine would have recognised my name from the letters she'd been asked to type. She must have mentioned to Luke that someone she knew stood to get a lot of money, maybe even shown him a copy of the letters, letters he'd then told her not to post. Therefore, letters I'd not known about until *after* Luke had picked me up in the bar. And Nadine would have been able to describe me to Luke, adding the details about what I'd been like at uni. *He hadn't remembered me at all.*

He'd cooked this whole thing up. Nadine knew Katie, would have known that we all went drinking in the Grape and Sprout after work. He'd only have to hang around for a few days before bumping into me. Having groomed himself into looking almost exactly as he had ten years ago. My skin flushed an unsightly puce. She must have known I'd had an insane crush on him. After all most of the English department did. She'd had to stay working here until she could confirm to Luke that I'd found out about the inheritance, knowing all the time that she'd have to meet me face-to-face. Why had she done it? Well, that was a stupid question, Luke could have persuaded the Pope to fall in love with him. Oh God, poor, *poor* Nadine. The cow.

"Oh, look, here's John come to take you down to the test site." Mrs. Parry was obviously relieved to be shot of me, although not as relieved as I was to be leaving. The final item had fallen into place. It really had all been about the money. Luke hadn't *accidentally* met me, hadn't recognised the woman he'd fancied at university—had, instead, scripted, staged and starred in the whole elaborate production.

It made me want to go out and get syphilis, just so I could give it to him.

Watching Ganda's road surface being tested made watching paint dry look like a fun way to spend an afternoon. Various cars drove up and down a polytunnel, in various lighting conditions, braking, turning and generally doing what cars do. Eventually, the lights were lowered down to night-time level and John the tester sidled up to me.

"Everything's fine at every stage, except this one." He pulled his cap firmly around his ears as though worried I might be about to slap his head. "Tell us what you think about this."

In almost absolute darkness, a yellow Mini started its engine. Sprinklers began to spit water, damping the road as the car accelerated along the track, its lights strobing on the glittering surface.

"Oh my God," I said. "It's like *Come Dancing.*"

Each individual sequin-spot of light gleamed but, magnified and prismed by the water droplets, the lights bled and merged. We are talking *serious* special effects here, ILM time. A fine, shimmering haze hung over the road surface wherever the lights shone. I could feel my vision flickering around the edges as my eyes tried to refocus, giving rise to a small, but insistent, headache.

"It's even worse behind, in the tail lights," John intoned gloomily. "One of the testers said it was like reversing over Liberace."

"What happens if they switch their fog lights on?"

The Mini driver complied. I should have been warned by the way John shielded his eyes and turned his head away.

"Oh. I see," I said, when my vision eventually settled down. "Oh dear."

"So, I don't think we're going to be recommending commercial production. Sorry."

"No, it's fine. I mean, I can see why you can't use it." I'd still got glowing shapes burned on my retinas. "Would it have any kind of application at all?"

"We might be able to do something with it—toned down a bit, obviously, as regards markings at the edge of pavements, but we're still thinking about that."

My image of my future life, which had been shrinking lately, squeezing Luke out, shrank a little further and Cal's white house fell off the edge. I mentally packed away the big straw hat and the floaty frock. "So you won't be wanting to buy the design then?"

"Depends. If we can use it for something, you might get a few grand. For the use of the patent. But, as it stands, nope, sorry."

Chapter Twenty-eight

"What, nothing *at all*?" Jazz coughed into his pint with shock. "Not a penny?"

"She's already had fifty grand," Katie pointed out. "So it's not a bad return, really."

"Of which she gave half to that wanker, Luke Fry. Why don't you sue, Will? Take him to the cleaners."

I refilled my wine glass. "Because, people." I took a drink. Once again I was enjoying being the centre of attention. "There would be no case to answer. I've been through it with OC. Everything I gave him, I did of my own free will. He never coerced me or bullied me."

"He did tie you to the bed though," Jazz said, with his head down to avoid Katie clopping him around the ear.

"As I *said*"—I carefully ignored him—"of my own free will. And I bet all the other women he conned would say that he never directly *asked* for money. They were so terrified of losing him that they'd hand over whatever he told them he needed."

"But if they could afford it, then it's their lookout. Ow! Fuck, Kate, that hurt."

"Good," Katie said, tightly.

"It's the way he *did it*, Jazz. Even if the women could afford it, even if they were fucking *millionaires*, no one deserves to be treated the way he treats women. Do you know, I don't think he even *likes* women very much?"

"Gift to Ash then." Jazz arched his eyebrows.

"Ash has got more sense. Anyway, I didn't mean he prefers men. I just think he sees women as glorified cash-point machines."

"Holes in the wall." Jazz guffawed and then choked. His pint might have gone down the wrong way, or Katie might have grabbed him under the table. I couldn't tell, but his face blanched and his voice was a little higher when he said, "Sorry."

"You do know"—Katie laid a hand on my arm—"that it's not your fault, don't you?"

"What, Jazz being a tactless prick? Yeah, I know. Twenty-three years I've been trying to civilise him, but he's still convinced that being diplomatic is having a qualification in watch repair."

"Falling in love with Luke, you dipstick."

"Oh. Do you know, I'm not sure that I really did?"

"But you were going to marry him." Both Katie and Jazz looked shocked.

"Yeah, well, when I was twelve I was going to marry Simon Le Bon and look what happened there." I sighed, remembering my adolescent fixations for any man in eyeliner.

"He had stupid hair. And he's got fat," Katie said as she collected her things together and picked up her bag.

"Yes, lucky escape for me."

"Anyway, guys, much as I'd love to sit around and discuss Will's appalling taste in men, I must be off. The boys have gone to the park with Dan, so I'd better go home and tame the mess while they're out." Katie got to her feet. "See you on Monday, Will. Later, Jazz."

After she'd gone, Jazz and I stared into our respective drinks. "So, you'll be up for singing on Sunday?" Jazz said, continuing a conversation we'd started when I'd first arrived at the Grape and Sprout, as though the last ten minutes had never happened. "It's kind of a one-off. A special. Just the band and us, down by the river, near the Millennium bridge?"

"Oh, right. Open-air thing? For passersby?" I didn't mind that so much. Singing outdoors made everything a bit less intense and the weather at the moment was fabulous. "Yeah, why not. Count me in."

"Good."

I sipped my wine and looked at him. Over the past few weeks, Jazz had changed enormously. Gone were the towering boots, the funereal clothing and the tatty goatee. Although his hair was still long, it had returned to its natural dirty blond colour. Jazz now wore smart casual clothes, jeans and T-shirts and trainers. From Goth to Gap in three months. "You really like OC, don't you?" I asked. It was the only reason I could think of for the radical self-redesign.

He nodded, almost miserably. "When Grace was born and I was there, it was..." Horrifyingly, there were tears in his eyes. Jazz, who'd not even cried when he'd trodden on his signed Green Day album in stiletto-heeled boots. (It was a party and he'd not noticed, walked around with the CD spiked on his heel for three hours.)

I quickly looked around, in case I'd fallen into a parallel dimension. "I think she's very fond of you, too. You've been terrific, helping out with the dogs and all that."

"Yeah. Mr. Terrific, that's me." It really wasn't like Jazz to look glum. He looked as uneasy with the expression, as Santa Claus would look with a machete. "Do you really think she likes me, Will? I mean, *you know*, like a proper bloke?"

Another crowd of people entered The Grape and the diverting noise prevented me from having to answer. There wasn't much I could say, really. How should I know how OC felt about Jazz? Her husband had only just dumped her and now she'd got a new baby. I doubted that the lonely-heart pages were on the top of her reading list at present.

"Jazz." I took his hand, charitably. "Even if OC isn't interested, there's a woman out there somewhere for you."

Jazz looked me in the eyes, searching my face. "But maybe not the one I want," he said softly.

"Oh, *Jazz.*" My heart contorted a little and I squeezed his hand. "Honestly, everything will work out."

Thwack.

My first thought was "gosh, exactly like in the comics", as a fist shot out from behind my shoulder, catching Jazz a blow under his chin, in classic He-Man-punch style. My second thought, of course, was "what the *hell?*" and I whipped around to find Luke standing there, with a gleam in his eye.

"Was he trying to get you back?"

Would I be horribly shallow if I admitted to a moment's quiet pride? No man had *ever* punched another guy for me. I was a fist-fight virgin! And now, here was Luke, defending my honour, or at least defending his woman from the predatory advances of her supposed ex-boyfriend.

"No, we were talking."

"You were holding *hands.*"

Jazz began climbing to his feet, clutching his jaw. I made frantic keep-quiet signals with my eyebrows which he, perhaps understandably, chose to ignore. "What the *fuck* was *that* all about?" he muttered through clenched teeth.

"You, schmoozing your way around my girlfriend! Can't you get it into your head that it's all over? Mind you, Willow, I didn't exactly see you shoving him away."

"We were *talking*, Luke. That's all. Jazz is going out with my sister." Jazz's eyes went big and round at this flagrant lie and he opened his mouth to contradict. I stood hard on his foot under the table. He winced, but at least closed his mouth. "Honestly." I put a pacifying hand on Luke's arm. "We came out for a quiet drink. Katie was with us too, until a minute ago, and Jazz asked about OC. She's giving him a bit of a hard time at the moment."

"I came to find out how it went at the council today."

Jazz opened his mouth again, and I had to get brutal. I drew back my arm and slapped him firmly round the face. "How *dare* you grab my hand anyway. *Were* you trying to make Luke jealous? If so, it won't work." Then I turned my head to one side, pretending outrage, and mouthed "sorry" hidden from Luke by my hair. Jazz obviously now saw the value in being silent.

"Well, I dunno. Willow." Luke scratched at his stubble and rubbed his knuckles. "I mean, how do I know I can trust you? How do I know that you're not going to go running off with psycho-killer boy here whenever my back is turned?"

I felt a sudden rush of indignation. Forgetting that the romance with Luke had been fake from the moment he'd pretended to knock into me in this very bar, I reacted like any girl would, being accused of infidelity. "I was *not* up to anything with Jazz. If I was, why the hell would I do it in here? Luke." I lowered my voice and moved closer to him. "*You* are the man I'm going to marry, *you* are the man I'm in love with. Not Jazz."

I was slightly surprised that the bar didn't fill with the smell of brimstone at the totality of the fib, or that Jazz didn't burst out laughing. But it's probably quite hard to laugh with a cracked jaw. Besides, I had to say *something*. The thought of Luke—filled with unnecessary hurt pride—dumping me just when I was sorting out the kind of revenge most women can only dream of, made me feel sick. Then I came up with something that would swing things my way completely. "Come on." I pulled at his arm. "Let's go somewhere and buy a bottle of champagne."

Luke was still looking stern, but his face softened. "You mean?"

"They've paid up." I put a little wobble of excitement into my voice. "The council wrote me a cheque this afternoon for four hundred and fifty thousand pounds. But, of course"—I let my voice drop, cast my eyes repentantly downward—"if you don't want to, I'll understand."

"I'm not sure." Luke ran his hands through his hair. "Can you really promise me, Willow, that nothing is going on between you and *him*?"

Jazz had regained his seat and his pint and was looking at me with the hurt air of a dog which has had its tail trodden on. But at least he was quiet. I beamed good thoughts at him. "I can totally promise you that."

Luke still looked stern, his mouth tight and his eyes narrow. *Would* he dump the prospect of nearly half a million pounds? Had we all underestimated him? Did he *really* have a sense of pride, of love for me, was I the woman he wanted for herself not her wallet?

"Well, all right. I do believe you."

Obviously not, then.

"I'm sorry, Willow. I'm under a lot of pressure at the showroom. The thought that you might be fooling around was unbearable." Luke smiled at me. "We'll say no more about it."

253

Hang on. Did that still make it sound as though I *had been* in the wrong? And with a daggy guy like *Jazz*? At least if he'd caught me with my hand in Cal's jeans I could have gone out with a sense of pride at my good taste. "We really weren't..."

Luke put his hand in the small of my back to guide me out of the Grape. "I believe you," he said, in a tone which made it clear that he didn't, but was being tolerant. We got to the Pitcher and Piano, and ordered a bottle of the finest champagne (£140, I was beginning to regret my lie about the money, I hoped he wasn't going to suggest we went on somewhere equally pricey for dinner) before I realised what he was doing. Making me feel guilty, unsettling me, forcing me to try to buy him back with grand gestures. He was bloody good at it, I had to admit, generosity itself with his "I really don't mind that you met up with your ex without telling me," and yet just the tiniest bit withdrawn. No handholding under the table, no suggestive winks or casual remarks about our future. Cool enough that, had our relationship been for real, I would have been more than a little bit panicky by now. Smooth. You had to admire it.

So, since I was pretending that our love affair was real, I also had to pretend that I wanted his approval again. I told jokes and took him to dinner (although it wasn't the hugely expensive one he'd clearly set his heart on, it wasn't exactly cod and chips twice). We ended the evening with many references to my condition "down there" and an encounter which, although not the full back against the wall shag, wasn't exactly cod and chips twice, if you get my drift. He dropped me at my door after an "I've forgiven you" snog and I dashed straight in to phone Jazz and apologise.

First thing on Saturday morning, I cadged a lift up to the farm on the back of Ash's bike. We were both glad to get away from home, where Grace had discovered the joys of colic and had therefore kept us all awake most of the night.

"It's not that I *mind*, as such, but it's not even my fucking baby." Ash pulled the bike up onto its stand and leaned against it in the lay-by.

"Ooh, not getting broody now, are you?" I nudged him and after a moment he nudged back.

"Not for kids, no. But, don't you ever think you're getting old, Will? With nothing to show for it?" He pulled off his helmet and ran a hand through his spiky brush of hair, making it stand on end and himself, in consequence, look about twelve.

"We're thirty-two, Ash. It's not exactly cardigan-time."

"Yeah, but, I was clubbing last night and, know something? For the first time I felt old. There's loads of guys there, all about nineteen, all totally fuckable but it's like there's nothing going on apart from clubs, drugs and sex." There was a pause.

"I'm still looking for the bad in that statement."

"Well, there *is* more to life than that, isn't there? I want to buy a house, Will. I want to live with someone, eat breakfast with them, get a dog. Be real. Don't you ever feel that you want to be real?"

I inhaled heftily. "I think it's called growing up."

"I guess. Right, I'm going, leave you here with Gorgeous Boy." Ash threw a derisive look at the Metro, slewed into its parking space in the worst example of parallel parking since the *Exxon Valdez*. "I'll see you back at the ranch house." Helmet on and engine started, he threw up the visor to yell, "Give him one from me," and roared off into the scenery, which briefly became less scenic with the addition of a Yamaha 750 and concomitant exhaust fumes.

As I crossed down over the field, I could see that the door to the barn was open a touch. Nothing visible inside, of course, he was too careful for that. All the machines were tucked away in the far, dark corner, ticking and flickering and purring to themselves out of sight of any casual passersby.

"Hello?" Forgetting exactly who I was dealing with, I tugged at the slightly open door. The resulting noise drove me to my knees, both hands clamped over my ears. The noise was so big it had character.

"Er, sorry, Will." Gradually I became aware that the sound had stopped and opened my eyes, to stare into the knees of Cal. "Wasn't expecting anyone, so the alarms were enabled." He helped me to my feet. "I should know better, really. Last time I was working with the doors open, the bloody goat got loose. I'm in the middle of a really tricky piece of analysis and suddenly it sounds like a buffalo mating with an elephant seal. I go outside to shoo her off, forgetting I've got my headset on and all the team can hear me shouting 'fuck off and leave me alone you evil bitch' with the full-scale racket going on in the background."

"Sounds nasty."

"It was. They thought I'd been raided. All shut their systems down, all off-line, couldn't reach anyone for a week." I was upright but he hadn't let go of my hand. "So. You came back."

"No. I'm a hologram."

"Won't bother offering you a drink then. Don't tell me, you're deeply in love with my goat and you've come to ask for her hoof in marriage?"

"I wouldn't take that thing's hoof in anything less than a curry." He was smiling down at me in a way that made me itch inside. "Cal, I think someone's calling you."

"What? Oh, yeah, right." He flipped the headset back up from around his neck, but even his voice was smiling as he spoke into it, "Yo, Zak! What's the news? What? Yes, Willow's here, how could you...oh, did I? Shit. Hey, down boy, that's for me to know and you to forever speculate on. Now..." Turning away from me he walked back into the barn but I didn't follow. I wanted five minutes.

I walked behind the barn and leaned on the paddock gate looking up the hill towards the moor. Winnie stopped scratching her bum on one of the fence posts and eyeballed me balefully. "I'll even miss you, you evil-smelling lawn mower," I whispered. As philosophical as I'd been about the lack of council funding coming my way, the thing I was really regretting was the loss of this place. Ever since the notion of buying it had come to me, the farm had felt like home. The smells, the dust, the dry rot and peeling paintwork, all had got under my skin and had become part of me, as much as I felt I had become part of them. And now, although Luke's treachery had allowed the desire for score-settling to fill me, the inability to buy the farm made me far sadder. "I wonder if that makes me really deep or incredibly shallow?" I closed my eyes and let my chin rest on the gate, the smell of pine resin trickled up my nose and made me think of forests and clean toilets.

"Penny for them."

I jumped.

"Sorry. You looked completely lost there. Making plans for turning all this into an herb nursery? Or just herself into goat-burgers and a bedside rug?"

I looked up at him, leaning beside me companionably. Those eyes were like a total eclipse. "I can't buy the farm."

His shoulders tensed, drew away from me. "Oh. Right." Our thighs had been touching, now there was a handspan between them. "Okay. Thanks for letting me know." And then he was turning, turning away from me and setting himself to limp back towards the barn. He looked beaten, defeated.

"I would if I could." I half-called after him.

A shrug. "Doesn't matter. Don't worry about it."

"Cal." I caught him up in the middle of the yard. "Look, I really am sorry."

A beat. Then he grabbed me by the shoulders, pushing me back against the wall of the barn, leaning his full weight into me, catching my hair in his hands and using it to tip my head back and up. I had time for a tiny whimper before his mouth came down hard on mine, kisses like bruises, tongue teasing, reckless, shuddering, *wild*.

"What the hell was *that*?" I asked, when he let me go, my face flaming flamingo-pink and my mouth doubling in size with the ferocity of the kiss.

"That, Willow"—Cal moved back lazily—"was goodbye."

"Good*bye*?" Confusion was streaming from every pore. "Why? What have I done?"

"I could live with you fooling with Luke, setting him up, maybe even one quick last fuck to keep him onside until the *denouement*, but I can't live with you deciding to write it all off. Or, rather, I'm going to have to, aren't I, but, well. Goodbye, Willow."

"But I haven't."

His eyes flared. "So, you've decided off your own bat that you don't want the place? Oh, come on. Give me some credit. I've seen the way you've been around here—you love it. You kind of *belong* here, somehow. I mean, even that fucking *goat* behaves for you. And now, suddenly, you don't want it? Yeah, right, there's a man behind a decision like that, and I can only think of one who'd let you pass up on your own happiness for the sake of his."

"Listen, you arrogant, sexist shit, not every decision I make revolves around men. You're so self-obsessed, what, you think

I've got a brain that doesn't work unless some guy's swinging his dick at me?"

On adrenaline-fired legs, I wobbled off across the yard, attaining a decent march by the time I reached the paddock. Winnie gave me an "oh God, it's you again" stare and clambered into the far corner, from where she watched me turn up the lane and head towards the hill with my fists clenched and my jaw rigid. How *dare* he? Was that what he really thought of me, that I was so gullible and trusting that I'd get back with Luke, after everything he'd done? I power-walked up the track, not acknowledging the nettle stings peppering the backs of my legs, or the tiny flag-wavings of butterflies celebrating the thistle flowers. *Bastard.* Did he see me as some weak-willed, pathetic little woman, having to have a big, strong man at her side in order to feel vindicated? Even if that big, strong man was a double-dealing fraud? That even *Luke* was better than nothing?

Halfway up the hill my anger and I ran out of steam and I sat down on the sandy bank overlooking the farm. I couldn't see Cal, no movement apart from the goat shuffling around her drinking trough and some bumblebees lazily torpedoing the gorse blossoms. Maybe he'd gone inside the barn and plugged himself in to his machines, called up the team and told them to stop their work on my behalf. Not needed anymore. With that scared, tortured look back on his face, the look he'd lost come to think of it, since I'd told him I loved him.

And then, with the perfect clarity of hindsight and the additional focus of the microscope of guilt, I realised.

This wasn't about me. It was about him.

Cal, with his fear of being rejected again. He'd let down his guard, let me in, showed me who he truly was. He'd told me things, trusted me, and I'd done the metaphorical equivalent of kneeing him in the nuts. He didn't think Luke was better than nothing, he thought Luke was better than *him!* His worst nightmare had come true, he'd been living in dread of this moment, and I'd done nothing to reassure him. Cal wasn't like Luke, wasn't tough, uncompassionate. He was scared, fragile, *damaged.*

And here was me, bringing my flamethrower approach to relationships.

I got up, dusted down my backside and left the hillside, cantering down the slope and arriving in the yard with a kind of braced-knee sliding stop. I'd been wrong. Cal hadn't gone into the barn. He was sitting on the edge of an old churn-stand, his weaker leg drawn up under his chin and his hair hiding his face. "Cal."

He jumped. "Oh, yeah, you'll be needing a lift back, won't you?"

"Um, no. Actually. I need to explain to you…stuff."

"There really isn't any need. You don't have to justify yourself to me, Willow."

But now I knew what he was doing. Not pushing me away, not withdrawing, he was performing damage limitation.

"Cal, listen. I didn't get the council money, all right? *That* is why I can't buy the farm. Nothing to do with anyone else." The quick hope on his face left me weak. "So, now you know. It's not that I don't want to, it's because I *can't.*"

"Oh." Cal wiped the back of his hand across his mouth. There was blood on it. It had been quite a goodbye kiss. "Oh, *fuck.* I'm sorry, Willow."

I did a shrug very similar to his.

"No, really. Oh, God. What have I done? I only wanted…look, I…shit." He lopsidedly jumped down from the stone platform and ran his hands through his hair. "What can I do to make it up to you?"

My smile started slow and I watched the answering fire spark in his eyes. "Are you *kidding*?" My voice was slow, too. "That kiss was the most erotic thing I have *ever* had done to me."

His mouth twitched. "You really had me going there, you cowbag."

"Well, you've got me going here, bastard."

"Then come into my tent and let me attend to you. I have scented unguents and liquors with which to pander to your every whim." He led me into the barn, one hand clamped around my wrist as though afraid I'd suddenly change my mind and run.

"Why the hell would you want to panda to me? Don't they sort of mate once every twenty years or something?"

"Ah, but they know the value of foreplay."

And with that, he proceeded to show me the value of foreplay, until I was drunk and drugged and intoxicated with it, and each time I threatened to crash he'd catch me up and lift me again until he finally whispered me into making love so completely that only the feel of the straw around me kept me earthbound.

We only realised how uninhibited we'd been when a distant and tinny round of applause broke out from the computer speakers and a voice said, breathlessly, "Sandman, whatever it is you're on, get me some."

"Shit, Fortune, you could have turned your 'phones off," Cal said languidly, lying beside me with his fingers tracing my ribs.

"What, and miss fifty quid's worth of entertainment? You should webcam, man. You'd make a killing."

"Ha fucking ha." Leaning across me, Cal flipped the switch that sent the machine into deaf-blindness. "Sorry. Forgot to turn the boys off."

"I think quite the opposite was true."

"Hmm, yes. Look, Will, I've been thinking,"

"What about?" I pushed his hair off his face.

"Mostly about how can anyone who's seen Johnny Vegas believe in evolution, and that Beatrix Potter must have been smoking some serious weed to come up with *The Tailor of Gloucester*. Oh, and that I love you. And, instead of giving up on the idea of this place, why don't we *both* move in here."

"What?" I propped myself up on my elbows.

"*I* don't want to sell, but I can't keep the place on because of the legwork, ha. *You* love it here. You could turn it into a going concern. I could drop the consultancy work and increase the, ahem, other stuff. What do you think? Between us, it shouldn't be too much of a job making the place habitable. I'll get a lift put in so that I can get all the way up to the attics, make some extra space that way."

I looked at the rough, whitewashed walls of the barn and out of the doorway into the yard. Tiny plants had forced their way up between the cobbles and down between the stones of the walls and were now blooming in random spurts of yellow in unlikely sites all around the enclosed space. It looked like an explosion in a sun factory. I loved every last weed-infested inch of the place.

"Oh, yes."

"Of course, there's a downside." Cal shook his shirt out and began putting it back on. "There's the fact that you'll be stuck with me, dragging myself around the place like a sexually obsessed Quasimodo."

"Quasimodo *was* sex obsessed."

"Was he? I thought he was just misunderstood and lonely."

"Yes, well, I used to think that about you."

"Ha. Fine, all right, dragging myself around *exactly like* Quasimodo."

"Except for the hump."

"Willow, will you please shut up? Thank you. Right, okay, so there's me, and then there's the winters up here."

I gave a little shiver. "Mmm. Snowed in with nothing but a bottle of whisky, and staying in bed until the snowplough gets through, wasn't it?"

"Disadvantages rapidly turning into an upside, and there's the goat."

"Just needs a firm hand."

Cal groaned. "Oh, stop. But you know what I'm saying? It'll be tough. And there may be winters so bad that you lose all the herbs."

"I'll make things with them. Candles, soap, that sort of thing. When the herbs themselves are out of season. That way there'll be back up."

Cal looked impressed at my forward planning. He would have been even more impressed if he'd seen the pile of magazines in my room. Shut up, not the bridal ones. I suspect he would have made rude remarks about grown women dressed as toilet-roll covers if he'd seen those. I mean the rural-small-business ones, the start-your-own-smallholding ones, the North York Moors' publications of rules, regulations and grants for new businesses within the National Park. Ever since the thought of buying this place had crossed my mind, I'd been researching.

I'm not stupid, you know.

Except, possibly, about violet-eyed, tight-trousered science graduates. Which really wasn't my fault. Besides which, I wasn't alone in that particular stupidity. Which reminded me.

"How's the planning going for next weekend?"

"Mmm? Oh, not bad. Ratboy's had a few bites. We're taking it from there. You found a hotel yet?"

"I've booked the honeymoon suite. It's absolutely fabulous. Katie came to look at it with me. There's a whirlpool bath in the middle of the floor and this huge four-poster all done up in silver gilt. It looks like the Beckhams' spare room."

"I find a perverted pleasure in hearing about the scene of your seduction of another man."

"You find a perverted pleasure in everything."

"True."

"Cal, look, I've still got nearly ten grand left in the bank. We could make a start on getting this place fit to live in before the winter, couldn't we?"

He gave a peculiar chuckling laugh. "Um. Willow. Have you been listening to me? I head up the best-selling anti-hack business in the world. Me and the boys, we save companies billions of dollars, not to say the world from nuclear meltdown and Doctor Who from the Daleks."

"So?"

"Do you have any idea how much they pay me? On average? I know things that could bring whole continents to their knees, ways to bring down the yen, the pound, how to transfer the funds of multimillion corporations into a Swiss bank account with my number on it. Believe me, they pay to keep me sweet."

"But." I looked around me at the crumbling plaster and the spongy beams. "Why do you live in a flat in York? And drive such a horrible car? And surely you could afford someone to come and help keep this place up, someone you don't mind knowing about what you do?"

Cal looked into my face, hooked my hair behind my ears. "Because, Willow, *I don't care*. Didn't care. When Hannah left me all the pleasure in it went *fooof*. The money was coming in and what could I do with it? I bought a flat with fewer stairs, but I *like* being in York. Love the place. And same with my car, you should have seen the one I had *before*. After that, what was there to spend it on? And if I'd found someone on the strength of how much I earned, what kind of relationship would that be? Money is not important, Will. I've grown up without...well, you can see what I grew up with, can't you? And Mary wouldn't take any. I paid to refence the field down by the river, but she'd had her stroke by then and she couldn't complain fast enough to stop me, so."

"So it never was about the money. Selling this place to me."

"*No!* I'd have given it to you, if I thought you'd take it. But if I had, how would you have run it, mmm? You would have had to carry on working at the paper for at least a couple of seasons just to fund your startup, and you'd probably have come to resent it, having to travel out here to dig and plant and stuff and then spend all week working to spend your weekends doing the same again, no. If you'd taken this place on your own, you would have come to hate it. But together..."

"Big finish music, maestro."

"What?"

"You're starting to sound like a romance novel."

"Sorry. All right then. But together, we can spend all our spare time arguing over where to plant parsley. Better?"

"There's no point arguing with you. It's like trying to juggle jelly."

"Ha. Come on. Let's go and walk the acres and you can tell me about your plans. And don't try telling me that you haven't made any. I know what you're like, Willow. You'll have been drawing up little planting maps since the first time you saw the place."

Maybe Ash had told him about the magazines.

Chapter Twenty-nine

Sunday afternoon, down by the river. The air was humid and heavy, lying over us like a damp flannel as the band set up the equipment. They'd brought a portable generator and a kind of small marquee, all paid for by Jazz, whose job, doing something unspecified and probably unspecific in an accountant's office, seemed to have paid some kind of bonus.

I lay on the grass and sweated like a horse. Ash was helping to hump speakers around, wearing a tiny vest and shorts and probably, knowing Ash, a film of baby oil just in case a tasty punter should wander by. Even Clay had been dragged away from his great allotment plans for the afternoon, with the promise of free beer (in a cool box under the shade of the marquee, again courtesy of Jazz, I was *definitely* in the wrong job) and Bree was somewhere on the periphery, trying not to catch anyone's eye.

I had a kind of fizz of anticipation in my stomach that owed nothing to my forthcoming performance. Yesterday, while Cal was occupied with some technical stuff, I'd browsed through some of the files we'd copied from Luke's laptop, reminding myself what a complete louse the man was, with his mass-produced I'll-love-you-forever letters and his varying accounts of what his job actually entailed. He'd been everything, from a hair-stylist-to-the-stars in LA (only needing the money to open his own salon over here) to a racehorse syndicate manager (just needing the money to buy his own dead cert horse and put it through training). Whilst I was surfing through the emails, sniggering at some of the more flowery phrases, I'd found a record of an online conversation he probably hadn't even known had been archived. I wouldn't have taken much notice, except that the date was familiar.

At first I hadn't known why, then it dawned. The twenty-seventh of May had been the first day of our weekend in Cornwall. The weekend that Luke had sent me off out to enjoy myself while he stayed in our room and "worked".

Worked, my arse. He'd been hooked up to the internet, trawling for his next target, and it looked as though he'd found her. Argento was (or so she said, wouldn't it be great if it turned out that she was a *he*?) living in Bristol, had recently broken up with her boyfriend of seven years and was beginning to put her life back together again. Luke had spent, the archive told me, five and a half hours talking to her. Perhaps grooming would be a more accurate description. He'd told her that he was newly single (his wife had, apparently, "left him for his best friend" and he was finding it hard to trust again), from Wales, and a personal fitness instructor. He'd obviously picked up on her clues. She felt "fat and undervalued" and was sure "her weight was what drove her boyfriend away in the end". But she also mentioned owning her own home and having a private income...and he'd talked about being in Bristol soon.

Bloody hell, Luke Fry was good at what he did.

My name, shouted over a power chord, pulled me to my feet and onto the stage. The crowd wasn't large, mostly families dotting the grass, enjoying the sunshine and ice creams. As we drove into the first number, others joined in until, nearing the end of the set, there were about a hundred people singing and clapping along with "Waterloo". Spread-eagled on a bank beside the river, Ash, Bree and Clay were sharing a beer. It was only then that it occurred to me to wonder where OC was. Was it too hot for Grace to be out and about?

An instrumental break allowed me a drink of water and a longer look over the crowd. I could see Cal leaning against the van that had brought the equipment, moving lazily in time with the music, drinking wine from the bottle. He saw me notice him and raised the bottle in salute. In answer I stuck my tongue out, then the band changed song and I hurried back to the front of the makeshift stage, picking up my microphone.

Feedback hummed in the air, as Jazz flipped a switch, turning off my mike and grabbing his own. "Just something, um, yeah, to wrap up the set, a song for my favourite girl in the world," he announced. The rest of the band and I exchanged a look—this definitely hadn't featured in rehearsals—and Jazz began to play alone, picking a tune out on his keyboard.

When it dawned on everyone what he was playing, they all joined in, bass first, then drums, then lead guitar. It was an old song, one we'd performed when we'd first got together, but was now so old-fashioned that we'd discarded it from the act in favour of The Human League and some of the less complicated Spandau Ballet. As I swung into backing lyrics, with Jazz fronting up, I saw what had triggered it. OC was pushing the three-wheeled, all-terrain buggy over the grass, Booter and Snag on either side like overweight dwarf huskies pulling a sledge. We were singing "Miss Grace"—satin, French perfume and lace indeed. OC stopped pushing, staring up at the stage, up at *Jazz*, with an almost awestruck expression. She pulled Grace free of her restraining straps and held her against her shoulder, swaying her in time to the song. I was sure she was singing along. When the song finished, Jazz brought his mike up again.

"I'd like to introduce you to Grace." He held out a hand. As one, the crowd swivelled until everyone was looking at OC and the baby. "And her mother, the most fabulous woman in the world. And I know it's soon, and I know you're not divorced yet, and I know everything's complicated but, Oceana, would you marry me?"

And the crowd, as they say, went wild.

I used the tumult to cover my escape, slipping off the stage sweaty and hoarse, and finding my brothers waiting for me.

"That went well." Clay pressed a beer into my hand and I rolled the chilled can around my hot forehead.

"All to plan, anyway." Ash shaded his eyes and looked over the crowd. "What's she doing now?"

"Crying, I think."

"Stupid bloody woman, doesn't know when she's well off. He's a billion times better than that prick she was married to."

"Excuse me? What *plan*? Did you and Jazz cook all this up between you?"

Even Bree smiled at that. "It was the best way. She needs romance."

I looked over at Jazz, his hair standing away from his head with the static in the air and the heat, holding Grace against him with one hand, and OC with the other. They were surrounded by people, and they were both smiling. It looked perfect, even though sweat was dripping from the ends of Jazz's hair and Grace was making a face which indicated that a full nappy was on the cards.

"Well, I guess being proposed to from a stage in front of a crowd is *pretty* romantic," I said, grudgingly.

Ash blew a raspberry. "Hark at her."

"How about cliffs at midnight?" Cal strolled up alongside us. "Would that be more your style?"

"I don't know. Is Cliff's some sort of bar?" I took the wine bottle from him and somehow everyone else slipped away and we were encased in our own little bubble of quiet. "It would beat down on one knee by a heap of dogshit anyway."

"Ah, anything would be better than being proposed to by a heap of dogshit." We'd not long been out of bed and he looked it, all tousled and unshaven.

"God, you're sexy."

"Look who's talking." As he pulled me against his hard body (oh yes, he was sexually insatiable, I'm not sure who's up for casting in the role but they'd better be able to portray the appetites of Peter Stringfellow), I looked up over his shoulder and found myself fighting free of his embrace.

"*Shit.*"

"What?" Hurt, Cal took a step back, let his hands fall to his sides. "What did I do?"

"Not you, over there. It's Luke! What the bloody buggery is *he* doing here? He's supposed to be in Wales."

"It's all right, he hasn't seen you. Us. He's far too busy with what he's doing."

From behind the cover of Cal, I peered out to where Luke was standing. He'd obviously been walking past and got caught up in the crowd scenes surrounding Jazz's proposal. "He wouldn't be here on purpose, would he? No, the gig wasn't advertised. Jazz set it all up by himself. Well, I know now why, but he's *supposed* to be in *Wales.*"

No, Luke was not in Wales. Instead, he was with a dark-haired woman. *Nadine.* Maybe he had seen me, and was working on his cover story for when *I* noticed *him.* I couldn't take the risk. I took another few steps away from Cal.

"Christ, I'll be glad when next weekend is over."

It was no good. I couldn't risk that Luke had already seen me. Thank God Cal and I hadn't been doing anything more than talking.

"Luke. Hello, I thought you were off to Wales this weekend." It was the devil that made me walk over there, face stretched in a welcoming smile. I could have just made a call-me gesture across the intervening space. But a little demonic part of me wanted to know how fast Luke really *could* talk his way out of a situation.

"Willow, how lovely to see you. We were on our way somewhere and we saw the crowd and...decided to come over."

"Yes, we've just finished. Hello, Nadine, fancy seeing you here, too."

Oh, Willow, you complete bitch. Poor Nadine, she's done nothing to deserve this. But Luke had obviously primed her. "Hello. I'm talking to Luke about showroom things."

I could have followed this up. I *could* have forced her to talk for ages, to elaborate on the story that Luke had told *her* he'd told *me*, whilst all the while knowing that she thought he was someone, some*thing* else. But she looked pale and her face was hollowed and scared-looking. She was wearing a summer dress and my already suspicious eye detected a small bump under the waistline.

"Look, Will, I'd better get on. Nadine is showing me where the council regulations say that I have to put my car park. There's been a bit of a mistake, you see. I *thought* I could have it round the side, but, apparently, I have to have it somewhere away from the surface drains."

He was eyeing me up and down as he spoke and I had a brief shiver of guilt. Was it obvious from looking at me that I'd spent the previous night wrapped around Cal? Did I look sexually sated? I thanked God for the blush-red cheeks that the combination of performing and the oppressive heat had brought. But no, it was just Luke. Ogling my breasts as though he wanted to rip my bra off there and then.

"Talk to the face, cos the boobs ain't listening," I muttered. "Nice to see you again, Nadine. I'll call you, Luke, okay?"

Nadine granted me a cool nod, sucking her cheeks in as she did so. Luke looked over at Cal. "I see you've brought a friend, too. You've got so many male friends, Willow, I'm surprised you've got time for me."

Oooh, Mr. Clever. Not only had he managed to spin an on-the-spot story, but he'd managed to draw attention to Cal in such a way as to make me feel guilty. He'd ended his phrase with a self-deprecating little laugh, but I knew it for the warning it was. "You mention Nadine, and I'll point out that you seem to be running around with half the male population of Yorkshire."

I'm sorry. My parting remark probably means that my karma is now in negative figures and I'm going to have to suffer reincarnation as a jampot cover, but I couldn't help myself. "I'll see you soon, Luke. I'm really looking forward to next weekend."

I saw Nadine blanche further and hurry away before she could throw up at me. Having spent the past twenty years as the thrower-upper, I was in no hurry at all to be on the shoe-splatty end of things. Although, I swallowed, experimentally. I couldn't actually remember the last time I'd thrown up. Cal and I had a relationship. God, yes, did we ever, and I hadn't been sick on him for ages. Maybe I had finally "grown out of it".

ജ

We all went back to the house. Cal had promised to cook dinner, Jazz and OC were high on each other, and even Grace was stunned into an unusual silence by the general air of bonhomie and levity which hovered around us all.

"I think"—Clay raised a glass—"that I'd like to drink a toast to Ganda, for all the changes in our lives."

"I'll drink to Ganda, but I'm not sure what you mean." I moved the bottle to one side, so that Cal could put down a steaming dish containing apple and ginger-wine pie. "I didn't get what he intended me to from his inheritance. I suppose you got the allotment, but OC got Booter and Snag."

"Which, kind of indirectly, got me Jazz." OC grinned. Since the advent of herself and Jazz as a couple, she'd become a lot more relaxed. Gone was the super-housewife personality. All right, she'd never be Slob of the Century but even so, only this morning I'd seen her throw a crisp bag at the bin, miss, *and not instantly get up to throw it away properly.* "It was when he kept coming round to help walk the dogs that I realised what a gorgeous man he really is."

"That and the hours of hypnotism he put in," Ash whispered to me. "It was like Derren Brown with spaniels."

"Sssh." I kicked his ankle.

"And Bree"—Clay nodded at his younger brother—"is writing a book based on all the stuff Ganda left him."

"It's from Ganda's diaries and letters. The story of an inventor and some of the crazy gadgets he comes up with, and how he finds his true love." It was the longest, most coherent sentence I'd ever heard Bree say.

"*Chitty Chitty Bang Bang*, anyone?"

"No, Ash, it's much more realistic than that. Anyway, I've got a publisher for it and they want to publish some of Ganda's other notebooks. Like *Country Diary of an Edwardian Lady*, only with gadgets."

Blimey. Bree was almost fluent now.

"What about Ash?"

"Ah, well, my theory all falls down there a bit. Still got the twelve pairs of waders, Ash?"

"Yep. But I'm taking them to the tip tomorrow, if anyone wants to come for a ceremonial seeing-off."

I caught Cal's eye and we grinned at each other. I hadn't come so badly out of the inheritance thing. Maybe the half a million pounds hadn't materialised, but I'd got Cal, I'd got a whole new life beckoning to me from fifteen acres of moorland and a small, white house. Oh, and a nose, in a matchbox.

ೞಗಛ

I couldn't settle at work on Friday. In fact, we were all edgy, twitchily enervated by the muggy heat, snappy with each other and miserable with overwork.

"The twins wouldn't go to bed last night, till midnight," Katie said. "They said it was 'too hot'. Were you hot last night, Clive?"

"I'm hot every night, darlin'."

I looked at her. "Why do you even bother?"

"I keep hoping he'll break his programming."

I fiddled with a notepad, tearing little strips off the corners, shredding them and starting again. I couldn't concentrate on work, even though I knew I should. I *had* to get this article in shape before the paper went to press on Tuesday, and there were still the pictures to sort out.

"Why don't you go home, Will?"

"What, and sit around thinking? Can't. I need to be occupied."

"Go round to your man's then. I'm sure he'll occupy you."

Clive went "hur hur" in the background. Katie reached out a foot, depressed the handle under his chair and watched smugly as the seat shot downwards, causing him to bang his chin on his desk.

"Cal's busy, sorting things out for tomorrow. I don't want to get in the way."

"Well, go and help your sister with the baby then. I'm sure she'd be glad of someone to take Grace out for a push so she can catch up with her beauty sleep."

"She's busy, too. She's moving in with Jazz."

"In with *Jazz*? Is she mad? His place is only a short hop from being an anthrax zone." Katie sighed. "I still think you should be somewhere else, Will. I'll finish the article for you."

"Do you know what to say?"

"Of course I do. Now, just go."

"If Luke rings..."

"I'll tell him you've gone home early to pack. All right?"

So I went home. The house felt strangely underoccupied without OC and Grace. Ash had gone off to the tip on Monday and not been seen since, and even Clay had gone out somewhere, so there was complete quiet as I let myself in.

Thunder rumbled. The humidity made my head ache and I rested my forehead against the cool wall of the hallway, slumping against it with my eyes closed. I stayed like this for a few minutes. I felt flat and dopey with the combination of muggy air and the logistics for tomorrow, so the quiet was welcome. Outside I heard the birds stop thrashing about in the hedge, an unnatural peace descending as everything hurried for shelter from the oncoming storm.

Thunder rolled again and I straightened away from the wall. As I turned to go through the kitchen to the back door, I heard a rattle behind me and swivelled in time to see an envelope flutter to the floor, landing with a tiny pfff alongside the mat and sliding a few inches on the wood boards.

I recognised the envelope without needing to pick it up. Another of those anonymous letters, probably still saying "you don't deserve it", although in a sudden rush of creativity the unknown sender had managed "I feel sorry for you" (very big of them) and a couple of "I hope you learn your lesson". Not exactly Shakespearian, but disturbing nonetheless.

This one, flopping to the floor like a dying goldfish, as my head pounded and the thunder bundled about, was the last straw. Angry, slightly scared and incredibly frustrated, I swept to the door and flung it open, leaping outside and intercepting the sender just before the garden gate.

"Ow! You're hurting me."

"Serves you right, Nadine. What the hell are you playing at?"

Sulkily Nadine rubbed her arm where I'd grabbed hold of her. "I'm not."

Sorry, do I sound unsurprised? I'd kind of, sort of, *almost* figured it out when I'd seen her desk, an imagination-free zone filled with cutesy toys and knick-knacks, all hailing from the fuchsia end of the spectrum. Who else would write such curiously childish notes? And then, as though my disbelieving stare finally shook something loose in her head, she burst out, "He's lying to you, he *doesn't* love you and he's not *really* going to marry you and he only went out with you so that you'd give him money. He loves *me* and we're going to have a baby and get married and—"

"Well, *duh*, dear."

Nadine stopped, mid-tirade. "What? You *knew*?" Her legs seemed to give way and her weight slumped against me. "But if you knew, then why are you going away with him this weekend?" Her head began shaking from side to side. "He won't sleep with you, you know. He's told me about you trying to seduce him, wearing stupid underwear and prancing about half-naked to try and turn him on, but he won't do it because he loves *me*."

I rolled my eyes and waited.

"And as soon as he's taken you for every penny, we're going to go to Canada and get married and have our baby and he's going to buy a design company so that I can work with him and he'll do the designs and I'll be his model and..."

Now *I* was the one shaking my head. "Nadine. Listen to me. Luke Fry is a liar and a fraud. I know you won't believe me because you love him, but come with me and I'll introduce you to someone who can prove it. If we *can't* convince you, then I promise I'll forget all about the letters and you can go back to him and start your new life in Canada, okay?"

"You're hurting me again."

"It's not far."

Dragging Nadine, who moaned and protested all the way, I headed for Cal's flat. When we arrived, I dumped her on his sofa and asked him to show her all the evidence we'd acquired against Luke Fry, and whilst I told her the story of how he'd used her, Cal dropped printed sheets in her lap. Everything we'd taken off his computer, all the letters he'd written to her, the emails, the files he'd held on me and the other women, the archived internet chats, everything.

At first Nadine wouldn't even look at the papers. She kept looking from me to Cal as though hoping that this was just a simple abduction. It was when I began to describe how Luke had pretended to buy the flat, and how we'd had sex there, that she flinched.

"I bet he told you that he refused to sleep with me, did he? What, that I begged, but he managed to keep me at bay with promises? And you were scared that he might give in, that maybe this weekend would be the one? Nadine, this weekend, after I'd given him the money, of course, he was going to skip out on both of us."

"No. We're going to Canada!" It was the first real reaction she'd shown.

"Look." I showed her the conversation with Argento in Bristol. "Here. Where he says he'll be coming to the South West on 'business'. That's next week. What's the betting that this 'phone call' he's talking about making to her was where he set up a meeting? He's going to meet her, Nadine—next week—with the money from me in his pocket."

"I...don't..." Protectively Nadine clutched at her bump. Then with a small sigh she fainted and slid to the floor in a strangely serene tangle of limbs.

Cal looked at me. "What do we do?"

"Leave her there for now. She'll be all right. But we *have* to get her on our side, Cal. If she goes to Luke and tells him that I know all about him, he'll drop from the radar so fast that even your boys won't be able to track him."

"And we're certain that she's not part of it? That he really *isn't* going to whisk her off to Canada for a good old colonial lifestyle in the Rockies?"

"What do *you* think? He'll have gone through any money Nadine had, and you've seen what he said to this Argento woman. Did that sound like a man who was planning to emigrate any time soon?"

"She's pregnant."

"Probably poor and pregnant by now. He's a wanker. Old news."

"I just meant, he is *such* a bastard."

I flashed him a quick smile. "Can I leave her with you for a bit? I've got to go and make some phone calls about tomorrow, and she might take the story better from you than me. She thinks I've got an axe to grind."

"I'll do my best. But what if she *won't* co-operate?"

"Then you'll have to use your charm, won't you?"

"Which one? The shrunken human head or the silver horseshoe?"

"Very funny."

"Willow." Cal reached across the prostrate body on the floor and took my hand. "You realise that if Luke even so much as *suspects* that you know about him, he might not just disappear. He could be dangerous."

The thought had occurred to me. "That's why I have to make sure that he is one hundred percent convinced of my undying devotion to him. Plus, of course, I have the world's most powerful aphrodisiac at my disposal."

"Mmm? It's working for me, by the way."

"Oh this one wouldn't work on you, you've got enough of your own. I'll call you later, okay?"

"Be careful." His eyes were guarded now. "I don't want anything to happen to you."

"Not, I would bet, quite as much as *I* don't want anything to happen to me. See you tomorrow." And I skipped off down the stairs, with the sting of adrenaline sharp in my mouth.

Chapter Thirty

By Saturday morning the storm had swept clear of York, leaving trails of gravel strewn with petals and branches about the streets as though a thousand careless landscape gardeners had passed by. I was up as soon as it was light, pacing about my bedroom, muttering to myself—there was still so much that could go wrong, so much that I couldn't leave to trust, to faith, to *Cal.*

But I had to, didn't I?

It had to work. It just *had* to.

At least I knew that Luke would be there. Whoever, *whatever* else might go wrong, Luke would be there. Yesterday's phone call had made sure of that. Although he'd been a bit cool to start off with.

"How did the gig go? I would have come and said hello as soon as I realised it was you, but you were...chatting to that man." A clever insertion of a pause, long enough to make me wonder whether he'd seen anything incriminating, until I realised we hadn't been *doing* anything incriminating.

"It was good, thanks. I thought I'd ring to let you know that the bank is releasing the money, so that I can write you out a cheque tomorrow, if you like. At the hotel? Are you still on for that?"

The word "money" acted on Luke like Viagra cream applied direct to his libido. Suddenly he was the besotted, devoted boyfriend, couldn't do enough for me. Did I want picking up? Could he bring anything? Oh, and by the way, the dress I'd worn on Sunday to perform in—stunning, made me look like Jessica Alba.

I didn't even know who Jessica Alba was.

 හ©ෂ

I set out for the hotel at ten. I'd booked the suite from lunchtime, but I wanted to get to the place early to spy out the land, wander round a bit, settle in. I wanted to be in control, confident and relaxed, when Luke arrived. I had to play perfect girlfriend a while longer. Accordingly, under my plain slip dress I was wearing the tightest black lace basque that I'd been able to find. The "God's gift to Men" picture was completed by sheer stockings, a pair of lace knickers which obviously weren't meant ever to be walked in and the highest heels this side of a transvestite's cocktail party. My hair was piled up on my head and secured with a few indolent pins which let random swathes tumble onto my shoulders, and when I walked into the hotel reception they clearly thought I was a hooker.

Having reassured them with my credit card, I found my way to the honeymoon suite and began laying out the first stage of my plan, although I had to take my shoes off to do it. The carpet pile was so thick that my heels kept snagging. The alluring knickers, which had looked so sexy on the rail, kept riding up between my buttocks, and the boning in the basque meant that I couldn't bend down without being suffocated by my own breasts. Obviously I hadn't missed my vocation as a top-class prostitute. Although, looking around the room at the velvet blindfold beside the bed, the serious handcuffs and silk restraints, the scented massage oils, maybe I had.

I'd finished and it was still only twelve thirty. Luke wasn't due until two. Somewhere, elsewhere in the hotel, Cal was hopefully putting the rest of the plan into action. I was slightly disturbed that I hadn't heard from him, nor seen any sign of his presence. The Metro definitely wasn't parked at the front. Maybe they'd worried about their profile and made him park around the back. Maybe he'd got a lift. Maybe the whole thing had fallen through and I was here alone. I shuddered. Don't even think it. Trust him.

I ought to have been hungry. Maybe I should eat something. If nothing else it would pass the time.

No. No room. My stomach was caught in the pincer movement of anticipation and fear, boiling and rolling with something that fell between both emotions and might even have been guilt. Was it fair to do what I was going to do? Was it right? Was it my place to deal out justice? Maybe those other women hadn't cared that he'd taken their money, maybe they'd shrugged their shoulders and got on with their lives?

Maybe this was wrong.

But then I thought of Nadine. He'd conceived a child with her, a woman he was planning to abandon. Brought another innocent person into his filthy schemes without caring that Nadine was going to find herself a single mother, without a penny.

A tap at the door and my heart nearly fell out through my mouth. "It's okay. It's only me." Cal put his head inside the room. "Just wanted you to know that I'm here. Everything is fine."

I ran over and grabbed him, hiding my face against his chest, feeling his warmth and the press of his bones against me. "God, Cal, I am *so* scared."

"Hey." And then he caught sight of the arrangement on the bed. "Hey. Whoo, where'd you get *this* from?" He held up the silk restraint. "Don't tell me, Ash."

I gave a shaky giggle. "How did you guess?"

"Well, I hope you washed it, is all. I'd better go, just in case. See you later."

"Yes," I whispered as he closed the door. Strangely, the fact that I knew Cal was here made me relax and I lay down on the bed, adjusting my underwear so that I could lie comfortably.

Bleeurgh. I woke up, blearily aware that one leg had gone dead because my suspenders were pressing against a nerve, and checked my watch. It was ten to two! I leaped up, rearranging myself, tweaking stockings straight and repinning bits of hair, fighting my cleavage back into the containment vessel of the basque. I felt smeared, distant, as though I hadn't properly woken up yet. My reflection reassured me that I didn't look quite as dislocated as I felt, although my makeup had fallen into my skin and my lipstick was nonexistent. I was reapplying the lipstick when the door to the suite opened, framing Luke.

"Hello," he said, his voice dropping down the register as he noted my appearance. "You look absolutely bloody *amazing*, Willow."

"Thank you," I sparkled at him, smoothing my skirt over my thighs so the bulges of the suspender belt stood out and the low neck of the dress pulled even lower over my chest. "There's a bottle of champagne in the fridge. Would you like to open it?"

"Not as much as I'd like to open you."

Nadine, think of Nadine. "Plenty of time for that in a minute. Let's have a drink first."

Luke's eyes were almost red-hot with friction, running up and down over my body, taking in my wasp waist and the way the high heels made my legs look forever and slender, veering back towards my breasts every time they got bored. "Yeah. Good idea."

Carefully I poured the champagne, watching in the mirror as Luke took in my back view and then glanced around the room. There was a noticeable flicker as he saw my bag with the cheque book right on top. "I thought"—I turned around slowly to give him plenty of time to change his field of vision—"that we might test out the bed before we do anything else." Now he looked at the bed and his eyes flickered again, seeing the props I'd laid out. It wasn't like me to instigate sex quite so blatantly. Had I panicked him? "Of course, if you don't want to..."

"Oh, it's not that, I'm just a bit... You always seem so *proper* about sex. I didn't think you were really into all the tying up and that, and now, here you are." He waved a hand at the blindfold I'd left on the bedside table.

"I thought you'd like it." Demurely I turned away, letting one shoulder drop so that my dress fell away to reveal the tight-fitting black underwear, making my skin look extra pale where my breasts spilled out over the top. "If it's too much, that's fine."

"Shit, Willow, I didn't mean that." Luke drained his glass and stood up. "It's a real turn-on knowing that you got off on it all the time. All that time you laid there, you were really getting kicks from it."

"Oh yes." I backed towards the bed. "Absolutely." Another shrug and my dress fell clear of my body, leaving me standing in black lace underwear and high heels, fingering the silk cords which tied the velvet blindfold. Honest to God, *Graham Norton* would have got a hard-on. "Now, come here."

Now, for reasons of good taste, decency and suchlike, I'm not going into what happened in the next half-hour. But for those of you shuddering and thinking of Cal, *sex never took place*, all right?

However. Time passed, and now Luke was beginning to fret for some sort of conclusion. He lay, naked and coated in aromatic oil, spread-eagled across the huge bed with his arms handcuffed to the bedhead and legs loosely tied to the foot, a purple blindfold across his eyes and a most impressive erection on his lower quarters. As I continued to massage the oil into his torso, he bucked and thrust beneath my hands trying to bring his groin into contact, moaning slightly and biting his lower lip. "Aw, Will, if you don't sit on me soon, I swear I'm going to coat the ceiling."

I smiled, although he couldn't see it. "Don't worry, the longer you have to wait, the more spectacular it'll be. I'm going to go and take this basque off in the bathroom, and then I'll come and attend to you properly."

"Christ." He shuddered and for a second I wondered if I'd misjudged. But he lay back and a lazy look came over his face. "Okay, but don't be too long."

"I'll just be a moment." I went into the bathroom and hastily climbed back into my dress, tweaking it down so that the whorish nature of my underthings was more-or-less concealed. Then I tiptoed out. Crept across the thick, plush carpet with half an eye on Luke in case he'd managed to escape his bonds, and turned the door handle to release the lock. "Hey Luke, I'm on my way," I murmured in my most seductive tones to cover the sound of the door inching open. I don't really think I needed to bother. He was so far gone in his own exotic fantasy that I could have driven a herd of wildebeest through and he wouldn't have noticed, straining his weight against the ties that bound him, jabbing his hardness ineffectually into the air.

"Come...*on*...bitch..."

"Would you like me to show you something, Luke?" I asked, teasingly. "Something that'll really *really* shock you?" Just another few seconds.

"Oh, God...yeah..."

The door closed again and my mouth went dry. Shit, come on, Willow.

"Okay." I climbed onto the bed and pulled the blindfold free. For a second Luke blinked, seeing me fully dressed again, then his eyes focussed and he glanced over my shoulder.

"Shit! You fucking *fucking* bitch!"

Behind me, the room was nearly full. To my left stood a young woman with an acne-scarred face and a blank expression, beside her a middle-aged lady in an unfetching pleated skirt and seventies perm. On the other side of the bed a girl who didn't look much out of her teens hoisted a child higher on her hip, two more women flanked her, both with equally pinched faces.

"Hello, Luke," said the girl with the child. "Say hello, Hugo." The child obediently removed the thumb from its mouth and burbled something. It had Luke's violet eyes and blond nearly-curls. "Looks just like you, doesn't he?"

I was impressed by her cool. And also, grudgingly impressed that Luke hadn't instantly lost his erection, although flaccidity was beginning to arrive, his willy drooping like a sulking Dalek.

"Smile."

Neil leaped forward from the throng and pushed between the women, clicking his camera over Luke's body.

"You *fucker.*"

"And another one, for the dailies. Can you pop it up a bit for me, give me the full-frontal look? Ah, perhaps not, all right, dahlin'?" Neil gave me a wink. "Will that do, love?"

"Perfect, thanks, Neil."

And there, in the second rank, stood Cal, with Ash, Katie, Jazz and Clive, all grinning fit to bust. "He ain't all that big in the bathroom regions, is he?" Clive nodded towards Luke's rapidly drooping appendage. "Wouldn't need a wide angle lens to get that one in."

"Nah, perfectly normal aperture, mate." Neil chuckled. "I 'ad to use a flash though, geddit! Flash?"

For some reason I found this hysterical. The tension which had been holding us all broke. One woman burst into tears and ran out of the door, clutching a handkerchief to her eyes. The acne-marked girl let out a sudden scream and launched herself at Luke with a nail file in her hand and had to be escorted out by Clive.

"I suppose you think you're so fucking clever, don't you?" Luke addressed the crowd, propping his naked body up on his elbows. "What *is* this, get-back-at-Luke day? You're bitches, all of you. None of you worth a fuck in bed. *You're* ugly, you're fat, you're too fucking old. I used to have to close my eyes to poke you...and *you...*" Now his attention was back on me. "If it hadn't been for the money, I couldn't even have got it up for you."

"Funny, *I* don't have that problem." Cal came and put his arm around me. "But then, I don't have difficulties in that department. I hear that you sometimes have a bit of a case of Mr. Floppy."

Luke looked as though he'd been hit. "Who?"

"Me." Nadine. I hadn't seen her. She'd been at the back of the room, behind Cal.

"Dee-Dee? Oh Christ, look love, I can explain."

"No, I really think you can't." She looked frail, greenish-pale with huge dark circles under her eyes. "But I've been listening to these other women, *they've* all explained things to me. Charlotte told me how you tried to accuse her of having an affair so that you didn't have to pay for Hugo. Melanie says you stole the money she'd saved to buy a house. Anna and Jemima said you were going to marry them, and you took their money. You swindled all of them."

"No, I..."

But it was hard to listen to any kind of rationale from a naked man tied to a bed. "Do you know what we're going to do, Luke?" Now I had his attention.

"Oh, let me guess." He narrowed his eyes at me. "Tell me to go away and never do it again?"

"Well, no." Katie stepped forward. "We're going to put all this in the paper on Tuesday, and Neil's got contacts in the National Press, so we reckon we'll be able to sell the story to *all* the dailies. Fraud Exposed—they'll love it—and the pictures, oh, obviously we'll have to have some fuzzy pixels over your fuzzy pixels." Katie started to giggle but managed to carry on. "So, we think, by the time you hit the tabloids, your name and, er, *face*, will be well enough known that you won't be *able* to do anything like this again."

"Probably get offered a deal presenting on Channel 4." Trust Ash to stick his oar in. "I hear 'Gay Guys Talk Sex' is looking for a front man. You'd be ideal. Every boy's wet dream." And he licked his lips, making Luke widen his eyes in shock and turn his head away.

"And, as a rather nice little by-blow, we should all come out of it with a bit of cash. Plus the *York Echo* is going to be the name on everyone's lips for at least a week. Not exactly cutting-edge journalism, but good on the CV."

Apart from the girl with the baby and Nadine, the women surrounding Luke hadn't said anything. They stood, as though modelling for Easter Island statues, grim-faced and totally still, staring down at him as dispassionately as women staring at the moon. Eventually the older lady with the bad perm spoke:

"Did you ever love any of us?"

Luke wouldn't look up. "Do me a favour."

"So it was lies? When you called me 'gentle soul'? You were making it up?"

"And when you said that you'd treated my mother, and she'd talked about me before she died?"

"You *gave* me the money, all of you. I never asked, made a point of never asking, you *wanted* me to have it!"

The women exchanged a glance. I half-expected them to join hands and start chanting, and Luke's head to explode.

"So you don't feel guilty?" This was one of the pinch-faced women. I saw that she wasn't as old as I'd at first thought, just drawn and miserable-looking. "Not even a bit?"

Luke snorted. "You could afford it. You don't know what it's like..."

Without another word, the women left the room. Luke looked astonished. "Where've they gone, then?"

"To leave you to your fate." Cal said. "You don't realise who that lady is, do you? Maybe you never knew."

"Jemima Horton," Luke answered smartly. "I never forget an heiress." He twisted sideways to conceal his groin from Cal's frankly amused stare.

"She's also the sister of the guy who owns most of Fleet Street. If you'd lied just then, told her that you'd loved them really, in your own way, that they'd been special to you, then she could have put in a word for you. Maybe stopped your picture being spread over the tabloids by Monday morning. As it is, I reckon you'll be lucky if they've stopped dragging up your exploits by this time next year."

"You're shitting me."

Cal's stare turned cold. "No." Then he turned to me. "Let's get out of here. It's beginning to smell bad." Everyone started to filter out, Nadine leaving after a long, long final gaze at Luke's naked body.

"Hey, Willow. You can't leave me here!" Luke writhed on the bed. "At least unlock the cuffs, eh, babe? Come on, for old time's sake?"

I hesitated. Tried to think of a pithy leaving statement, but settled for "fuck off, Luke" before following Cal out of the door and into the corridor, where I leaned on the wall and panted with relief.

Cal held my hand until I calmed down. "You were incredible there, Will," he said. "Just incredible."

"I didn't do anything, it was the others. How the hell did the boys manage to find them?"

"Give Dix anyone's email address and he can find their phone number. Don't ask how, best not to know. We got hold of most of the women that Luke had done the bad thing with, these five were the only ones keen enough to stand up and be counted. Oh and Nadine, of course."

I shook my head. "Poor Nadine."

Cal smiled. "Oh, I don't know. She was getting on quite well with Clive while we were waiting for you to give the nod. I don't think she'll be alone for too long."

Katie and Jazz bounced up alongside us. "Way to go, Will." Jazz high-fived me. "That'll show men that they can't fuck you for money."

A momentary silence. "I don't think that's *quite* what you mean." Katie pulled a face. "But we understand."

"I think," I added.

"Right." Cal rubbed his hands together. "I've got this shockingly good recipe for Lamb Passanda that I'm really keen to try out on people who aren't likely to die of it, so, all back to our place?" And he closed his arm around my shoulders, leaning on me slightly to keep his balance.

Ash came alongside me. "So, where've you been then, you dirty stop out?" I asked.

"You are *so* not going to believe it." Ash leaned down to whisper. "But you know what Clay was saying? About Ganda's inheritance?"

"What, the waders stuffed with tenners were they?"

"Better than that. While I was dumping them this guy came up to me—oh, gods, Will, he was *gorgeous*—and asked if he could have them. Turns out, he's a shoe designer, right. His name's Simon, he lives in Leeds, he wants to work on some designs based on my rubber waders and, I can hardly believe this myself, *he's invited me to help him.*"

"And you know what about shoe design?"

Ash shrugged. "I can learn. Anyway, for Simon I'd learn to slaughter pigs with my teeth. I really think"—and he lowered his voice even further, with a furtive glance at Cal—"that he might be the One."

Without looking over, Cal squeezed my shoulder, very slightly. "I think that's fantastic, Ash," I said honestly.

"Fantastic? It's a bloody miracle." We'd arrived at the cars by now. "Are you really going to leave that guy naked and tied to the bed, Will?"

"Of course. He deserves it. Why?"

My brother gave me a sidelong glance. "Do you think we should scare him a bit more? Just to make sure?"

"What are you planning? Ash?"

"I'm not going to *do* anything." Ash turned round and headed back inside. "He is *so* not my type. I'll just, you know. Where's your guy with the camera?"

"Neil? He's over there. Ash?"

"We wouldn't want darling Luke to go off and get himself some lucrative TV work now, would we? I reckon a few secret, incriminating photos might make sure that *that* little scenario never comes to pass." And Ash pulled off his shirt, motioned to Neil to follow him, and disappeared back towards the Honeymoon Suite.

"You've got to admire a mind as devious as that." Cal gave my shoulder another squeeze as we found the Metro hidden away behind a convertible Mercedes.

"Yep. Not just bent, totally warped," I said, happily. "Right. To the Lamb Passanda, Jeeves, and don't spare the horses."

Cal doffed a nonexistent hat and muttered, "Yes, milady."

Sitting in the front of the Metro, as we led a procession of cars down the hotel drive, I closed my fingers around the matchbox in my bag and heard the slight, distinct rattling of the nose within. I slid open the tray a fraction and smiled inside.

"What are you grinning at?" Cal risked taking his eyes from the road for a second.

"Just my good-luck nose."

"Hey, don't try to outweird me."

I closed the box up and let it fall back to the bottom of the bag. "Wouldn't dream of it, Cal." I rested my head. "Wouldn't dream of it." But in the back of my mind a tiny thought took wing. Ganda had known what I needed. Somehow. And it wasn't what I thought I *wanted*. Wasn't money, it wasn't Luke— it was this skinny, dark-eyed lunatic currently hunched over his steering wheel, blowing imaginative curses at the traffic and occasionally throwing brilliant glances my way. Ganda had known, and somehow he'd got it for me.

As Katie would have said, I was one lucky, lucky bitch.

About the Author

Jane was born some time ago, and has found living to be habit forming. She resides in North Yorkshire in Britain with her partner, Kit, five children, two dogs, four cats, two guinea pigs, a rat and some Giant African Land Snails. At least, that was the count this morning, there's probably a hippo and a couple of anteaters as well, by now. She writes for her own amusement and has become quite used to her children banging on the office door and asking, "What's so funny in there?" She has hobbies, of course, like any well-rounded individual, these include: the search for clean trousers, interrogating trees and laughing manically at passing motorists. She hopes one day to identify her true planet of origin.

To learn more about Jane Lovering, please visit www.JaneLovering.co.uk. It's a nice place, and you can wear your slippers. Send an email to mail@JaneLovering.co.uk or join her Yahoo! group to get the latest news on Jane's books, win stuff and chat with other readers as well as Jane herself, if she's having one of her lucid moments. Just go to http://groups.yahoo.com/group/janelovering.

If you fancy some salacious gossip, a bit of gratuitous blogging and some lovely pictures, go to www.myspace.com/janelovering. Your brain will love you for it.

Can KD convince Kelsey they were made for each other before she marries the wrong guy?

Born Again Virgin
© *2007 Sami Lee*

When she started a new life in the small town of Holly Hill, Kelsey Simmons made a vow to give up sex until she found The One. Now, finally, she has Mr. Right set firmly in her sights. She's got the perfect plan to catch him. Trouble is, her intended target dodges cupid's arrow and it hits Mr. Wrong smack in the rear.

KD McKinley isn't looking for love. He's just renovating Kelsey's house to help out his ill stepfather. But smart and sexy Kelsey proves impossible to resist. Pretty soon, KD is reconsidering the whole white-picket-fence thing. However, his Miss Right thinks he's all wrong and KD isn't sure he can convince her otherwise...

Available now in ebook and print from Samhain Publishing.

Did you ever want to live a different life? Or actually have a life?

Ellie's Dream
© *2007 Margaret Wilson*

The last thing Ellie Newman expected to see was her husband wrapped in the arms of a blonde. Talk about a wake-up call.

With her son almost grown, her job a bore and a husband whose hobbies don't include her, she is ready for a change.

Out of the blue, Ellie gets a chance to live another life when she goes to New York City for the summer to escape her problems. She gets a job of sorts, pet-sitting for her friend's cousin.

She loves New York. The parks, the food, the museums, the clubs all beckon. The only annoyance is Seth, the beast who unexpectedly shares the apartment.

Seth wants her to leave. Women are trouble and he needs to focus on his music. But she is hard to ignore, especially after they discover a mutual love of jazz. Ellie is up for a fling. After all, who can resist such a bad boy?

Ellie's Dream is about finding your heart, finding your passion and letting go.

Available now in ebook and print from Samhain Publishing.

Enjoy the following excerpt from Ellie's Dream...

Seth and Marshall pushed their way through the crowd to the edge of the dance floor. They looked around for Ellie and Jamie. Marshall spotted them and pointed them out to Seth. Their bright red heads made them stand out in the crowd. As the couples moved, Seth caught glimpses of Ellie's milky white thighs playing peek-a-boo with that ridiculous excuse for a dress. Then he noticed Jamie's hands firmly gripped her sweet little bottom. And worse, Ellie hung on to his ass for dear life. Their hips moved together like a well-oiled machine.

"I had no idea Ellie danced so well," Marshall shouted in Seth's ear. "They look amazing together."

Just then the song ended and Jamie dipped Ellie back, her long white arm arched over her head as one shapely leg wrapped itself around Jamie's hip. Jamie ran his lips down Ellie's neck, over her chest and stopped at her waist. Seth's hands clenched. Jamie righted Ellie and caressed the leg still wrapped around his hip.

"What's the matter?" Marshall shook Seth's arm. "You look like you're ready to explode."

"It's hot in here," Seth said through clenched teeth. Jesus, Jamie still had his hand on Ellie's ass. Seth wanted to punch him out, gay or not. He was hot and hard. All he wanted to do was throw Ellie over his shoulder and get her out of here. Get her alone, rip that dress off and see what lay underneath. He shook his head to clear it and took a deep breath.

As they returned to the table, Ellie saw Marshall at the edge of the dance floor. She pointed him out to Jamie. "I think he came to see you." Then she noticed Seth behind Marshall. "Do you think they're checking up on us?"

"Looks like it. Seth seems quite smitten." Jamie steered her toward the two men. "This could be our lucky night."

"Maybe for you. I've been talking you up to Marshall." Ellie clutched Jamie's arm. "He really likes you."

"He doesn't even know me," Jamie shot back.

Ellie whispered in his ear. "He could get to know you."

"What's up?" Ellie asked. They stopped in front of Marshall and Seth.

"We wanted to get out of the apartment, get a drink." Marshall held up a bottle of water.

"I love Latin music," Seth added.

"But it's not live," Ellie protested. She pointed to the DJ. "I thought you'd prefer live music?"

"Did you see us dance?" Jamie put his arm around Ellie. "Ellie is a terrific partner." He placed his hands on her hips. "She really moves these."

Ellie wiggled her hips. "I need to find the ladies room. Get me some water, Jamie?"

"Sure, I'll meet you back here." Jamie kissed Ellie's cheek.

When Ellie left the ladies room a few minutes later, Seth was standing outside the door with a bottle of water in his hand.

"Thanks." Ellie took the water. "Where is everybody?"

"They seemed to have a lot to say to each other, so I left them alone." Seth pointed to a dark corner where Ellie could barely see her friends. They were huddled together, heads close.

"It looks like I've been dumped," Ellie said with a smile.

They made their way to the edge of the dance floor. Ellie sipped her water and looked around. The club was getting very crowded. A tall man with dark hair appeared at Ellie's side and asked her to dance.

"My wife is taking a break right now." Seth drew Ellie to his side. "Thanks for asking."

The man held up his hands and moved away.

"Wife," Ellie sputtered. She shook off Seth's arm. "I don't need a chaperone."

"He's a creep and that dress of yours is bound to give him the wrong idea." Seth drew her close again. "It's giving me a lot of ideas." His fingers brushed her thighs.

"It's the perfect dress for salsa." Ellie pushed his hands away.

"So let's dance." Seth held out his arms.

"You can dance?" Ellie looked at him uncertainly.

"I was raised by a gay Hispanic musician who hung out with drag queens." He looked her up and down. "You may not be able to keep up with me."

"I bet I can." Ellie put her empty bottle on a table and grabbed his hands. "Ready?"

Dancing with Seth was very different than dancing with Jamie or even Sergio. It was sexual, very physical, with Seth completely in command. After a minor test of wills, Ellie gave in and let Seth take charge. His body was strong and fluid and he stared into her eyes as they moved to the frenetic beat. Ellie had the time of her life. After two energetic mambos, the DJ slowed the tempo down to a samba. Seth pulled Ellie close.

"Maybe we should sit this one out," Ellie whispered.

"Not a chance. This is the most sensual music there is." He dipped Ellie.

Ellie sighed and let Seth take over again. She remembered the dance classes she and Patti took together because their husbands were too busy. She tried to show Charlie the steps but he never seemed able to spare the time. She wanted to call Patti and describe the club and how much fun she was having.

She was startled out of her daydream when Seth kissed her neck, sending a shiver right down to her toes. She pushed away from him.

"You have to stop this." Ellie fought to catch her breath. "I like you, but we can't be lovers. I'm married."

Without a word, he led her off the dance floor to a dark corner. He pressed her against the wall and braced his hands on either side of her.

"If you were my wife, I would come after you wherever you tried to hide. I'd take you home and do whatever it took to make you want to stay." He lowered his eyes and looked at her body. "And I'd take you dancing so other men could see how lucky I was, but then I'd have to take you home early because I'd need to make love to you." He closed his eyes and took a deep breath. "But that's just me." He started to back off.

"One more thing." He lowered his mouth and kissed her deeply, passionately, using his lips and tongue to excite her. He broke away leaving Ellie's head spinning. "I'd kiss you like that every day, so it's clear where you belong." With that he grabbed her hand and marched her over to the table where Jamie and Marshall sat.

"See that Ellie gets home safely," Seth said to the two men.

GET IT NOW

MyBookStoreAndMore.com

GREAT EBOOKS, GREAT DEALS . . . AND MORE!

Don't wait to run to the bookstore down the street, or
waste time shopping online at one of the "big boys." Now,
all your favorite Samhain authors are all in one place—at
MyBookStoreAndMore.com. Stop by today and discover
great deals on Samhain—and a whole lot more!

Samhain Publishing

WWW.SAMHAINPUBLISHING.COM

Printed in the United Kingdom
by Lightning Source UK Ltd.
129282UK00001B/88-96/P